Watchers

Watchers

*In a society where people are illegal
Is anyone beyond hope?*

SHEILA JACOBS

**Authentic
LIFESTYLE**

First published in 2003 by Authentic Lifestyle

07 06 05 04 03   7 6 5 4 3 2 1

Authentic Lifestyle is a division of Authentic Media,
9 Holdom Avenue, Bletchley, Milton Keynes, Bucks MK1 1QR, UK

Distributed in the USA by Gabriel Resources,
P.O. Box 1047, Waynesboro, GA 30830–2047, USA

British Library Cataloguing in Publication Data

A catalogue record for this book is available from the British Library

ISBN 1–86024–289–8

Cover design by David Lund
Printed in Great Britain by Cox & Wyman Ltd, Reading

Dedication

The Lord has done this, and it is marvellous in our eyes
(Psalm 118:23)

*Special thanks to Alison Hull, Malcolm Down, Colin Nutt,
Wendy Jackson, Austin and Judith Mudd, Sue and Laura Bayliss,
Yvonne Knight and Mary Jacobs.*

Government memo to
Head of Security Department (Watchers)

PRIORITY

Summary of Watchers' brief

1. Keep order in the New Towns (Clean society). If any trouble occurs, sort it.
2. If anyone is seen/caught/known to be (by informant) breaking one of the rules (see Free Living in the New Towns Manual, sections 1–85), make decision according to the Law – death penalty or social exclusion (if you must kill them, do it somewhere it won't be seen – we don't want to frighten the general populace).
3. Social exclusion: (commonly termed Dumping) de-Code them before entry into the old city, now used as an Exclusion Area (prison).
4. Remember death penalty for certain groups is mandatory: e.g. any religious group that will not conform to the state religion.
5. Watchers have the authority to check for the Code in any person at any time. Anyone not having the Code in the New Towns will be questioned, dumped or terminated according to the Law.
6. Illegal/Unclean (city scum) – Watchers' brief is to kill the old and sick and trouble-makers (or *anyone* during a population cull).

Give all Watchers a copy of this brief

Keep Watchers as happy as possible (women, drugs, Credit, whatever). Don't cross them, don't stop them – and watch out.

1

Rescue

The old city. Half-demolished buildings with exposed rooms; rubbish and rubble-strewn roads ending abruptly in gaping holes. Derelict, dead, and filthy – so filthy.

The driving rain, washing the streets, would never cleanse it of its dirt. Not if it rained for a year. Not if it rained for a lifetime.

'There.'

The blip on the car scanner indicated that this was the place.

'He's in that doorway.'

The armoured vehicle slowed down, and its searching beacon threw a shocking beam into the darkness. There was no electricity anywhere in the city. No light. No life. At least, no life worth living. It was darker than the pit of hell – if Mike believed in hell. He didn't. He grabbed his rifle and sprang out of the car.

Chain-link fence, once ten metres high, lay ripped up and pulled down, but nothing stopped Mike. The looming half-burnt out building seemed to rise up in front of him like some half-dead enemy, protecting the Unclean.

'Watchers!'

Who said that?

The pathetic baggage, clutching a carrier bag, scrambled to its feet in the doorway. It put up a hand, shielding eyes from the searchlight's intensity.

'Mercy!'

'No mercy, old man.' Mike raised the rifle, admiring its silent efficiency as the victim slumped to the ground.

He walked up to the body and, in the brilliance, he could see that this Unclean wasn't really very old at all. He was hardly more than a youth.

'Check, Jay.'

Jay was out of breath. 'He's dead, isn't he?'

'You know the rules. Just check him!'

'OK, OK.' Jay bent down, the flat-line on his Laserscan rifle corresponding with Mike's own.

'What's happening with you tonight, Jay?'

'Not feeling so good, I guess.' Jay stood up. 'Unclean terminated. Check.' He stared down at the body. 'Man, what's worse, bringing them here or culling them? I don't know.'

'That's our job.'

Jay shuddered. 'How old are you, Mike? Older than me – much older. You ever wonder why you've lasted this long? I look in the mirror and wonder how come I'm still out here, and I'm only twenty.'

Mike wasn't sure how to reply to that. He was still thinking about what to say when there was a sound of shouting some way off.

'Five minutes west. Come on.'

Jay didn't move. 'Our shift's nearly over.'

'What?'

'Look, why do more than we have to? Why risk it? By the time we get back to the Gate, our shift will be over.'

'I can't believe I'm hearing this.'

'OK, whatever. Can we just go?'

Mike grabbed his partner's arm.

'If you've got a problem, deal with it. I need to know I can trust you.'

'We've been partners for a year now. You know you can trust me, but you enjoy this and I don't.'

'You better hope I didn't hear that.'

'Why?' But Jay knew why.

The shouting was getting louder. Jay was heading back to the car. Mike watched him. He had to be able to rely on his partner. His life depended on it. He couldn't afford to have a partner whose nerve had left him. He should report Jay's less than enthusiastic commitment to the job.

'No one gets out, Jay. No one stops being a Watcher.'

'Yeah, well maybe some do,' Jay called back over his shoulder. 'I've put in for a transfer of duties.'

And no Watcher was transferred anywhere, ever, thought Mike.

Jay's question repeated itself in his mind. 'How old are you?' A feeling Mike was accustomed to having only in the middle of a sleep period rose up inside him. He remembered his age. Why hadn't some Debtor killed him by now, some kid who should never have been born, some old man who couldn't afford to live any more, someone who couldn't get the Code, and had been banished to this living death?

They'd get him one day. Or maybe the Watchers themselves would do it, as soon as he stepped out of line, said the wrong thing – lost his nerve. Mike took his helmet off and ran a hand through his hair. Thinking of age made him nervous: not that he would ever admit it to a living soul. Maybe that was why he was especially glad to execute the elderly. He replaced his helmet, looking with distaste at the lifeless form in the rain. He hated all the dross in this forsaken place.

Yet for all his loathing of the old city, Mike felt part of it. Right now, he liked the feeling. Cleanse the city. A feeling of power washed away any temporary fear. It was only when he was back in the New Towns that he really felt uneasy. Somehow, Mike belonged here.

Then the Watcher of all Watchers realised that he himself was being watched. A noise in an alleyway brought a deft movement as he levelled his Laserscan and yelled a warning.

'Stand still for scan check!'

'You can lower that thing. I check out. I've got the Code. I'm not an Illegal.'

'Stand still!'

The figure stood still. The small screen on the Laserscan converted her identification code into a name. By now, Jay had driven the car up close, the searchlight fixed on his partner and the girl.

'See, I never let you down.'

Mike glanced at him. 'Look who we've got.'

Jay looked at the identification. 'That can't be right.'

'What's up?' asked the girl. 'Don't you like my name or something?'

'Shut up,' said Mike. 'Double check it, Jay.'

The girl didn't seem afraid. It was unusual. Everyone feared Watchers.

'It's unreal Mike, but this is Sunny Cain.'

Mike lowered his weapon. The girl was slight and thin, wearing only a shirt and pair of jeans. Her long hair hung in wet strands.

'What are you doing here?'

There was an explosion – it wasn't far away. A wall of flame lit up an old church tower. Mike's priority suddenly became to protect the girl. 'All right, Sunny Cain, let's get you out of this place. Let's move.'

Once in the car, they roared through the pitted streets, jolting through loose rubble that was once a fine main road.

'Are you injured?' Jay asked. 'Miss Cain? Are you injured?'

'No, I'm just great.'

'You're just lucky,' said Mike. He turned to the girl, who was sitting on the hard ledge behind his seat. 'What were you doing in the old city?'

Sunny leaned forward. 'You're Mike, aren't you? Mike Merrick.'

'You haven't answered my question.'

'I often see Jay – it is Jay, isn't it? – at the Relaxation Centre. Do you remember me, Jay?'

'Er – yeah,' admitted Jay. 'I think – yeah.'

'You'd have recognised me if I hadn't been so wet, wouldn't you, Jay? Once seen, never forgotten. I'm afraid you haven't caught me looking my best, Mike. I never see *you* at the Relaxation Centre. Why's that?'

'What were you doing in the city?'

'What are *you* doing here? Targeting anyone who hasn't got the Code? Keeping down the Unclean population? Doesn't that give you a kick? You know, it's funny we've never actually met before. I mean, my father is your boss.'

Something clicked into Mike's brain and he turned away from her in disgust.

'She's playing a game – get into the old city, see a little danger. Some of your privileged friends never get out, you know, Sunny Cain.'

'But I did. You've rescued me, Mike.'

'Jay, maybe we should stop the car right here and let her live out her little fantasy.'

'You won't do that,' said the girl, confidently.

'No, we can't do that,' agreed Jay, ramming his foot onto the accelerator, not at all sure his partner wouldn't order him to stop.

'I've met some people.' Mike heard Sunny's voice low in his ear. 'If you only knew what I know!'

'Who've you met? Names?'

'Oh, I've got a name.' She sat back, smiling. 'A name you'd die for.'

'What name?'

Sunny Cain just smiled. Mike wasn't in the mood to play games. He looked away.

'You're wasting my time.'

'I wouldn't waste your time, Mike.'

Jay was amused now. Mike didn't feel amused or flattered.

'Sunny, if you've got a name, let's have it. If you haven't, OK. If you want to pretend you know something and you don't, all right. But remember it's the law – you must give full details of all meetings with Illegals to Watchers.'

Jay expected him to add 'or else', but he didn't. The coldness of his voice wasn't lost on Sunny. She didn't like being rejected.

'Oh I've got a name, all right. Trouble is, I can't seem to remember it now.'

Jay cursed and manoeuvred the car around several burnt out wrecks of old trucks as they headed towards the regular lights of the highway ahead. Another explosion lit up the sky and, for a moment, it seemed like a new and violent day had suddenly arrived.

'Gate,' Jay spoke into the vehicle's intercom. 'Gate. Request Gate open.' He gave identification details. 'And we picked up a passenger. Sunny Cain. Yes, as in Stirling Cain's daughter. Yep. You heard right.'

The city wall loomed nearer, that great greyness that kept the Unclean from the Clean. Guards were visible now, as the Gate slowly opened.

'I've seen you around, Mike,' said Sunny.

Mike didn't reply.

'You're attractive, you know.'

Still no response.

'My father's afraid of you. Why's that?'

'You tell me.'

She was quiet for a moment. 'Ever been across the water?'

'Across the water? The sea? No. Why?'

Now it was Sunny's turn not to reply.

The car slowed down as they reached the Gate. Jay leaned out and spoke to the Gate guards, and they gazed in at the passenger. Sunny folded her arms across her body and complained that she was cold.

The Gate heaved shut behind them, and Jay breathed a sigh of relief as they pulled onto the wide, broad, well-lit highway. In the distance, the tall buildings of the New Townships became visible.

'Light!' said Jay.

'Glad to be home?' Sunny asked him.

'What about giving us that name?'

'That's if she's got a name,' said Mike.

'I've got a name.'

Mike laughed his sudden, disarming laugh. 'Is there anything in your head that isn't made up? Got to go to the city to get a buzz.'

'Don't judge me, Mike Merrick. You're just the same.'

'No, Sunny Cain. Not the same at all.'

A large black limousine was gliding silently towards them, looking as if it were part of the real night, the night which had been pushed back by the artificial lighting; night which had escaped its boundaries and had slunk back onto the highway.

Jay stopped their vehicle.

'OK, game over.' Mike stepped out of the car and called to the driver of the limousine. 'Here she is. Take her away. Go home, little girl.'

'I remember the name.'

'There's no name.' Mike turned back to the armoured car.

'David Drum. That's a name, isn't it?'

Mike spun round. 'David Drum? What David Drum?'

'Just David Drum.'

'David Drum is dead.'

'Maybe it isn't the same one.'

'You're lying.'

'I'm not. They talk about David Drum in the city. And they don't talk about him as if he's dead. They talk about him as if he's alive and helping people to escape!'

'You're wrong. You're wrong, Sunny.'

She leant against the limousine. 'You wanted a name, and now you've got it, you don't want it after all. Is there no pleasing you?'

'You've got to be wrong.'

'David Drum is alive and well and helping people escape, I tell you. They call it going over the water.'

Mike slung his hands onto his hips. David Drum! One of the leaders of that renegade sect . . . what were they called? That sect that refused to take the Code, the sect that were banned years ago when all religions were herded together under one banner . . . what was that group that wouldn't conform?

'No. John Woodley, Stephen Lewis, Kurt Dane . . .' Kurt Dane. That was a name he hadn't thought of in a long time. 'And David Drum. All dead.'

'Maybe not as dead as you think.' Sunny moved closer and whispered, 'I'm going to be at the Relaxation Centre tomorrow around four. Perhaps I'll remember even more when I'm relaxed. Think so, Mike?'

And with that, she smiled again, and walked to her father's limousine.

'David Drum! That's not possible.' Not possible.

Was it?

2

Assistance

'You're not serious. Mike? Come on.'

Mike was pulling off his body armour. He chucked it, and his helmet, to his partner. Jay shook his head.

'You're crazy.'

'Maybe.'

'You'd risk it – just because of what that girl said?'

It was raining harder now.

'Mike, I do remember her . . . at the Relaxation Centre. She was trying to talk to me . . . I was with Juno. You know, she's probably lying about the name . . . trying to get your interest.'

Mike handed his rifle to Jay. 'Probably.'

'You don't need to do this.'

'Yeah, I do.'

The large white armoured Aid vehicle pulled up at the Gate. Mike hailed it, and called out to the driver.

'Picking up tonight?'

'Yes.'

'Good.'

Jay shook his head again.

'Crazy. What if one of them recognises you? What if you find yourself face to face with someone you've dumped, de-Coded . . . you haven't got your Laser-scan . . .'

'They won't recognise me. Too much fear for that.'

'I don't know. If one of them – '

'You worry too much. See you later.'

'Yeah . . .' Jay didn't look too sure. He got into the armoured car, revved it, and pulled away as Mike climbed into the back of the Aid truck. There were several people inside but no one would look at him. Mike didn't care.

'OK, go.'

Someone rapped on the panel that separated the driver from his passengers. The truck roared into life and they were through the Gate.

One of the passengers was looking at Mike now.

'Merrick.'

'Doctor Stone! Well, doctor. Didn't know you'd be out here tonight.'

'Isn't your shift over?'

'Monitoring my movements? Not sure I like that idea.'

'I monitor who goes in and who comes out. You know that.' The doctor glanced at the boxes littering the back of the vehicle. Mike leaned forward and fixed Stone with his most intimidating gaze.

'If it wasn't for us, you wouldn't be delivering anything to them ever again.'

'It undermines their trust.'

'Too bad.'

'They'll know you're a Watcher.'

'They won't.'

'Stay inside the vehicle.'

'Don't tell me what to do.'

The doctor spoke through gritted teeth. 'You'll ruin everything. Everything we're doing.'

'Shut up.'

A couple of the other passengers exchanged glances and Mike smiled to himself. They were priests, these long-robed characters with their serious faces. Mike had about as much time for priests as he had for the Unclean.

'Where are you picking up from?'

'The river.'

'Hey, that's quite a trip ... pity I left my Laserscan behind. We could've spent some time seeing if everybody's codes checked out.'

The priests, the doctor and the other Aid workers were visibly disturbed by that thought.

'We all check out,' said a priest.

'Yeah? Well, that's good. Got nothing to fear, then, have you?'

One of the Aid workers spoke in a low voice.

'Doctor Stone, we can pick up by the old cathedral.'

'That's five minutes away,' said Mike. 'You getting nervous? Got something to hide?'

'No.'

'You sure?'

'He just doesn't like the company we're keeping,' said the doctor.

'That's a shame. You're stuck with it.'

Doctor Stone nodded at the Aid worker. 'Yes, we'll pick up at the cathedral. Tell the driver.'

A few minutes later, the Aid vehicle stopped, the back doors crashed open, and hectic activity began. The priests and the Aid workers started to shift the boxes, throwing them out to the clamouring mass of hands and arms that reached for them.

'We could do with some help,' the doctor said to Mike.

'I think you manage pretty well.'

'If you help,' Stone replied, in a low voice, 'they won't think you're a Watcher.'

Much as Mike hated the idea of assisting in feeding and giving out medication to the Unclean, there was sense in what the doctor was saying. Mike lifted a few of the boxes and shoved them with some force at the priest waiting to receive them and pass them on.

The crowd was milling about, muttering and crying. 'Thank you . . . thank you!'

'I only wish we could bring in more!' The doctor was moving around the gathering mass of people who washed up against the sides of the vehicle like an Unclean sea. 'Yes . . . yes . . . be patient . . . there'll be another drop at three, by the river . . . and another at six, right here. Don't be afraid.'

Mike stood at the back of the vehicle. The truck's lights lit up the old cathedral; derelict, with what was left of its ancient spires sticking up like some weird skeleton into the night sky. The gaping hole in the walls looked like the entrance to a tomb.

Mike's gaze locked on to a half-visible shadow. Just by the cathedral was an armoured car and Watchers ready to take out any of the Illegals who became a little too keen to get to the Aid. They knew this – this rabble who weren't fit to live. In between their grabbing and grasping, there were frightened glances over shoulders. Mike almost laughed to see them trying to act with such restraint when they were so utterly desperate.

'I know, I know . . . I don't like it either, I can assure you!' Fabian Stone was doing what he did best. He was *caring*, lightly touching hands and heads like some ancient saint from the cathedral, awarding benedictions to the faithful. 'Yes, I know . . . I'm sorry they have to be there, but you know what it's like for us . . . we don't want them there, but it's the government . . . I know . . . truly . . .'

A woman rushed at him. For a moment, Mike thought she was going to attack the doctor, but she was sobbing into his neck, her thin body pressed against him, matted hair in his face. Mike couldn't watch that; it turned his gut over.

'Bless you . . . I know,' said Stone, and one of the priests picked up the refrain.

'Bless you. Yes, bless you.'

The priest gently removed the woman from the doctor's person, comforting her.

Mike folded his arms and leaned against the side of the vehicle. He wished they'd get to the point where they'd pick up . . . cut all this sentimental trash and get to the crux of the visit.

'I'm a doctor . . . let me help you.'

Stone was still at it. Mike wondered if he could report him, back in the Towns, for taking too much time.

'Food, medicine . . . I can't stay . . . the fire? No, I can't help . . . you know that . . . you know we're not allowed. If only we were . . .'

Mike looked at the Watchers' car. The windscreen wipers moved once or twice, clearing the rain.

'We've got permission to get four out for reassessment. Two men, two women. Got to be under thirty-five.'

At last.

Mike jumped down from the truck and waited.

Someone pushed a young girl forward.

'Got to be healthy. Bless you . . . I can't take her.'

The sobbing woman was bringing a skinny young boy to the doctor. He wasn't much older than the youth Mike had killed an hour ago.

'Yes, fine. Yes, we'll have him.'

'Oh, doctor!' the woman bleated. 'You're a good man!'

Mike turned away. This was really getting on his nerves. As he turned, he saw one of the priests putting an arm round another boy, glancing about, realising the Watchers couldn't see what he was doing, then covering the boy with his robe, and almost throwing him into the back of the truck. The man – his father? – who had been with the boy, cried, and put out both hands to the priest in gratitude.

Fabian Stone was talking to an old man.

'Yes, I know you're afraid . . . Watchers, yes . . . your eyes . . . you're nearly blind. Let me see if we can help. Maybe we'll take you too, eh?'

'He might be blind,' Mike said in Stone's ear. 'I'm not.'

'So report me. That's what you want to do, isn't it?' Stone shouted to one of his workers. 'We're taking the old man.'

Is this getting out – is this going over the water? thought Mike. Maybe Sunny Cain had got it wrong after all; maybe she'd got her ideas mixed up in the excitement of her adventure. But then – there was the matter of that name . . .

They'd selected the second male for reassessment. He was a thin-faced, scrawny looking man in his twenties, but he'd do. Mike's warning glance stopped the Aid workers from putting him in the truck.

'Hey, you all right?' he said, lightly – as if he cared.

'I can't believe it!' The young man was shivering in the rain, his long hair plastered to his cheeks. 'I'm getting out. I'm getting out!'

'Yeah, it's your lucky day.' Mike smiled tightly at a few of the Unclean and hoped with all his being that they wouldn't start falling on his neck and thanking him. That really would be too much.

He put a hand firmly on the man's chest and pushed him so that his back was against the truck.

'OK, listen. Answer a question and you've got re-assessment.'

'But they just said – '

'Yeah, just answer this question first. Right?'

'Well – yes – of course – anything . . . *anything*!'

'What do you know about David Drum?'

'Nothing.' The answer came much too fast.

'Right. What do you know? Come on.'

'I can't – I can't remember.' His shivering intensified; his teeth were chattering. 'I'm getting out. It's really happening. I'm getting out.'

'Yeah, yeah . . . David Drum.' Mike increased the pressure on the young man's chest. He was aware of one of the priests standing close to him, but that wasn't going to stop him. The young man frowned suddenly.

'I thought you were a doctor? An Aid worker?'

'Never mind who I am. You're getting out, remember? So long as you tell me what you know about David Drum.'

'Everything all right? We've got to go!' The doctor was behind Mike. He sounded nervous. Very nervous. Mike cursed and relaxed his grip.

'Maybe I'll come talk to you later,' he told the young man.

'OK. OK . . .'

'Bless you, my son!' said Stone, grasping the young man by his bony shoulders. 'A whole new life awaits you.' And he gave Mike the blackest glare Mike had ever seen outside of the Watchers.

Seconds later, they were in the truck, the whole lot of them; the thin-faced young man, the skinny boy, two girls, the old man and the kid who'd been 'rescued' by the priest. The priest kept a protective arm round him; he was hardly more than ten, maybe twelve, with huge, terrified eyes. There was a strange atmosphere of shock and elation and fear. Doctor Stone was smiling graciously and saying kind words. One of the girls was crying, and the thin-faced man kept muttering, 'It's really happening. I'm being re-assessed. I'm getting out.' The stench in the truck was overpowering.

They reached the Gate, and the truck's doors were slammed open.

'Mandatory check,' said one of Aid workers, smiling at the Unclean. 'Don't be afraid.'

Gate guards were there now, peering in, checking what the doctor was telling them. One of the guards immediately recognised Mike.

Mike looked round at the others in the truck. 'Well, thanks for the ride. Here's where I leave you.'

'Merrick!' said another guard, as Mike jumped out of the vehicle. 'Don't you ever take a break? That was pretty risky. If that city scum had recognised you, or found out you were a Watcher – '

'They didn't.'

The guard shook his head and laughed. 'One of these days – '

'Yeah, one of these days.'

Another guard was speaking.

'Can you step out of the vehicle for a moment, please, Doctor Stone?'

'Oh no!' said someone from inside the truck. 'Oh no . . . don't let it go wrong . . . not now.'

'You were going to pick up four. There are six Illegals in there.'

'Yes, it's all right.'

'If he says it's all right, it must be all right,' said Mike, coolly. 'He knows what he's doing, our good doctor here.'

Doctor Stone span round and stabbed a finger at the Watcher.

'You nearly wrecked everything!'

'Keep pointing at me and you'll find out what wrecked really means.'

The doctor stopped pointing, but spat his words out furiously.

'I saw what you were doing. If any of them had seen it, it would all be over.'

'Oh, relax. It didn't happen.' Mike turned away. 'Anyone give me a lift into Town? I've had enough of travelling with this – doctor.'

'I'm going to report you.'

'And I'm going to be paying you a visit in a few hours.'

Mike watched the Aid vehicle speed off towards the New Towns.

'Want us to take him the next time he comes through, Mike? We can make sure he disappears,' said a guard.

'No.' Mike ran a hand through his wet hair. 'You can leave Doctor Stone to me. Now, have I got a lift?'

'OK, Mike.' And one of them muttered, 'Wouldn't like to be that doctor. Not in a thousand years.'

3

Suspicion

'Something's wrong.'

'What?'

'I said, something's wrong.'

The fair-haired young man looked up at his companion.

'What do you mean, wrong?'

'I've just got this weird feeling, Gideon. This weird, weird feeling . . .'

'Uh-huh?'

'That guy . . . the Aid worker.'

'Which one?'

'The big guy.'

Gideon smiled at the gaunt-faced girl he was helping. 'Sorry, Lou. Is the bandage too tight? I'm sorry.'

He finished what he was doing, and stood up. His dark-haired companion was leaning against the doorframe, staring out into the street.

'I've seen him before.'

'We've seen them all before, Tris.'

'Something's not right.'

The girl pushed past Gideon, pausing for a moment to rest a grateful hand on his arm, and smiling at him and his companion.

'Thank you.'

'You're welcome, Lou,' said Gideon. 'Wish we could do more.'

18

The rain lashed the people, scurrying here and there with their items of food, clothing, medicine. But no sooner had the Aid vehicle roared away than there was nothing in the street to say it had ever been there. No people. No boxes. Even the Watchers' armoured car had quietly backed away and disappeared. Nothing was left – just the rain.

'Well, one thing's for sure. They bring good quality bandages.'

'Yeah, good *Town* quality.'

'I wish I was a real doctor. I wish I knew more.'

'I've got a feeling they wouldn't admit you to the Town University, Gideon.'

'No.' Gideon smiled, faintly. 'That's right enough.'

'Right? I can't see anything right in any of it.'

Gideon put his head on one side. 'What's up? You're really edgy.'

'It's that guy. I told you.'

'What about him?'

Tris bit his lip. 'If I didn't know better, I'd say he was a Watcher.'

'Oh – that's not possible.'

'All right, it's not possible.'

'What would a Watcher be doing with the Aid workers?'

'The unseen presence . . .'

'Yes, but they don't usually help unload the boxes!'

Tris sighed. 'OK, maybe I was wrong. It's been a long night.'

'If he was a Watcher, maybe he likes doing voluntary work in his off-period.'

'That's not funny. You can't joke about them.'

'I know. I'm sorry.'

Tris turned and rested his back against the doorframe, his good-looking face creased into a troubled scowl.

'It'll be dawn soon. Tris? Tristram?'

'I heard you.'

'We should have heard from Zach by now.'

'Give it a few minutes. If we don't hear then, we'll go looking.'

'Maybe he got rescued.'

'What?'

'Maybe Zach got the chance of reassessment.'

'No, he didn't. I saw who they took. I was right there.'

Gideon started. 'You mean, you went right up to the truck?'

'Yep. Right up.'

'You like taking chances, don't you! What if one of them decided to trade a little information – '

'They were too busy trying to get the Aid to worry about me.'

'Still, I don't think David – '

'Don't tell him.' Tris looked at his friend. 'That's how I managed to get a good look at this guy. I *have* seen him before. I can't think where, or when. But I am just about one hundred per cent sure he's one of them.'

'They all look the same to me. Anyway, you can't tell what they look like in all that armour and the helmets. I think we should try to find Zach.'

'Yes. You're right, he *is* late.'

Gideon hesitated by the door. 'I don't know if it's wise to tell them about this . . . I mean, don't tell the city people. If they believed a Watcher was with the Aid workers – well, you know what could happen.'

'Mmm. Oh yeah – one of the people they took – it was Mole.'

'Really?' Gideon's face fell. 'Oh . . . I had some high hopes in that direction. We talked for ages the other night. I mean, really talked. He was asking lots of questions.'

'He was being *asked* a few too, as far as I could see.'

'Was he? That's strange. They don't usually do anything other than put them in the back of the truck.'

'And guess who was doing the asking?'

'Your big guy?'

'Yep. Couldn't get that close . . . there was a priest, and that doctor . . . but something was going on.'

Gideon looked worried now. 'Don't like the sound of that.'

'No.' Tris shook his head, slowly. 'Like I said, something's wrong.'

'Perhaps we should back off for a bit after this.'

But as they exchanged knowing looks, they knew they wouldn't back off unless they really had to.

Above the cityscape, the sky was lightening, slowly, slowly; the rain was easing off as a new day began. They were just about to leave the building, but then they saw two familiar figures sprinting towards them down the street, a young woman and an older man.

'We've got trouble!' the woman gasped, almost falling in through the door.

'What's new?' asked Gideon, ironically.

'It's Zach.'

'Where is he?'

'He's dead.'

'What!'

'In a doorway. Watchers.'

'Oh *no*! But why? Zach wasn't old . . . he wasn't sick . . .'

'It's a cull.'

'No, the cull's over . . .'

'Not for some of them.'

'Zach would never have been trying to attack them.'

'It's still a warning, isn't it? After that big riot? They're not going to let anyone forget.' The young woman could hardly get her breath. 'Edward saw what happened.'

Edward was red-faced with running and anger.

'Just randomly picking people off. Just finding a living body and *doing* it.'

'Oh, no!' Tris was sick at heart. 'You mean they're taking out just anybody?'

'Anybody.' Edward's voice was brimful of hate. 'You know, I've got a dream – a real ambition in my life. I haven't got much but I have got this . . . you know what I'd really like? I would *really* like to get my hands on one of them. A Watcher. I mean it. And I'm not the only one. They're evil. They *love* it. And Zach's dead in a doorway . . . and Mole's missing.'

'Mole got out,' Gideon told him. 'He was taken for re-assessment.'

'Oh!' Edward's face relaxed and he shut his eyes. 'Lucky guy. Lucky, lucky guy. I always told him he was going to get out. I hoped he would. Oh, that's – that's wonderful.'

'You could get out, too, you know, Edward,' said the woman, quietly.

He opened his eyes and smiled at her. 'You mean, with you people?'

'Yes.'

'Shanna, I know what you're saying, and I know you care, and I don't know why you keep coming back here, and the city people think – *most* of them think – you're good people, but listen: the Towns have got what we want. Not the Deadlands.'

'Try it,' suggested the woman. 'You might be surprised.'

Edward smiled again. 'You just don't get it. You can't give us what we want. *They* can.'

'Not many people get reassessed,' said Gideon. 'The chances are so slim. And they rarely take anyone old.'

'They did tonight. Took an old blind man.' Tris turned his back on the rest and his voice was bitter. 'True compassion.'

'Is that right? They took a blind man?' Edward's eyes darted round the others. 'Then there really is hope for us all.'

'Not in the Towns. Can't you see that?' Tris was exasperated. 'Reassessment! What a generous offer, when there's space for a few to be re-introduced to the Towns ... so long as you never get sick, or old, or poor, or anything else again, eh?'

'No. It's not like that. People who get reassessed don't come back here – ever! They're too careful; they know how to avoid it. New identities ... a new start ... your old identity, your old life, is gone, forgotten!'

'We can offer you a new life. We can, Edward,' said Gideon.

'No! Not like this! You've never lived there. I did – for forty years. Forty *years*! Do you know what real luxury is? I had it! You don't know what you're talking about. I'd do anything to get back there. I would.'

'And live alongside the Watchers?' said the woman, in a low voice.

'Yes! Yes – you have to.'

'And yet you hate them.'

'Of course I do! *Everybody* hates them!' Edward's eyes narrowed. 'We're going to get a bit of revenge soon, anyway. We'll have some payback ... for Zach, for everyone.'

'What revenge? You planning something?' asked Gideon.

'I can't say. I can't tell anyone.'

'You mean you can't tell *us*,' said Tris, still bitter.

'All I can say is that we're going to catch us a Watcher.'

'Oh, man – that doesn't sound too wise!'

Edward came up close to Tristram and stared in his face. 'Since you met up with David I think you lost your guts. You used to be a city kid. I've seen you take down Watchers in your time.'

'Not any more.'

'Yeah, I never could understand that. You're good . . . you could help us.'

'I *try* to help you! But not like that!'

Edward's lip curled into a sudden vicious sneer. 'What use are you, then? Really? Care, care, care. But you don't even bring us food. At least they do *that* from the Towns.'

'We do what we can,' Gideon said, calmly.

'You know, some of them out there don't understand you. Some think you're government spies. Maybe *you* should watch out too.'

The young woman touched him. 'Edward, you don't think that? You don't think we're spies?'

'No.' Edward put a hand to his eyes, his flash of temper evaporating. 'No, Shanna. No. Look, I don't know *what* I think. I'm tired. So tired. I've got to go.'

The tension lifted as Edward left them.

'That went well!' said Tristram, sarcastically. 'We were hoping Edward would want to go across the water, weren't we? Great.'

'We were hoping Zach would go, too,' said the woman.

'And Mole.' Gideon wiped a hand wearily across his face.

'Man, tonight's turning out *just* fine!' said Tristram.

'There's still Lou,' said Gideon.

'Yeah.' Tris sounded cynical. 'Unless the Watchers get her as well.'

'Tris thinks there was a Watcher with the Aid workers,' Gideon told the woman. 'Good job no one else spotted him, isn't it?'

'Good job? You sure about that?'

'They're human too, Shanna.'

'Barely. They say Watchers haven't got a soul.'

'That's ridiculous,' said Gideon. 'You can't believe that.'

'The city people believe it.'

'City people!' Tristram walked to the door. 'We can offer them everything and they don't see it. They want *that*.'

'They don't understand,' said Gideon.

'We've got to *make* them!' Tris slapped his palm onto the doorframe.

'Come on, Tris. That's all they can see – the Towns. How good it is there. You heard Edward. They feel re-assessment is the only way out . . . the only escape from this place, and from the processing plants: except for the ones who want to take what they can by force.'

'You know, maybe tonight wasn't a complete failure.'

The two young men looked at the woman and she shrugged as she continued.

'I think I've got a new contact.'

'You're just saying that!'

'Tristram! What do you mean?'

'You're just saying that to cheer us up.'

She smiled at him. 'Tristram, I'm glad you've still got your sense of humour.'

Tris wasn't at all sure he'd been joking. However, Shanna thought he had been and she was still smiling at him – which he liked.

'Someone wants to get out. Urgently.'

'They all do, Shanna,' said Gideon, 'till they find out we're offering them the Deadlands.'

'Or they decide we're spies after all and they can't trust us,' said Tris, 'or they get reassessed or wiped out in doorways.'

'Come on, boys . . . don't give up. There's plenty of respect for us out there.'

'Yeah.'

'Well, I'll follow this contact up, anyway.'

'You do that.' Tristram couldn't help adding, 'Let's hope something really happens this time.' And he stepped outside into the new morning.

Its very bleakness cast an oppressive greyness over everything. Water was lying in great puddles in the pockmarked street. At least the Aid meant that the people didn't have to drink it; there was always plenty of bottled purity from the Towns, packed with antibiotics.

Tris, hoping the rain had freshened the air, took a deep breath – but the explosion earlier on had deadened the atmosphere and his mouth tasted acidic. A group of women were hurrying towards him, panic-stricken. Voices had been heard under some of the rubble . . . yes, people had been caught in the explosion . . . some of the disabled had lived right there . . . the old tower had gone down . . . fire . . . the result of all that dumping of toxic waste here so long ago.

Could they help? Could they help? Come quickly – tugging at his arm. *Please* help; we know you care!

And they ran to help. As they always did.

4

An Interview

'You know your trouble, Mike.'

Mike glanced at his partner.

'My trouble?'

'You don't know how to relax.'

'I didn't come here to relax.'

Mike turned back to the window, leaning against the wall, surveying the scene in the courtyard below. People were laughing and talking. Handsome young men in togas, pretty young women in sarongs. A girl was sitting on the low wall beside the pool, dangling a hand into the ripples made by the fountain, the sunlight catching her hair which blazed like copper round her slim shoulders. As Mike watched, a man approached the girl. She smiled at him.

'*Everybody* comes here to relax, Mike.'

The man and the girl were leaving the courtyard together, heading under one of the many rose-covered arches leading to the Guest Rooms.

'Mike? I said, everybody comes here to relax.'

'I heard.'

'Everybody – but you.'

Mike looked again at his partner, who sat up, and stretched. The girl who had been giving him a massage whispered something, and Jay laughed.

'No, I'm trying to be faithful to someone. I'm sorry.'

A smile played around Mike's mouth as Jay continued to apologise. The masseuse didn't seem to believe he didn't want her further attentions.

'Tell her, Mike. I'm being faithful to Juno. She's really got to me and she wouldn't like – no, I really mean it – no.'

'What about your partner?' The girl fixed her large blue eyes on Mike. Mike had seen that particular shade of blue in many eyes over the years. And that particular body-shape. It was one of the most popular designs Credit could buy. 'Are you being faithful to someone?' the girl asked him. 'Maybe you would like – '

'No.' Mike turned back to the window. 'Not today.'

'Mike, ease up. Come on,' said Jay.

'You know why I came here.'

'But we're off duty.'

'I can't let this go. It's too important.'

'It's all you think about – work.' Jay yawned. 'Forget about it.'

Mike shook his head. How could he forget?

'Anyway, it's gone four. She's not around.'

'She could be anywhere here.'

'But you left a message for her in reception. She'd know where you were.'

'Yeah.'

'Maybe she's changed her mind about whatever it was she was going to tell you . . . if that's what she was going to do. I'm not sure that's what she had in mind for you, Mike.'

'Well, if she comes looking for me, tell her I'll be here at six.'

'What? Are you going somewhere?'

'Uh-huh.'

'Is this to do with last night?'

'Yeah.'

'Want back-up? Mike?'

'No.'

'Wait!'

Mike smiled as Jay swung his tanned legs off the couch; it was carried out with such an air of reluctance. Mike put his hand up.

'You said it. We're off duty. Stay here.'

He heard Jay's comment as he left the room: 'He's just not comfortable here. I'm sorry. No, of course it isn't your fault.'

The warm red brickwork of the corridor walls, and the mosaic tiles on the floor, were meant to give a feeling of charming old-world comfort; a sanitised version, of course, cleaned up, shot through with scented spray. Jay was right; Mike wasn't comfortable here. Truth was, he felt exposed – like the brickwork.

He went down the wide staircase to the large reception area, bathed in a flattering half-light and full of marbled pillars, leafy vines and small fountains which *tinkled*. Mike momentarily thought of rain, which didn't *tinkle*. And the thought of rain brought to his mind the picture of a boy lying dead in a doorway.

Occasionally a soothing voice would drown out the tinkling as the loudspeaker system advertised relaxation therapies, along with details of where they might be found within the Centre.

'Any messages for me?'

The girl at reception shook her head. She smiled at him.

'No, nothing for you, Mike . . . well . . .'

'Well?'

She had something to say and didn't appear to want to be overheard. Or perhaps she just wanted him to get closer. Mike leaned across the reception desk.

'I've got a friend . . . she likes the look of you, Mike . . . how about a party, just the three of us? Got some Stardust . . . make it good . . .'

'Mmm. I've got a better idea.'

'Have you? Tell me.'

'Go see my partner. He was just saying, he never has any fun these days.'

Mike removed himself from the desk and walked to the elevator. He hit the button and looked over his shoulder at the girl.

'Don't forget. Go see Jay. Tell him I sent you.'

Then the elevator arrived and he stepped in, closing the doors before anyone else could share the ride. He was going to a level that few were allowed to access.

He tapped in the code, and the elevator jolted. Down, down, down . . . down to the lowest level. When the doors opened, the brightness of the corridor made him blink; the light was harsh, the walls brilliant white. He walked to the end of the corridor, to another reception area, but this was very different to the Relaxation Centre; there was a clinical atmosphere, a bank of computer screens and several people engrossed in whatever those screens were showing. There were no girls offering Watchers a good time.

But there were Watchers.

'Hey, Mike.'

'Val, Rico.'

'Aren't you off duty?'

'That's right.'

The two Watchers grinned.

'You want information? Better enjoy the scenery.'

'Slow today, huh?'

'You got it.'

'Mike!'

He turned. The young nurse behind him smiled warmly.

'Are you well?'

Instead of answering with the customary 'Very well!' –

the standard greeting in the New Towns – Mike just said, 'Uh-huh,' and let his gaze linger for a moment. She *was* cute . . . blonde, with those very familiar bought blue eyes.

'I thought you were off duty today, Mike.'

'I am.'

'You should be relaxing.'

'Yeah. I guess.'

'Where's Jay?'

'Trying to be faithful to you.'

This brought a few deep laughs from the other Watchers. The nurse didn't seem to mind the laughter. Mike thought she probably trusted Jay. That was a bit of a novelty. He wondered how long they'd let Jay have Juno. Watchers weren't expected to have long-term relationships. It was said to be unhealthy for them . . . they were meant to be single, unattached – no favourites. It wasn't unusual for a Watcher to have a girl outside the Relaxation Centre, but the practice was not encouraged; still, it happened. Any girl who stuck around too long was always paid off sooner or later . . . and if she hadn't been particularly willing, she just disappeared. Mike couldn't remember how long Jay had been hung up on this nurse. But she seemed to like him, too, and that was dangerous . . . for her, and for him; what if he wouldn't let her go?

'Look, Mike, you'll be waiting forever. Can I help you?'

'I need to find new arrivals.'

'OK. Hold on.'

Juno went to one of the terminals.

'How did you get her to do that?' asked the Watcher Val.

'Just got it, I guess!' Mike shrugged.

'Yeah, right. Wouldn't mind *that* myself.'

'Jay's girl.'

'Well, when Jay's done.'

'Here you are, Mike.' Juno nodded at the screen. 'New arrivals . . . rooms five through nine. This level.'

'Thanks.'

'Be well, Mike.'

'Yeah. See you, guys.'

Mike made his way to rooms five through nine. They were situated almost at the end of another long, white corridor. He looked through the small glass panel of each until he saw what he wanted. Was the door locked? Yes. Of course.

'Hey!' he called to a medical orderly, who was checking a data sheet as he walked down the corridor. 'I want to see one of your . . . patients.'

The orderly stopped, and looked at the Watcher.

'All waiting for assessment.'

'Number five.'

'Not possible.'

'Now.'

'I'll have to confirm this with the doctor.'

'You do that. Open the door first.'

'I can't.'

'Open the door.'

'I've got to check first. You need permission. Would you like me to explain procedure?'

'Would you like me to explain what will happen to you if you don't open this door *now*?'

The orderly set his mouth in a firm line. But, as he considered who and what Mike was, he thought better of continuing with his protestations, and produced a bunch of electronic keys. He unlocked the door to room five.

'You've got a bad attitude,' Mike told him. 'That can be kind of dangerous, you know? Better change it. Understand?'

The orderly hurried away as Mike entered room five.

'Remember me?'

The thin-faced young man was sitting on the edge of the bed; his knuckles were white and he looked scared to death.

'Treating you well?' asked Mike, shutting the door.

'Yes. Oh, yes. Wonderful.'

Mike glanced around the blank little room.

'Well, that's just great.'

'Yes.'

'Given you a change of clothes, I see.'

'Oh yes. It's wonderful.'

'And a haircut.'

'I'm being assessed.'

'Yeah, I know.' Mike moved towards him, casually. 'Feel like talking to me?'

'What about?' The young man seemed to have trouble focusing on the Watcher.

'About last night.'

'Last night?'

'I asked you a question. You said you recognised a name.'

'Did I? I can't remember.' He began rocking slightly, backwards and forwards.

'Keep still and talk to me.'

'I can't remember.'

'David Drum.'

He kept rocking.

'I said, David Drum.'

'What?'

Mike moved closer.

'What do you know about David Drum?'

'I don't know him.' The patient stood up, suddenly. 'Are you here to re-Code me?'

'Not exactly.'

The young man was pacing, now. 'I wish they'd hurry up.'

'Talk to me about David Drum.'

'No one talks about that. Not to the Clean. Not even to the Aid workers.'

'Oh yeah?'

The door slapped open.

'Thank you for your interest in the patient. Now get out.'

'Doctor Stone . . . I haven't finished with your . . . *patient* . . . yet.'

'Yes you have.'

'You know, doctor, it's really not wise to annoy me. And you've been doing a lot of that lately. Maybe we should have a little chat about it. Huh?'

'What's happening?' asked the young man. 'Is everything all right?'

'Yes, everything's fine.' Doctor Stone didn't sound quite so calm as usual as he tried to reassure his patient. 'Do you need anything? No? Be with you shortly! Don't worry.'

'Must you lock me in?'

'Yes . . . I'm afraid so. It's for your own good. We have a lot of *undesirables* hanging around the MedCent. You never know who might just wander in . . . you know?'

The doctor locked the door.

'All right, Merrick. My office.'

'I hope that's a request.'

Doctor Stone silently indicated a room further up the corridor. Once inside, with the door closed, the doctor quickly snapped down some blinds which covered the window to the corridor. It was a small, very white, claustrophobic room. The only furniture was a chair and a large desk with some paperwork scattered on it, a computer, VidPhone, and a name plaque – 'Dr Fabian Stone' – with a quotation underneath it. This took Mike's eye because the quote wasn't the MedCent's well-known and well-used motto – 'Wellness and Wholeness, Health and Youth'. It simply said, 'You shall not die'.

Mike picked the plaque up and waved it in the doctor's face.

'What's this? Your hope for the future? Keep annoying me and it isn't going to happen.'

The doctor glared and snatched the plaque from the Watcher. He placed it on his desk with, to Mike, ludicrous precision. He still had his back to the Watcher as he began to speak.

'If this is about last night . . . I haven't reported you. But next time, I will.'

'You think that's what I'm here for? To find out if you reported me?'

Mike put his hand down on the desk beside the doctor. His voice was low.

'You think I care?'

Doctor Stone looked at him. Mike wasn't sure whether he saw fear in those slate-grey eyes, but he very much hoped so and decided to work on it.

'Merrick, I will *not* have you harassing my patients.'

'Going to try stopping me? How do you plan to do that, then, doctor? Enlighten me.'

Fabian Stone, not happy with the Watcher's very close proximity, tried to step away. But Mike wouldn't let him.

'Come on, I want to hear this. I'm interested.'

'I just don't want you bothering my patients.'

'Don't you? Well, that's too bad, doctor. I'm kind of good at "bothering".'

'What do you want from number five? He's got to rest . . . we're assessing him. You know what that means.'

'Oh yeah. I know what that means.'

'Couldn't we – look, Merrick, couldn't we come to some arrangement?'

'Arrangement? Well, let me tell you how it is. I'm not done with number five. OK? I'm coming back later and I don't want to find him drugged up, gone, or anything else . . . get it? I said, *get* it?'

The doctor managed a quick nod of the head.

'You know,' said Mike, standing away, 'you've got a stressful job. You want to do something about the pressure. You're trembling. Can't be good for the heart, can it?'

'Are you leaving?'

Mike was silent for a moment. Then he said, 'How old are you?'

'What? I'm – I'm thirty-eight.'

'I can check.'

'I know what you can do.'

'And I'll tell you what *you* can do. You can sort out the attitude of some of your staff members. Remind them that Watchers have access to *all* patients. No arguments, no stalling. OK?'

Doctor Stone nodded again.

'I'm so glad we understand each other. We do . . . don't we?'

'Yes – yes. We do.'

As Mike left the office, he glimpsed a half-open door to another room. The orderly with the bad attitude was talking to someone. Mike couldn't see who, but he heard a tremulous old voice: 'You're really going to give me new eyes?', and the orderly's reply: 'Yes, you're a pioneer! You're the first. The first of many, we hope.'

Yeah, thought Mike. You hope.

5

Age

Back in the Relaxation Centre, there was a different girl at the reception desk, but still no messages for Mike.

He ran a hand through his hair. What should he do next? Where was Sunny? She must be here by now. Maybe she was outside. He walked through the reception area and stood under the archway leading to the courtyard.

Sunlight shone down on the courtyard through the fine pseudo-glass covering the complex. Guests stood around, drinking in the Relaxation Centre's perfectly controlled environment. There was another girl on the low wall beside the fountain. Another Daughter of Love provided, they said, by some sort of supernatural love force. What was the name of that force? Mike couldn't remember. He didn't believe in forces of love which provided girls – and boys – any more than he believed in hell; the government was the provider. The women were well paid to be with the guests, but sleeping with Watchers was the highest earner. In fact, the Watchers themselves joked that they were providing a pension service for the girls' future security. And then, of course, there was the Stardust: available only for the Watchers, those pink tablets heightened the whole experience. Yes, the government certainly knew how to take care of its Watchers; they said it was a reward for all their hard work.

Mike didn't see any sign of Sunny. But he saw someone else.

'Mike!'

Stirling Cain, short, heavy and bejewelled with an unnatural thatch of blond hair, crossed the courtyard and put a thick arm round Mike's shoulder.

'Well, well. We don't see you here very often, my friend.'

Mike didn't like to think that Stirling Cain thought of him as a friend.

'It's good to see you here enjoying yourself.'

Mike didn't answer. He was wondering what he should do to encourage his boss to remove the arm that was now firmly placed around his back.

'You *are* enjoying yourself, I suppose?' Cain noticed Mike's discomfort and took his arm away. 'I don't think I've *ever* seen you let go . . . now look at that!'

Mike looked. 'James Oakley? Ferryman. So?'

'Oh, not him. He's very nearly as miserable as you. Over there, in the corner – talking to that Son of Love.'

Mike recognised with dislike the elegant affectations of the Watcher Rohan Adams. Rohan had been good-looking once. That ugly scar across his right cheek ruined his chiselled appearance.

'Now, he's not afraid to have a good time.' Cain sighed. 'Mike, I *want* my Watchers to enjoy themselves when they aren't working. They deserve it.'

'Rohan,' said Mike, 'deserves a lot of things.'

'I'd love to team you up with Rohan again, you're both so good . . . but I want you terminating the city scum, not each other.'

Cain beckoned Mike to follow, and walked to the fountain. He sat down heavily beside the Daughter of Love.

'Yes, later.' Cain put a weighty hand on her knee.

Mike felt compelled to sit beside his boss, and leaned forward, his arms resting on his knees.

'You're going grey.'

Cain was staring at Mike's thick black hair.

'I'm thirty-three,' said Mike.

Cain shifted uncomfortably and licked his lips. Mike smiled, and looked down at his hands.

'Thirty-three? Surely not. No, no. I would have said twenty-five.'

Mike smiled again and raised his eyes, meeting his employer's gaze.

'Oh yes, Mike. I would say twenty-five, easy.'

'Would you?'

Cain nodded and Mike noticed the blond thatch of hair beginning to darken on the too-smooth forehead. Cain wiped his brow.

'Getting hot, isn't it?' observed Mike.

'Twenty-five. Oh yes, Mike, I would say twenty-five . . . I *will* say it . . . more . . . I could take ten years off your age . . .' Cain slapped his palm onto Mike's leg. 'Yes Mike, if you like, you're twenty-three. How's that?'

'I'm thirty-three.'

'And I'm forty!'

Cain had been approaching that when Mike had started working for him, sixteen years before. Cain wiped his brow again. Mike had never seen him look so frightened.

'Do you know,' he said, 'I'm beginning to enjoy myself now.'

Cain eyed the Watcher, the man who executed the elderly.

'Well – that's fine. Excellent. Remember what I said. You may want my help one day soon. Very hard to get Credit you know . . . shouldn't be, but it is . . . once you've passed a certain milestone. I mean, some people even have

to go so far as to have their Code changed. It isn't strictly
legal, you know.'

'Yes,' said Mike, 'I kind of know that.'

'I'm beginning to feel almost worried myself, and I'm a
young man.'

'You're forty.'

'I am.'

Mike nodded and looked away. 'You're forty.' He
glanced back at his boss's flushed face. 'For now.'

'What?'

'Got to face facts,' said Mike, standing up, 'none of us
are getting any younger!'

'You don't want to believe everything you hear.'

'I don't.'

Cain stood up. 'Mike, let me do something for you.
You're my best Watcher. You deserve something. What
would you like?'

Mike's mind was blank. What would he like?

'A girl. You could do with a *good* girl. Yes . . . that's just
what you need. You don't like any of them here? No
problem. If you've seen someone you like – anywhere –
just say the word, and you've got her. Get yourself some
Stardust . . . enjoy yourself! You want a girl, Mike? Any
girl – I mean it – wherever, whoever. Just name her and
she's yours.'

'Yeah . . . OK.'

'Good!'

'Your daughter.'

'What!'

'Sunny.'

Mike watched the shocked expression on Cain's
features turn to distaste.

'Mike, Sunny's only fifteen.'

'I know.'

'Surely there must be some other – '

'No.'

'Sunny!' Cain sat down, wiping a hand over his face. 'Well, all right, but keep it quiet. I don't want this broadcast.'

'You don't want *what* broadcast?'

'You know . . . Mike, there are those who don't approve . . . government's daughters don't usually . . . well, not with *Watchers*.'

'No, not with *Watchers*,' agreed Mike, with irony.

'I don't know where she is. She was here earlier.'

'And now?'

'Not sure. I'll find her and send her round to you – if you really want her.'

'It's all right, Cain. I only want to talk to her.'

'Talk!'

'Talk,' said Mike, with a shrug.

Cain blinked a few times. 'Oh! This must be about her little trip into the city. That's why you want Sunny. It's work, isn't it!'

'What else?'

Cain stared up at the Watcher. 'Work! Don't you ever think of anything, other than what you do?'

'What else is there?'

'All this.' Cain gesticulated wildly.

'Oh yes, all this. Well, you should be glad I do my job so well. You pay me to do it.'

'The government pays you, my friend. Central office! I'm just your supervisor.' Cain shook his head. 'Supervisor! I couldn't supervise you. You just do it and I tell them what you've done.'

Mike was going to point out that Cain used to do it too, years ago, and that he was the only Watcher who ever retired and became a government official; although there were people who didn't think the head of the Watchers really deserved the kind of privilege normally given to *decent* members of the government. Still, Mike decided to keep that observation regarding Cain's past for another time – a time when he might need a little extra leverage.

'We're agreed? Take Sunny. Do what you like.'

'You know, if she keeps going into the old city she'll wind up dead.'

'Yes – yes. Very dangerous. That's true. I must do something about that. I'll speak to her . . . sometime soon.' Cain caught the eye of the Daughter of Love. She glanced down, and showed him what was in her open palm. Two little pink tablets. Cain's face brightened. 'Ah – Mike! I know where Sunny might be, if you want to find her quickly. She might be in the temple with Father.'

'All right.' Mike turned to leave, and then remembered something. 'Jay's put in for a transfer.'

'I know – first he puts in for a transfer of partners, now it's a transfer of duties. It's impossible. You know that. Can't happen.'

'I'd be grateful.'

There was silence. Then Cain said, slowly, without looking at Mike, 'Would you?'

'Yes.'

'Well, in that case . . .' Cain reached out a hand, and the girl took it. Cain smiled benevolently. 'I'll see what I can do. Can't promise anything, of course. Have to call in quite a few favours. Not easily accomplished . . . but for *you*, Mike . . . I'd rather like your gratitude.'

'Yes,' said Mike, 'I'm sure you would.'

Mike watched Cain and the girl walk away under one of the rose arches. He frowned and wondered why Sunny hadn't mentioned the name 'David Drum' to her father, because if she had, Cain would most certainly have told Mike about it. Mike was suddenly aware of his reflection in the pool. He ran a hand through his hair. Was he going grey? The fear that sometimes woke him in the middle of the night suddenly gripped him; it caught him by surprise. How had he lived so long? His best years were going, nearly gone, and they all seemed to merge into one. He didn't want to be old.

He sat down beside the pool and thought of Cain's offer of an extra ten years. But a new Code wouldn't make him younger. Laserscans might read it as younger, but he would know the truth. The weakness! The terrible weakness . . . smiling faces saying they were sorry, but Credit wasn't available . . . being thrown in the back of an armoured car, being dumped in the city . . .

He watched the guests wandering about, Credit-full and privileged, without a care in the world. They could live like this because the Watchers did their job thoroughly, removing the dross so there was no threat to orderly living. How would these guests react if the wild and the violent and the old and the sick and the unfit-to-live turned up here, in the middle of their society? They had the Watchers to thank for everything – and yet they merely tolerated their security force, privately thought them disgusting, wouldn't let their daughters anywhere near. What was it Mike had heard, a long time ago? 'A necessary evil.' Necessary evil! If there were no Watchers, thought Mike, what then?

Mike walked out of the courtyard, under a portico covered in pink blossom. The blossom wasn't real. The sickly scent caught in Mike's throat. Walkways guarded by white trellis led to more pools. Quiet, flower-strewn squares led off the walkways, squares which held marble statues of what people called a god. Old gods, new gods – here was Apollo, here Hermes, here Auran. Ah yes, Auran – the chief deity of the moment, the most popular, with his handsome smiling face, holding out hands full of Credit. How did you ever get out of this maze of gods?

Mike spat on the ground. He was no more interested in gods than he was in the so-called force of love.

'Michael! Well, here you are – and what are you doing?'

Mike waited for the familiar voice to address him again. It did, buoyant and free with intoxication.

'Spitting. That's illegal, you know.'

'So tell the Watchers.'

Rohan Adams laughed. 'Are you worshipping Auran, or are you trying to find your way out? What, not having a good time? There's a surprise.'

Mike faced the Watcher Adams. 'Following me, Rohan? Why's that?'

'Just wanted to confirm something.'

'Oh?'

'Jay's put in for a transfer.'

'Transfer of duties, yes.'

'Couldn't handle working with you, either, then.'

'Couldn't handle working with you, that's for sure.'

'I regret that. I liked him.'

'Yes, that was the problem.'

Rohan Adams' pale eyes glinted. 'Don't much like your tone, Michael.'

'That's good. You're not meant to.'

Rohan Adams took a step towards Mike.

'Oh, go on, Rohan! Do it! Just give me an excuse.'

Rohan fingered the scar on his face and stepped back. 'You should learn to relax. You're not as young as you were, Michael. You need more rest . . . otherwise you might start getting careless. And when you get careless . . .' Rohan raised his eyebrows.

'Step up again and you'll find out how careless I've become.'

'You know, Michael, I feel you would benefit from a visit to Father.'

'Really?'

'Perhaps he could re-birth you. You could find out if a past life has blocked some of your karma. Why, Michael, you could go along and find out just who you are!'

'I know what I am.' Mike turned away – and then turned back. 'Rohan, I think you should know – I requested you as my new partner.'

The smugness evaporated from Rohan Adams' face. 'You're joking.'

'You better hope so . . . still, you haven't got a partner at the moment, have you? Who was it, now . . . that young guy, new Watcher . . . what *did* happen to him?'

'He made a mistake. A very costly mistake.'

'Yeah, I heard that. Fished him out of the river, didn't they? What did they say about his injuries? Let me try to remember . . .'

'He let me down. He disappointed me.'

'Mmm. I bet he did. Good job there's me between you and Jay and the river, huh?'

With that, Mike walked out of Auran's square, out of the complex, out of the Relaxation Centre, out of what he considered to be the choking atmosphere of perfume and hypocrisy.

Where was Sunny? The temple? Mike spat again. He didn't want to go there but he was driven to find the girl. And so he headed towards the religious centre, fixing his thoughts on the job, the work, and pushing away the persistent echoes of Rohan Adams' mocking voice: 'You're not as young as you were, Michael. Not as young as you were.'

* * *

'The Festival of Auran.'

Shanna pulled a face. 'Ugh.'

'Well, it coincides with what the city people are planning.'

'That's just horrible.'

'What, the Festival, or what they're going to do?'

'I meant the Festival. Edward told me about it.'

Tristram sat down next to her, cradling a cup of water in his hands.

'I mean, I know the priests help out with the Aid and everything, and the people say they're so good, and kind, and all the rest of it, but do you know what they *do* at the Festival?' Shanna shuddered. 'No, I can't tell you. I can't even bring myself to talk about it.'

'OK.'

'I mean, do you know what they *do*, Tristram?'

'No. You're not telling me, remember?'

'And all in the name of that god thing.'

'Auran.'

'No wonder some of the people in the city have a weird attitude when you start to talk about belief and why we come here and do what we do. They must think we're like – that.'

'Explains a lot. I didn't know anything about Auran until you just told me what you didn't tell me!'

'He's one of the new ones . . . a new god. I wonder who dreamt him up?' Shanna frowned. 'How did you get them to tell you about the plan to trap a Watcher? I couldn't get anything out of Edward or any of them.'

'Lou . . . the girl Gideon's been helping . . . she told me.'

'Oh? Perhaps she likes you, Tris.'

'No, I think she likes Gideon. Quite a lot.' He smiled easily at her. 'He says she listens to everything he's telling her about why we do it.'

'Well, there's nothing we can do in this particular situation. We can hardly warn them – even if we wanted to.'

Tristram's smile faded. 'Would we want to? There's the question.'

'Gideon would if he could.'

'I know.'

'You know where the trap is?'

'Oh yes.'

'Will it work?'

'I don't know.'

Shanna stood up. 'Oh well.'

After a few moments, Tristram spoke again. 'We might be able to do *something*.'

Shanna said nothing. Tris got to his feet and stood behind her.

'I know how you feel about them. I feel the same. I'm no different to you.'

'Yes you are,' she answered. 'You struggle more with it. I don't. I'm not going to pretend.'

'Struggle? Oh yes, I struggle, Shanna. You don't know how much.'

'Did you ever kill a Watcher?'

Tristram's response was quick and sharp. 'I never trapped and tortured one.'

'I'm sorry. I shouldn't have said that.'

'It's OK . . . I'm sorry too.' Tris shook his head. 'So what are we going to do?'

'I don't know, Tristram. I just don't know.'

'Tell David?'

'Yes . . . I guess. Tell David.'

6

Sunny

The white marble building shone with a pure brilliance
in the early evening light. Mike looked up at the massive
temple, dominating the skyline of this part of the New
Towns. Spotting a man in a white robe, arms spread out
in welcome as he greeted women who, with armfuls of
almost realistic scented blooms, ascended the temple
steps, Mike felt an overwhelming feeling of contempt. He
really didn't like priests.

Still, Sunny might be in there. So Mike walked across
the pavement to the temple steps, and met the gaze of
the priest. Mike saw revulsion and fear in the priest's
eyes. Was this the one who had snatched the boy from
the city streets? No. But he'd been in the truck the night
before.

'Welcome to the Temple of the Free Church!' the priest
said, with a very wide and very false smile.

'Yeah, all right.'

'Er – you're not – er – coming in? Are you?'

'Looks like it.'

'Ah . . . that's just . . . fine. Um . . . Can I help you?'

'Out here on the steps, you mean?'

'Well . . . there are people in there . . . praying.'

'And you think if I walked in I might give them
something to *really* pray about.'

'This is a sanctuary, my son.'

48

Mike lowered his voice and the priest had to crane his neck in order to hear him. 'I'm not your son. OK?'

'Er – no. No, of course not. Quite. I – er – apologise.'

'I'm looking for someone.'

'Well, that's not – '

'I believe she's with Father.'

'This is a sanctuary.'

'Then I'll see Father.'

'You need an appointment.'

'He'll see me.'

'He is preparing for the Festival of Auran tomorrow. He will not see you.'

Mike put a hand on the priest's arm and applied a little pressure. 'You will *ask* him to see me.'

The priest's too-taut features were almost as white as his robe. Mike's size and stance and grip were just as threatening as his known occupation.

'Very well. If you insist.'

'Oh . . . I do.'

'All right. All right. Wait here.'

The priest disappeared through the white panelled doors of the temple, closing them behind him. Mike didn't like being shut out like that. He pushed the doors open and walked into the temple hall.

It was huge, high-arched, with row upon row of carved wooden seats. The great altar, set on a marble dais, was radiant with gleaming cups of gold and silver. Raising his eyes to the ceiling, Mike saw a bold mural stretching the length of the hall, depicting life in all its fullness – he could hardly miss the mass of naked people and vines. There was a gallery, too, but no windows. Light emanated from the many statues; statues of the very same gods which could be found in the Relaxation Centre complex.

'He will not see you.'

The priest, emerging from a curtained doorway behind the altar, was trying to cover his agitation with a serene smile, but failing.

'However,' he went on, 'he suggests you enter any prayer or request on the Sacred Paper which will be offered at the altar tonight in the usual way.'

The usual way. Mike laughed out loud. His laughter echoed round the temple and made the women, who were arranging the flowers by the altar, clutch at each other.

Perhaps hearing the laughter, another priest appeared from a side door. He saw Mike, recognised him, and turned round, but froze to the spot when Mike announced, very loudly,

'I'm looking for someone!'

'Lower your voice!' hissed the first priest. 'Have you no respect?'

'Not much. Your friend over there looks kind of worried, doesn't he? Why do you think that is?'

'We aren't accustomed to . . . to . . .'

'To having Watchers walk into the temple.'

'Well, not quite in this way . . . still, you'd be surprised how popular religion is becoming with the – er – members of our security force.'

'You know, I *would* be surprised at that.'

'I'm telling you the truth. Several of the security – er – team – are proving to be most ardent worshippers.'

'Oh yeah? But they don't usually come in the front way, huh?'

'Well, it does tend to worry the other members of the congregation.'

'Don't move!' Mike ordered the second priest, who had been quietly edging back out of the side door. He froze again when he heard the Watcher's voice. 'Maybe I should go question *him*, huh? Think he'd be more – sensitive – to my request?'

The first priest became even more agitated. 'No! Look, my s – look, I told you, Father – '

'Is she with Father? Or not? It's that simple.'

'I can't say.'

'Priest . . . I know where that side door leads.'

'What door? We've got many doors.'

'Don't mess with me.'

'We haven't done anything illegal.'

'You mean, like, taking the boy?'

'The boy? What boy?'

'You know what boy.' Mike indicated to the second priest. '*He* did it . . . you were in on it . . . and there was another priest, too, wasn't there?'

'Doctor Stone said – '

'Doctor Stone isn't here.'

'Watcher!' said one of the women, just loud enough for Mike to hear. 'How dare he come to this sacred place?'

'It's all right, sister,' called the priest. 'What beautiful flowers! May Auran bless you.'

The woman glared at Mike.

'Is she the one you're looking for?' whispered the priest. 'I've got no information on her, but I can find some.'

'No.'

'You're disturbing the atmosphere . . . it's not good.'

'Disturbing the atmosphere . . . mmm. Maybe I should come disturb the atmosphere more often. You think?'

The priest bit his bloodless lip anxiously. 'Oh, all right, all right. There's no one with Father. No one.'

Was he telling the truth? Mike didn't know.

'I see you are not a believer,' remarked the priest, as Mike moved away from him. 'But we all have our paths to follow. Your path is obviously not to worship the gods in this life.'

'Oh, I'm sure of that,' replied Mike.

'And remember what Father has said. Your prayers and requests, on the Sacred Paper . . . there's a supply of the Paper at the entrance to the small shrine in the temple garden and a hole in the wall for you to – '

'You know, I get the feeling you're not keen for me to return.'

'The gods read the Sacred Paper – '

Mike beckoned the priest to come closer and he came, very reluctantly.

'I know who reads it, and it isn't the gods. Remember who you work for. I know how you come by your information.'

The priest opened the temple doors.

'No need to raise your voice. That's not doing any of us any good, is it? As a matter of fact,' he said, quite loudly now, 'I think the Watchers do a fine job, sending the lost and the sad and the bad and the poor suffering elderly and terminally sick to a glorious new incarnation.'

'. . . and the young and the Illegal. And sometimes even priests.'

The priest seemed to have some trouble swallowing. 'Well, thank you so much for your presence in the temple. What an honour it was . . . Indeed, some say you are more than men.'

'And most say we are less.'

The priest opened the doors even wider. Mike felt frustrated but he didn't have the authority to make a member of the government talk to him if they didn't want to. Still, he got a kick out of eyeing the priest with menace as he left the temple.

'You have anger. We could help!' called the priest.

'Anger? Mmm. Plenty of that!' Mike assured him. 'And I don't need any help with it.'

'Well, the offer's there . . . we don't turn anyone away from the Free Church. Not even – not even – '

'You know, you should thank me for my anger. It helps to keep the Towns safe, doesn't it?'

The priest didn't seem to know how to reply, and Mike wasn't going to hang around waiting for any more false compassion. He was glad to get away from the temple, and those priests . . . yes, they were well paid in Credit and changes of Code for their help in pinpointing and catching Illegals. But for all their usual assistance, Mike utterly despised them for their deception. He decided to go home and wait for Cain to send his daughter there.

In the street, he hopped onto a Town Car, found a seat, and watched the Town go by. A tiny child was crying, and Mike looked across the wide aisle. An older woman put an arm round the little girl.

'Watcher! She's legal. We've got nothing to hide.'

Mike half-smiled, and looked away. He noticed the woman and child got off the car at the next stop.

He was the last passenger when the car finally ended its outward route. It stopped where the habitable buildings did. Ahead stretched the broad highway which led straight to the next New Town, and from there, to the next and the next, spreading out like a spider's web.

Mike's ground floor apartment was in a featureless grey building right away from the rest of society. The Clean didn't, after all, want Watchers living among them. The *decent* people of the Towns barely tolerated them even at the Relaxation Centre, but, as the government admitted, you had to give them *something*. Still, the government also thought it best to keep a little distance – it would be unthinkable for Watchers to make any real friends within the Clean community . . . just in case a friend's status suddenly changed and it became necessary to take a trip to the city. As the government said, it was very unfair to place any Watcher in that position – they were human beings, after all.

Mike stood at the door, and the scanner acknowledged his Code. There was the customary delay before it opened, and Mike turned and stared at the old city, just visible beyond the highway. A thin wispy yellow vapour trailed across the evening sky from the processing plant just out of Town. Mike kicked at the gravel path. Some of it showered onto the synthetic grass.

The door clicked. Mike went in. And as he caught his likeness in the mirror on the wall, he felt suddenly, unutterably, tired. Was it his age? Perhaps he really should rest more; it was just so hard for him to switch off. Still, he figured he might as well try, and headed for the bedroom.

'What the – ' His hand went to his thigh as he pulled a knife.

'It's illegal to carry a knife. It's illegal to have a weapon in the Towns. Honestly, Mike, I should report you to the Watchers.'

'Sunny!' Mike put the knife away, almost consumed with anger. 'I could have killed you!'

She was in his bed.

'Really, Mike, you do get so wound up, don't you?' She smiled at him. 'Come and relax.'

'How did you get in here?' Mike looked about the room, saw a pile of her clothes on a chair, and threw them at her. 'Get dressed.'

'Oh, Mike!' she wailed, her fair hair falling about her shoulders, 'Don't you ever want to have any fun?'

She sidled into the kitchen, eventually, fully dressed. Mike leaned back against the worktop, his temper under control. He wanted to know how she got in, but he guessed she could probably get in anywhere; anyway, now she was here, he could ask her about David Drum.

'Don't you like girls, Mike?'

Mike folded his arms.

'I like to pick my own girls.'

'But you don't, do you? Haven't – not for a long time.' Sunny ran her hand along one of the work surfaces and raised her eyes to meet his.

'How do you – that's none of your business!' For a moment, he thought she was pretty – green eyes dominating a heart-shaped face. Natural colour, natural body; she hadn't quite reached the age yet where she needed anything enhanced.

'You wanted to see me, though, didn't you? You came to the Centre.'

'You knew I was there?'

'I got your message. Just thought this might be a little more private. You know, I found some alcohol under your bed. It's illegal to have alcohol outside the Relaxation Centre. You like breaking the rules, don't you, Mike? Come on . . . let me thank you *properly* for rescuing me.'

'Sunny, the information. I need to know what you know.'

'Perhaps if you're really nice to me I'll tell you everything.'

Mike lunged forward and grabbed her by both arms. She squealed in sudden terror.

'Listen to me, little girl. I'm losing my patience.'

'Mike, don't!'

'You can either tell me everything now or you can get out. Don't play games with me.'

'Let go!'

'Why didn't you tell your father about the name?'

'Let *go*!'

Relenting, he let her go. 'Why didn't you tell Cain about David Drum?'

'I'm going. You hurt me. I'm not telling you anything.'

'Well, that's withholding information.'

'What information?' She tossed her hair and looked petulant. 'I haven't got any. Anyway, you've upset me now, and I'm leaving. Look at my arms. They're red where you hurt me.'

'You had the name – what else do you know?'

'You should be careful how you treat me, Mike. I know that much. You see, I'm really clever. I've got many talents. I'm good at telling stories, for instance. I could tell my father anything about what happened here today and you'd be in real trouble, wouldn't you?'

Mike laughed suddenly. 'You have no idea!'

'You'd die! Do you find that funny?'

Mike laughed again, and Sunny stared at him in bewilderment.

'Do you want to die, Mike?'

'Oh get out. I've had enough of you.' He turned away from her.

'You do, don't you? Mike? Why do you want to die?'

'I said, get out!' Mike's fist connected with the worktop.

Sunny said nothing, but made a move towards the door. Mike went with her to make sure she actually left and didn't dart off into another room to appear later as an accompaniment to his nightmares.

'Mike, maybe I could come back sometime when you're feeling – '

'I don't feel, and you're not coming back.'

'What if I got some Stardust?'

'Out – now.'

Sunny hesitated. 'OK. But I'll tell you one thing – '

Mike's hopes rose.

'You've got the most gorgeous brown eyes.'

* * *

'You're late!'

Sunny ignored Rohan Adams' remark as she ran up the steps of the temple.

'Father's waiting for you,' said Rohan.

'Get out of my way.'

'I said, you're late. He's not going to be happy about that.'

'How do you know I'm late?'

'Just warning you, that's all.'

'It's nothing to do with you.'

'You know it is.'

Rohan Adams stood aside, and Sunny pushed open the great white doors.

'You won't keep me waiting,' said Rohan, 'when the time comes.'

'You do talk a load of –'

Rohan Adams caught her arm, stopping her from entering the temple.

'I'm close to Father, remember. Very close.'

'So am I!' She yanked her arm from the Watcher.

'One day you'll be kneeling at my feet.'

'Anybody would think you were Father,' said Sunny, scornfully.

Rohan Adams smiled. It was an unpleasant smile, and Sunny was suddenly scared.

'It's amazing what the gods reveal,' said Rohan. 'The past, the future . . .'

'I'll tell Father.'

Rohan threw his head back and laughed. 'There's nothing you could tell him that he doesn't already know.'

'I hate you, Rohan Adams.' She slipped into the temple. 'I really hate you.'

'Maybe so. But you'll still kneel.'

7

Encounters

Doctor Stone fingered the plaque on his desk. He nodded vigorously.

'Yes . . . yes . . . I know . . .'

The person on the other end of the VidPhone squawked at him and he kept nodding.

'Yes . . . I know . . . very inconvenient. Have to get some new specimens but they don't want us taking anyone fit enough for the processing plants . . . no, it ruins them . . . the toxicity . . . yes, I *know* people are relying on surgery . . . yes, I know what you want . . . but you'll have to wait. What? Well, I can get young ones, but they're insisting I use the poorer specimens and some of them *are* poor, I can tell you. Most of the fitter ones are kept for the labour-force, but there's such a shortage at present – the Watchers have had to put down some riots lately – yes, there was that big one – and let's just say they've been a bit over-zealous and the young, fit – '

The office door opened, very slightly.

'Get out!'

It banged shut.

'What? No, just an orderly. Yes . . . I can probably get . . . yes . . . well, I've had to cut back on *that* kind of research. They only permit me to use the over-forties at present . . . of course I'm not happy about it! Do I *look* happy? What? Oh, that . . . Yes, the old man died . . . it didn't work . . . the eyes didn't . . . yes, I know it's irritating. But what can I do? My hands are tied, thanks to the – '

The door opened again.

'I said get *out*! What's the matter with you? Are you stupid?' Doctor Stone shook his head and fixed his gaze on the VidPhone. 'No, of course I wasn't talking to you. What? Well, there's no need to be like that . . . it's not *my* fault . . . you want to lay the blame on anyone, you look at those cretinous sub-humans in the armoured cars . . . what the – '

The door slammed, someone moved swiftly to his desk, a hand came down, the VidPhone link was severed and the doctor had a bloody nose.

'Merrick! You've broken my nose!'

'I wanted the one in five kept alive. I *told* you I hadn't finished with him!'

'What! Do you mean he's *not* alive?' The doctor scrabbled around, trying to find something to stem the blood-flow. Mike waited whilst the doctor grabbed several sheets of paper in a futile attempt to cope with the problem. 'This is a – this is outrageous! I'll have you for this, Merrick!'

'Don't threaten me . . . what did you do to him?'

'Nothing! Nothing!'

Mike shoved the doctor against the wall.

'I didn't! I didn't do anything to him! I didn't want him dead – he wasn't in brilliant shape, but I'm desperate – '

'Want *me* to show you desperate? Huh?'

The doctor was panicking. 'No! Look, I don't know what all this is about! Rohan Adams – '

'Rohan? What's he got to do with it?'

'Adams wanted to talk to him. That's all.'

Mike released the doctor.

'What? Why?'

'Why? Why? How should I know?' The doctor wiped the blood on his sleeve. 'Put "why" and "Watchers" in one sentence – I've got no answers!'

'Why would Adams be interested in that Illegal?'

'I don't know . . . he asked to look at the ones we picked up the other night, and he wanted to spend some time with number five. Just like you did.'

'When was this?'

'About half an hour ago. Oh! My nose . . . do you know what this nose cost?'

'Tell me about number five.'

'What's to tell? Young, early twenties, not particularly strong, but he'd do. His heart, lungs, everything worked . . .'

'Anything unusual about him?'

'The only unusual thing about him was that he attracted a lot of attention from top Watchers.' The doctor dabbed at his nose. 'If this was Adams – oh, it really is too bad. Government interference in medical matters! I'm going to lodge a complaint.'

The door was open again now. The orderly with the attitude peered in.

'Doctor Stone? There's been an accident in room five – oh!'

'Stay there! Don't move!' The doctor snatched several more sheets of paper and held them to his face. Now that he had a witness, he was bolder. 'Merrick, this time I *will* report you. You – you're all animals! Do you know what kind of material I have to work with because of you? So heavy-handed in the cull, there's hardly anything out there I'm permitted to use that's any good! It's causing a great deal of anxiety, you know, in high office! And when I *do* get something, this is what happens! You –'

'Where's Adams now?'

'How should I know?'

The orderly was staring at the doctor's nose, and then he noticed Mike's attention was directed towards him.

'He – he left!' the orderly stuttered.

'Did he say where he was going?'

'No.'

'Shut the door. Let's find out how sure you are about that information.'

'Tell him!' spat the doctor. 'I don't want any more trouble! Tell him, if you know!'

'I don't! I swear. I don't! He didn't say anything. He just left!'

Mike looked at the doctor. 'You want to do something about all that blood. It'll frighten the patients.'

As Mike walked away, the doctor pushed the orderly aside and shouted after him.

'Stick to doing what you're meant to do . . . leave the fit and the young ones alone!'

The elevator took Mike up to ground level. His mind was buzzing with questions, and he wasn't thinking about what he looked like – the doctor's blood was splashed all over his shirt. As the doors zapped open, and as he stepped into the MedCent's deep-carpeted, plush public seating area, he was suddenly aware of his appearance – several people uttered small cries of dismay, some walked out – quickly – and one or two of them ducked down behind seats, kneeling in spilt coffee.

The MedCent had already been crackling with the nervous tension of those who had been unable to buy their way out of the compulsory yearly health check; there was always the underlying fear that if you failed the test, you would never return from your routine check-up. Having a Watcher appear from the elevator covered in blood didn't help. Mike cursed, took his shirt off, and rammed it into the nearest waste disposal bin. The black T-shirt underneath didn't show the stain – much. It was illegal for Watchers to walk about in society with anything about their persons that might cause the general populace distress.

'Guy just came down in the elevator. Tall, light-coloured hair, scar on his cheek. Anyone see where he went?'

No one spoke.

'I said, anyone see where he went?'

A woman pointed to the entrance.

'Which direction?'

'I'm – I'm not sure.'

'I saw him as I came across the plaza,' volunteered a man, nervously. 'He was heading towards the temple.'

'OK.'

Mike walked to the sliding panel of smoky pseudo-glass. A metallic female voice said, 'Be well!' as he crossed the threshold. And then he stood on the smooth pavement they called the plaza.

The plaza was one of those clean, wide areas with creamy pavement blocks that were scattered through-out the New Towns. Here was a fountain ... more tinkling ... and there, on the wall of one of the towering buildings, the constantly displayed video advertising campaign. 'Be well ... working together for *your* health, prosperity and well-being,' and two women in a so-called conversation extolling the delights of Town living: it was a feel-good thing that made Mike sick and he tried to ignore the upbeat, cheerful, relentless drip-drip-drip of those sugary voices as he made his way past the government block and the Relaxation Centre, and headed across the plaza to the temple.

As he walked, he was deep in thought and oblivious to everyone else. As it was a Festival day, no one was supposed to work, but many did ... it wasn't illegal. Anyway, a lot of the population had to; society was very harsh towards those who hadn't 'provided' for

their future – amassed enough Credit either to avoid
debt when age meant you weren't so easily and readily
employed, or to buy a furtive extension to life – the
ultimate, illegal and unspoken ambition of them all.
There was little sympathy for those who couldn't provide for their future security; it was even said they
deserved all they got. And what they got, of course,
was the old city. Anyone who didn't like the way
things were, simply disappeared; there were lots of
Watchers about, and the government paid well for
information.

Certainly, life in the Towns had its attractions. If you
were healthy and young (or your Code said you were
young) life was generally good – very good indeed for
those in the positions of privilege to which all aspired.
The constant seeking after prosperity was excellent for
the economy; and anyway, what was the alternative? Still,
there was a constant feeling of almost tangible fear in the
New Towns, which Mike rather enjoyed; after all,
Watchers had a lot to do with it. But he enjoyed nothing
else and loathed the slick greetings of Clean people
brightly, and just with that *hint* of desperation, chanting,
'Are you well?' '*Very* well!' as they hurried about their
business. 'Be well!' they said to each other. 'Be well!' –
and a child, excited by the Festival day, ran straight into
the Watcher.

The mother's face was a study in horror as she realised
what had happened. Mike looked down at the boy – he
was about nine years old.

'I'm – I'm sorry!' the mother blurted. 'It's my fault. I
should have kept him closer to me. I'm sorry.'

'Control it. OK?'

'Yes. OK. OK.'

The sun beat down as Mike ran up the temple steps.
He had hoped he wouldn't have to come here again so

soon. The expression on the priests' faces as he strode into the temple mirrored that sentiment.

The temple was awash with flowers – but few people. That evening, the climax of the Festival of Auran would take place. Mike wasn't sure what happened at the Festival but he had a good idea. He guessed most of the worshippers were trying to reserve their energy for what would probably be a lively few hours.

One of the priests – the one he had spoken to before – was talking to a very familiar figure, near the altar. The other priests discreetly faded away as the Watcher walked up the centre aisle.

Rohan Adams, quizzing the priest, had his back to Mike.

'So, any more information? Any more of his Sacred Papers? What's the matter? Look at me.'

'Did you say I was getting careless, Rohan? Keeping your back to the doors . . . now *that's* careless.'

'I heard you come in, Michael.' Rohan looked at him, briefly. 'We all did. Not exactly quiet, are you?' He turned to the priest. 'Oh, stop looking so worried. He's not going to do anything to you. Go away. I'll speak with you later.'

The priest scuttled off.

'All right, Rohan. What's going on?'

'What's going on? The Festival of Auran . . . might just catch the start but I'll have to leave when my shift begins. A shame, but there it is.'

'You know what I mean.'

'I heard you were here before – only yesterday, in fact. Suddenly found a spiritual side?'

'I'll tell you what I've suddenly found. I've found a dead body in room five at the MedCent.'

'So?'

'So, what were you doing there?'

'Michael, I'm not completely happy with the way you're addressing me.'

'Answer my question.'

Rohan narrowed his eyes. 'Who do you think you're talking to? Some Unclean city scum?'

Mike moved closer to him – and Rohan glanced upwards. For a moment, Mike thought Adams was shooting up a prayer to one of the myriad of gods, but as he looked up, he saw the two Watchers Val and Rico standing in the gallery.

'Isn't it intriguing,' commented Rohan, with a smile, 'how very popular worship is becoming with Watchers!'

'They'd be glad if I took you out right now.'

'Perhaps.' Rohan's cold eyes glinted. 'But can you be sure of that, Michael? Really, *really* sure?'

'I guess we could find out. Huh, Rohan? What do you say? I'm willing to chance it. Are you?'

Rohan glanced up again. Val and Rico had vanished.

'All right, Rohan. What's really going on here?'

'Michael, you really are uptight these days.'

'Let's have it.'

Rohan sighed deeply in a very affected manner. 'Have what?'

'David Drum.'

'Who?'

'David Drum. Come on. You've heard that name before.'

'Have I?'

'Long time ago.'

Rohan turned away. 'I'm not in the mood to talk about the past.'

'Who did it – a long time ago? Was it you?'

'Hmm . . . a poor memory. Not a good sign, Michael. Could be your age, couldn't it? Well, you'll have to excuse me. I have to see Father.'

'David Drum, Rohan. What do you know?'

Rohan Adams' voice was quieter now, and very level. 'I said I'm not in the mood to talk about the past. Perhaps your hearing is going as well.'

'It seems pretty strange to me that you'd target the Illegal in number five unless you knew . . .' Mike wheeled round and fixed his eyes on the priest, who was hanging around by a flower-strewn statue depicting the smiling, benevolent Auran, '. . . unless you *knew* I'd been questioning him about something you were interested in.' It had slipped into Mike's mind: that priest had been standing nearby when he'd been talking to that thin-faced young man in the city.

'I am just about fed up with this . . . with you. You may have a poor memory, but I don't. I tend to remember people, and events, and conversations, and actions, and attitudes, small slights, wrong words, and *enemies*, in incredible detail. I think it's a gifting, don't you? It helps, you know, Michael – when it comes to *dealing* with people.'

'If you've got such a fantastic memory, you'll remember David Drum.'

Rohan averted his gaze and nodded towards the priest. 'I'm coming now.'

'No you're not.'

'Michael, take your hand off my arm.'

'Or what?'

'Take your hand off my arm *now*.'

'Talk to me.'

'Your hand, Michael.'

'Talk.'

'Is your memory so far gone that you can't remember that it's illegal to stop anyone from keeping an appointment with Father? I would *very* much like to –'

'Yeah, I know you would.' Mike released him. 'I haven't finished with you, Rohan.'

'Goodbye, Michael.'

'I mean it. We're not done.'

'Oh, I think we are. Yes, I think we are.'

* * *

Someone was behind her. Before she could turn, Sunny felt the hand on her shoulder, and jumped.

'Don't be afraid. It's me.'

'Oh.'

She watched Mike leave the temple.

'He's the one.'

'Good choice, Sunny. Yes, good choice.'

She stepped out from behind the curtain and frowned, because Rohan Adams was standing in her way. She tried to walk past him, but he stopped her.

'Was it you?'

'What?'

'You said something to him. Didn't you?'

'What about?'

'You know what about.'

'No.'

'Are you sure?'

'Don't talk to me like that,' said Sunny, haughtily. 'My father is a powerful man.'

Rohan Adams sneered. 'Powerful?' A malevolent smile spread over his face. 'You have no idea of power, Sunny Cain . . . No idea at all.' And he disappeared behind the curtain for his audience with Father.

* * *

Something about that encounter had left Mike feeling drained. He was hungry – he couldn't remember the last time he'd had a meal. So he grabbed some fast food from one of the super-clean little cafés in the plaza and sat down beside the fountain.

The advertising was still going on. The women were continuing their interminable conversation.

'The MedCent do everything they can . . . antibiotics in the food and water . . . always working to cure sickness . . . going to them and giving Aid . . . yes, even to those who don't deserve it!' 'Still, we provide them with constructive work to help society.' 'Oh, yes! They can really be productive and live useful lives!'

They meant the processing plants, of course. It was laughable. Mike nearly choked on whatever it was he was eating. The plants produced the stuff that was made into food . . . Vermalyde. It was a marvellous invention and nobody had to eat animals any more – which was just as well, because there weren't many around: people said they were full of dirt and disease, but at least no one had to be cruel to them and use them for food any longer. (They didn't use them for experiments, either, but nobody thought about what they *did* use.) The only problem was – and the nice Clean ordinary people didn't know it – Vermalyde had a toxic effect in its raw state that had unpleasant consequences for anyone who handled it for too long. Which was why they always needed new labour from the city.

The thought of this made Mike suddenly lose his appetite. Tasteless, bland trash. He threw it in the nearest bin and wondered what to do about Rohan Adams. There was something weird going on; something didn't feel right. He was certain there was something he should know that he didn't know and he hated that feeling; but how to get any information from Adams? That would be difficult. He'd have to handle that very carefully.

'I don't know one person who is really sick, do you?'
'No. And I don't know anyone who is really poor.' 'And
everyone seems to be getting younger!' Laughter. 'Be
well.' 'Yes – be well!'

8

The Return

'Get your hands off the grille!' The hands disappeared as the passenger in the back of the armoured car obeyed Mike's order. He turned to his partner. 'You OK tonight?'

'Yeah.'

'Sure?'

'Uh-huh.'

'The rest did you good, then.'

'I guess.'

'Did you see the girls?'

'What girls? Oh – *those* girls. Yeah – thanks, partner! I had a job to get rid of them, convince them I wasn't interested.'

'And you weren't?'

'Mike! Do you know how hard it is to be faithful?'

'No. Never tried it.'

The armoured car drew up at the city wall just as the Gate opened and two vehicles came out.

'New recruits for the plant,' said the Gate guard.

Jay watched the vehicles speed away. 'Did they have much trouble?'

'The usual . . . think they had a few problems, but some of them are actually keen to go. Amazing, huh?'

'Yeah, well. Perhaps they figure it's a better bet than *this*.'

'They're crazy.'

'Come on,' said Mike. 'Pass us through.'

'It's bad tonight,' commented the Gate guard.

'It's always bad,' replied Jay.

Gazing into the looming city, Mike could see several fires. Flames were licking up the side of a tall building. The places that weren't lit rested in darkness. It was unpredictable, that dumped waste . . . and not many people knew that the stuff was the result of the first few attempts to create Vermalyde.

'I hate this night shift,' muttered Jay.

'Be great if the whole place went up, eh?' the guard grinned.

'No,' said Mike. 'You'd just have a whole new set of problems to deal with.'

'How many places are there like this? What do you think, Mike?' asked Jay.

'Old cities? Too many. Too few. I don't know.'

Jay wiped sweat from his forehead. 'It's a hot night. It's always worse on a hot night.'

Was that fear now, in Jay's voice?

'Come on. Drive.'

The Gate was open. Jay was hesitating.

'What's up?' asked Mike, not looking at him.

'Nothing.'

'Jay?' Now Mike looked.

Jay glanced into the back of the car.

'It's just a hot night.'

'Jay,' said Mike, 'drive.'

One of the passengers began to sob.

'Quiet!' ordered Mike. 'And get your hands off the grille! OK, let's go. Take the left turning – to the river.'

'To the fire.'

Again Mike looked at Jay. It was more than a hot night that was making Jay jumpy.

'Move, Jay. Do it.'

Jay obeyed.

'Over the water!' Mike exclaimed, suddenly. 'Can you believe it? I tell you, I can't.'

'What?'

'It's not possible to get out of the city by water. There are barriers up and down the river – no one could get through. Sunny said David Drum was helping people escape over the water. What does that mean? Across the sea? I've thought about it. They couldn't do it. They'd never even get out of the city by water.'

'I think you should forget this.'

'No way. I've got to tell you – '

More sobbing.

'. . . sometime.' Mike frowned. 'Hey, would you say Val and Rico are pretty tight with Rohan?'

Jay shrugged.

'Mmm. Got to talk to you after the shift.'

'I'm seeing Juno after the shift.'

'She can wait.'

'She's thinking of leaving the MedCent. Doesn't like some of the stuff . . .'

'What, just *some* of it?'

'She wants to get out.'

'Yeah?' said Mike, with absolutely no interest.

Jay wiped his brow again. 'Do you ever want to get out, Mike? Get away?'

Mike stared at him. 'Where to?'

'I don't know.'

'Jay, you and I are going to have a long talk after this shift.'

'Oh yes . . . the name.'

'Not just about that. You've been with that girl too long.'

'Don't even suggest it.'

'What?'

'I'm with Juno, Mike, that's it. But I'll talk to you about

the rest . . . this name . . . got to tell you, I think your source is unreliable.'

'Sunny Cain? Unreliable isn't the word I'd use . . . I can think of a few others.'

'She just likes you. That's all there is to it.'

'No. Jay, believe me – '

'Can't you just believe someone would *like* you?'

Mike ignored that remark. He tapped his fingers impatiently on the car dashboard.

'I wish I could remember the name of that sect.'

'What sect?'

'David Drum . . . Kurt Dane . . . they were involved in that – what was it? What *was* that sect? Illegal religious group – had the death penalty. I just can't get the name.'

'Christian.'

'That's it.'

Jay turned the car. As they got closer they could clearly see the blazing tall building. There were screams and shouts and a drumming noise coming from that area. It was as if the inhabitants of the city were celebrating the destruction. The car stopped.

'Now what?'

'I'm not getting any closer to that building, Mike. If it falls, it will fall into the road. There must be another way to the river.'

'You know there is. Do you seriously want to try it?'

Jay tightened his grip on the steering wheel.

'If you want to go to the river, we've got no choice.'

As he spoke, part of the burning building crashed down. They weren't close enough to see where it had fallen, but they could guess.

'No choice. Request back-up assistance.'

Jay did so, but the answer crackled back over the intercom – other units were taken up with various trouble spots in the city.

Jay looked silently at Mike.

'Come on then. What are we waiting for?'

'Can't we dump the load here, Mike?'

'Got to be central, you know that.'

'This is central.'

'You're losing it, Jay.'

Jay fixed his eyes on the road, turning the vehicle into a side street.

The sobbing started again.

'What's wrong? Don't you like a thrill?' Mike called over his shoulder. 'Plenty of thrills here.'

'She's scared,' came a man's voice.

'Scared!' Mike looked round, taking in with one sweeping glance a middle-aged man, a woman, and a teenage boy shut behind the large metal grille in the back of the car. 'Shouldn't have got into debt, should you?'

The man grasped at the grille.

'I told you! Hands off that!' said Mike.

The man spoke with increasing desperation. 'Do you know how hard it is to get Credit after you're forty-five? How are you meant to live? How?'

'Keep your mouth shut,' replied Mike, checking his Laserscan rifle, 'or you won't have to live at all.'

'Please. Don't de-Code us.'

'That's the rule. Got to neutralise the Code in the Unclean.'

'We're not Unclean. Do you know who I am?'

'An Illegal about to be de-Coded.'

'Please!' begged the man. 'We can't live without the Code!'

'I don't think you get it. You're in the old city. You don't need the Code here. You're all Illegals.'

'But we weren't!'

Mike set the Laserscan to neutralise. 'Sit as still as you can.'

'Don't,' said the man. 'Don't.'

'Stop panicking. It isn't set to kill!'

'No, but – '

'I'm a good shot.' Mike de-Coded the three passengers. 'Spot on, first go. Not bad for a bumpy ride, eh, Jay?'

The woman began to sob hysterically. 'But how will we live?'

'If you don't shut up, I'll solve that problem for you!' said Mike. 'And get your hands off the grille!'

'Mike,' said Jay, 'have a heart.'

'Have a *what*!'

'They're frightened.'

Mike sat back, stunned. 'Of course they are! They're *all* frightened, always – they're *meant* to be frightened!'

'I know. I hate it.'

'Sooner you're transferred the better.'

'Can't be soon enough for me.'

The woman screamed as the car's front wheels slid straight into a hole. The engine raced, but the car wouldn't move.

'Request emergency back-up *now*!' said Mike.

'Emergency back-up! Unit needs assistance!' Jay shouted into the intercom.

Mike looked out into the dark, narrow street.

'I don't like this.' Mike reached for Jay's Laserscan and handed it to him.

'What's happening?' cried the woman.

'Look, Jay. Trench. They've dug right across the road.'

'It's a trap.'

'Looks like it.' Mike gazed up at the dark buildings either side of the street. There was no sign of movement, no noise – except for the distant drumming and yelling.

'I should have seen that, easy! I wasn't concentrating. I wasn't concentrating!' Jay slammed his palm onto the steering wheel.

'Try the Gate again. There has to be an available unit to assist.'

'What are we going to do? What are we going to do?' the man was gripping the grille, his eyes full of fear.

'I'll tell you what you're going to do. You're going to shut up.'

'It's no good,' said Jay. 'No available units.'

'That's not possible. There must be one.'

'No available units, Mike.'

'Then we're on our own.'

'Oh no we're not.'

A group of shadowy figures were slowly approaching the car.

'Searchlight's out,' said Jay, frantically flicking the switch.

But even without the car's bright searchlight, it was possible to see the figures were carrying clubs, metal bars, wooden staves, anything they could use as weaponry.

The passengers saw them, and the woman screamed again. Something hit the vehicle from behind and exploded.

'Watchers, Watchers, get out of there!'

'Mike, the Debtors. Let them go!' said Jay.

Mike looked round at them. They were frozen now with fear, transfixed by the flames which danced around the rear of the car.

'Can't do it. If I release the back doors, we're dead.'

'If we sit tight, we're dead.'

Mike thought quickly. 'All right.' He called to the passengers. 'You're free to leave . . . As soon as the doors open, go – might deflect some of the attention,' he said to Jay.

'Go! Out there!' shrieked the woman.

'They don't want *you*!' said Jay. 'They want *us*!'

'But the flames!'

'Jump through them. Jay, when I say "go", we go too. You ready?'

Jay nodded, and rubbed a hand over his face.

'You sure?'

'Yes. OK.'

'Now – go!' Mike hit the red button in front of him and the back doors swung open. He and Jay leapt out of the vehicle. Mike fired behind, Jay fired ahead. It was enough to keep the attackers back; some were hit by Laserscan fire, falling to the ground, others darted away into the buildings. Mike didn't see what happened to the Debtors.

Rocks began to rain down on them from above. Figures emerged from the buildings. Mike fired again and rolled into the trench for some sort of cover. One of the rocks hit the car's remaining light. Everything was dark except for the fire.

Other figures were in the street now, and they had their hands on the armoured car, rocking it backwards and forwards, yelling, howling.

Where was Jay? Mike couldn't see him.

For a moment, Mike imagined that he saw a familiar and very welcome sight – an armoured car – at the end of the street, but it could only have been part of the weird shadow thrown by the flames, because it vanished.

All was confusion. And then suddenly, everything changed. The rocks stopped falling. The howling ceased. All was quiet, except for the cracking and spitting fire.

They weren't rocking the car now. They stood back. Some faded away. Mike couldn't see what they were shrinking from. Why had they stopped their attack? Perhaps he hadn't been imagining that armoured car. A unit must have come to assist . . .

'Mike – help me.'

That was Jay's voice, weak, but nearby.

Mike scrambled out of the trench, and fell beside Jay. Nobody touched Mike, no one tried to attack him, but he wasn't taking any chances. His Laserscan was still poised to take out anyone who came too close.

'Jay!'

He touched his partner, and felt a warm stickiness.

'Oh Jay, no, don't do this.'

'Just want Juno, that's all. I love her.'

'All right, all right. It'll be all right.'

'Can't handle it, Mike.' Jay coughed.

'You'll get your transfer. It'll be all right.'

Mike watched Jay's life ebb away in the firelight as blood trickled slowly from his mouth.

Mike sprang to his feet.

'Where are you?'

His voice echoed around the street. He levelled his Laserscan but he could see no one.

'You want me too, don't you? Come on! But I'm going to take a few of you with me.'

Somebody jumped on him from behind. Mike, completely taken by surprise, crashed to the ground, landing heavily on his shoulder. He heard the bone snap but felt no pain – he was too pumped up with adrenalin for that.

The man standing over him, holding Mike's own Laserscan, had him totally at his mercy. Mercy! How many times had people begged Mike for mercy?

Mike tried to say something, but the words wouldn't come.

This was the end. He knew it.

9

Escape

The man threw the weapon down and knelt beside Mike.

'What the – '

'I'm sorry. I had to get the weapon away from you.'

Mike had expected to be shot, not given an apology.

'Can you move?'

'What's going on?'

The pain suddenly kicked in. Mike tried to focus but found it difficult.

The man called to someone. 'David!'

David? What David?

Mike tried to get up, but the man swiftly sat astride his chest so he couldn't move. Everything seemed to be happening a long way off; Mike couldn't hear properly.

'He's in shock.'

There was another voice now, older, deeper. 'How bad is it?'

'Pretty bad. Something's broken – shoulder I think.'

'This really isn't our problem, Gideon.'

'We can't just *leave* him here!'

'What are you suggesting?'

'Let's get him to safety.'

'Do you know what you're saying? Think about what you're doing!'

'They'll *kill* him – or worse – if we don't move him! We've *got* to do it.'

Silence.

'Can he stand up?'

'Can you stand?'

'Not with you on my chest.'

'Try to stand, Watcher, but take it easy,' said the older voice. 'And I mean *slow* . . . we don't want to have to break anything else.'

The man got off Mike's chest, but even if Mike had wanted to move quickly, he soon found he couldn't – the pain was too intense. He was helped to his feet and supported by two pairs of hands. A tidal wave of nausea hit him.

'Steady, Watcher – Gideon! Shoulder's probably bust but look at this.'

'Uh-oh. We've got to move him *now*.'

'All right. Be quick. They've backed off for a moment but it's asking a lot of them. They respect us, I know, but I'm amazed they've stopped at all.'

Mike clutched his shoulder. 'My partner.'

'Your partner is dead.' Gideon put a strong arm round Mike's waist. 'I'm sorry.'

Mike was in so much pain he didn't feel his legs would support him. His two helpers were insistent as they urged him across the road towards one of the buildings. Through the waves of nausea, he knew he had to move; if he stayed where he was, he was as dead as Jay.

'The Laserscan.'

'Leave it,' said Gideon. 'Come on. We've got to get out of the street.'

Mike stumbled through a doorway. It was very dark, and he was led slowly down what seemed to be a never-ending flight of stairs, pain ripping through his shoulder with every step.

Gideon knocked on a door. It opened. There was light. The door shut behind them.

Mike snapped out of shock. His hearing returned to normal.

There were two other people in the room besides himself and his rescuers.

'Mike!'

Sunny? No. It couldn't be Sunny Cain.

Someone brought a chair.

'Sit down, Watcher.'

'His name's Mike,' said Sunny.

A man was squatting by the chair, and Mike was able to see him clearly by what he realised was candlelight. Gideon was young – about Jay's age. He had a mop of golden hair, which fell almost over his eyes. Mike thought he had seen him somewhere before.

'Let's see your shoulder, Mike.'

'What's he done to his shoulder?' Sunny was squealing. 'Why's there so much blood?'

'You a doctor?'

'I wish,' said Gideon. 'But I can help you.'

Mike shut his eyes and gritted his teeth. 'That'll have to do.'

'Get that body armour off him,' said the older voice. Mike looked at the speaker. It was a stocky, bearded man.

Gideon produced a knife.

'It's all right!' he said to Mike. 'I've got to cut it.'

All Mike could think, as the body armour was cut away, was that Gideon shouldn't have a knife.

'It's not his shoulder. It's his collarbone. Right clavicle. Clean fracture.'

'OK,' said the bearded man. 'Where's all that blood coming from?'

'There.'

'Is that a stab wound?'

'I don't know. I think he's fallen on something. Whatever it was, it's gone right through a gap in the armour. Could've been a lot worse, though. As it is, we can stem the bleeding.' Gideon spoke to Mike. 'This is going to hurt.' And he deftly moved the arm to an angle across Mike's chest. Mike nearly passed out. He heard a strange sound, like ripping material, and was aware of someone taking his helmet off. When he'd recovered his senses, he realised there was a sling around his neck. His arm was tightly bound. Gideon, standing tall in the room now, was staring intently at him. The young man's shirt was torn. Apparently he had made the sling out of his own clothing.

'I'm sorry, Mike. I had to get the weapon away from you. I didn't mean to break your collarbone.'

Mike couldn't remember anyone apologising so profusely to him – ever. Even the scum of the city never apologised; they begged, they cried, they yelled abuse. They didn't say 'sorry'. Mike would've been almost embarrassed if he hadn't been fighting the urge to vomit.

'OK, let's think about the next step,' said the bearded man.

'We've got to get him away, now. She could stay here for a while, but not him. We couldn't keep him in the city even for a night.'

'I hope you're not thinking what I think you're thinking!' said another voice – a woman's.

Someone brought Mike a cup of water. He didn't ask where the water came from. No one ever touched water outside the Towns . . . but Mike needed to drink. The water was clear and clean and refreshing; it lacked the metallic taste of the water he was used to.

Then he realised that a small hand was grasping his own.

'Mike, it's me! It's me!'

'Sunny?'

'Oh Mike! They've killed Jay.'

'What are you doing here?'

'Mike, you look terrible. Terrible! I thought you were going to die.'

Mike removed his hand from Sunny's, and met Gideon's steady gaze.

'Get me back to the Gate.'

There had been low whispers in the room until he said that.

'I don't know why you helped me, but just get me to the Gate, and I'll see to it that you're not touched tonight. You'll be left alone until you can disperse.' The candles flickered in a sudden draught, casting eerie shadows on the damp brick walls. No one said anything. Mike cursed. 'Are you deaf? This is the first time in all my life I promised anyone that! Don't you understand? I'm offering you your *lives* tonight!'

'We're offering you something, too, Mike,' said Gideon, quietly.

Mike would have laughed if he didn't feel so sick and angry.

'You! What can you offer me?'

'Gideon!' said the bearded man, sternly. 'That's enough.'

'It's OK. Let me just say something to him.' Gideon crouched in front of Mike and looked at him out of earnest eyes. 'Mike, listen.'

'Get me to the Gate.'

'If you go back, they'll fix your collarbone, and in a few weeks from now, you'll be doing this again. I mean, how long do you think you can go on?'

'What?'

'Do you know what the average lifespan of a Watcher is?'

'Of course he does!' exclaimed the bearded man. 'And it's younger than him! He must be *very* good at it!'

'I am.' Mike ran his free hand through his hair, but that habitual movement jarred his broken clavicle and he couldn't speak again for a few minutes.

'We can offer you life, Mike,' said Gideon. 'Don't choose death.'

'Choose death? I figure if you were going to kill me you'd have done it by now.'

'I don't mean that.'

'What are you talking about?'

Gideon and the bearded man exchanged glances.

'What Gideon means is that we can take you back to the Gate.'

'No. That's not what I'm saying.'

'You've already said too much, Gideon, my boy. Do what the Watcher wants. Take him back to the Gate.'

'How?'

'Contact Tris.'

'Too dangerous. I'm not happy about going anywhere near that Gate . . . and where else could we leave him?'

The woman came forward now. She was young, but Mike was too caught up in his own torment to notice much more about her. 'Gideon, use your brain! We can't do what you want to do! We can't! He's a *Watcher*!'

'He's a human being. He's caught up in all this hell as much as the rest.'

'No!' said the woman. 'He *is* this hell.'

'Gideon's got a point.' The bearded man sounded anxious. 'We can't dump him near the Gate without being seen.'

'And we can't leave him here. He wouldn't stand a chance!' said Gideon.

'Some would say he doesn't deserve a chance,' muttered the woman.

'But not us. Eh, Shanna? Not us.'

A name buzzed into Mike's brain. He was swallowing down the sickness when something occurred to him. He saw in an instant that for all the apparent failure of tonight, something might yet be gained.

'I've got a question.'

'Let's have it, Watcher,' said the bearded man.

'Do you know anything about David Drum?'

Mike didn't miss the change in tension in the atmosphere. It had been snapping, but now it was as if his rescuers were frozen.

'David Drum?' said Gideon, eventually, 'David – '

'No.' The bearded man cut in. 'We don't know any David Drum.'

'You do!' exclaimed Sunny. 'You said he was alive! You told me!'

'No, Sunny, we didn't say that!' the woman murmured.

'You did! You said he could help me!'

'Well, that's just great!' The bearded man turned away, slinging his hands onto his hips.

Mike struggled to clarify his thoughts. This was far, far better than he had hoped. Excitement dispelled the nausea. He believed, with mounting certainty, that he had stumbled – literally – upon people who knew David Drum. Obviously these were the very people Sunny had said were helping people escape 'over the water' and the reason she wasn't forthcoming with the information was because she wanted to 'escape' herself! He couldn't imagine why – *she* hadn't been dumped in the city – but that didn't concern him. He had to think quickly about what to do next.

'You get people out of the city.'

The bearded man wheeled round and faced him. 'How do you know that?'

'You said so yourself. Just now. *He* said it. Gideon.'

'Great, just great.'

'You were offering me life a few minutes ago. Is the deal off?'

'You think it's a "deal"?'

'I don't know what it is. But I'm interested.'

'You're *what*!'

'I want to go over the water. That's what you call it, isn't it? That's what you call escaping from the city?'

'He knows about us!' the woman exclaimed.

'Right, OK.' The bearded man put a hand to his eyes. 'He knows about us. Think. *Think*.'

'Are *you* David Drum?' asked Mike.

'It's a code word,' said Gideon, 'David Drum is dead.'

'Oh, *Gideon*! Keep your mouth shut! Gideon, you're – oh, God! God! What a mess.' The bearded man put his hands to his face. 'OK. Now we've got a changed situation. We've *got* to take him!'

'You must be joking!'

'No, Shanna, I'm not. We can't leave him, we can't dump him, he knows about us – '

'And he wants out,' said Gideon.

'This is complete madness!' cried Shanna.

'It isn't. It's a risk. Maybe the biggest risk of our lives – and his.' Gideon looked at Mike. 'Are you saying you want what we're offering?'

'Do I have much of a choice?' said Mike. 'Do you?'

Apparently not.

'All right, Shanna.' The bearded man shook his head. 'Contact Tris.'

'Have I got a say in this?'

'There's no time to argue. Just do it.'

'It's one thing to try and stop the people doing what they wanted to do, but you can't seriously expect – '

'Shanna!'

'I don't want to do this!'

'All right! That's noted. Now *go!*'

The woman left the room.

'Gideon, this is all down to you. You're *never* coming to the city again. You've jeopardised everything. Everything. You're just so – thoughtless!'

'I'm sorry,' said Gideon, 'but I believe – '

'You believe! Well, that's just fine, then, isn't it! Everything's spiralling out of control, but *you* believe! That kind of naïve thinking got Kurt killed.' He held out a hand suddenly. 'I'm sorry. I shouldn't have said that.'

'It's OK. You're probably right.'

'Well, Watcher, whether you want a new life or not,' said the bearded man, 'looks like you've got one. Passage out of the city.'

'Kurt,' said Mike. 'Kurt Dane?'

'You know the name?'

'Oh yes.' More than that. He remembered Kurt Dane.

'My father,' said Gideon.

'Your father . . .'

* * *

'They've got him! They've got him in there!'

Edward looked at the mob.

The cry went up: 'Kill him! Kill him! . . . Get him out here . . .'

'We'll get our revenge tonight!' Edward's face was set and hard in the firelight. He glanced down at the body of the Watcher lying at his feet, and spat. 'Filth. Murdering filth.'

'David Drum has got the Watcher!' he yelled.

The crowd's cries increased.

'David Drum . . . David Drum . . . David Drum must give us the Watcher!'

There was a lone voice, shouting clearly: 'They help people . . . they help us!'

The crowd's cries lessened until there was almost silence.

Edward looked again at the body of the Watcher. He would have so much preferred this filth to be alive . . . alive for just a little while longer . . .

'I say David Drum is no friend of ours if they don't give him to us!' Edward roared.

'We'll kill them too!' shrieked a woman.

'Kill the Watcher! Make him pay! Kill David Drum, if we have to!' Edward raised his arm; in his hand was a sharpened metal bar. 'Kill them all!'

* * *

A gentle tapping on the door made them all jump.

'David Drum! David Drum!'

Gideon's voice was low. 'Who is it?'

'A friend of David Drum. I've come to warn you. Get that Watcher away from the city or they'll kill him.'

There was a sound of scrambling footsteps as the 'friend' raced away.

'It's Lou!' said Gideon. And he went after her, catching up with the girl at the top of the steps.

'Lou! Lou, stop!'

Her words tumbled out quickly. 'They got one of them . . . they want the other one. They thought *you'd* killed him, and then – I don't know what happened out there. They wanted them both. But – it was strange, they didn't . . . they stopped . . .'

'I know.'

The girl glanced fearfully over her shoulder. 'But Edward . . . Edward started talking. He said if you get that Watcher out, David Drum is no friend of ours . . . he

said they want that Watcher to pay. You've got to escape
– they'll kill you too! They'd kill *me* if they knew I'd
warned you!'

'Lou – you've got to come with us.'

'To the Deadlands? No. I can't. I just can't do that . . .
You helped me, Gideon. Thank you. I'll never forget you.
And I'll remember everything you told me. I promise.'
She disappeared into the darkness. And Gideon felt a
strange, sad certainty that he'd never see her again.

* * *

Mike tried to stand and found his head swimming. Blackness surrounded him like a shroud. He heard Gideon
come back, and speak, and he sounded far away.

'No, don't think about it. Just do it.'

'Do what!' gasped Mike.

Something was being tightened round his eyes.

'I'm sorry.' That was Gideon again. 'We can't let you
see our escape route.'

Mike heard a noise: grinding, grating, like a heavy door
being carefully manipulated open. What door? Not the
door to the steps, but Mike hadn't noticed any other doors
in that room – but then, he hadn't noticed much at all.
You've *got* to keep alert! He told himself. The name Kurt
Dane seemed to float before him.

'David – take the torch.'

David! The bearded man *was* David Drum!

'Come on, Sunny. Can you manage? Be careful there.'

'I'm scared!' cried the girl. 'Mike! I'm scared!'

'Nothing to be scared of,' said Gideon. 'Come on.'

Strong arms helped Mike along a cold, narrow passage.
There were rocks, debris and choking, dusty air. They
seemed to walk for miles, coughing, coughing, coughing,
and Sunny, somewhere in front of Mike, crying and

whimpering. Mike felt uncoordinated and unreal, but somehow his legs kept moving. All the time he kept trying to think: he was on the edge of something very big; no, not on the edge, right in the middle. Here was David Drum, and people who probably belonged to that long-outlawed sect, helping to get Illegals out of the city! There must be more than these few . . . how large was this operation? How many cell groups might there be, scattered – where?

They stopped.

Mike's heart began hammering. Were they going to leave him in this passage? He might never find his way out – he'd be buried alive – and even if he *did* get out . . .

He grabbed the nearest arm.

'Mike?' said Gideon.

'Let's do it. Let's go over the water.'

10

Over the Water

'Gideon – all clear!'

'There are steps here, Mike.'

Mike felt Gideon's steady hand on his back as his foot kicked against the first of the steps. As they went upwards the air became warmer. Mike heard a familiar yet unexpected sound – a gentle, rhythmic lapping. He could taste salt. They were outside.

Mike made a move with his left arm, but was apprehended by a firm grip.

'Keep the blindfold on, Mike.'

There was a noise, a clicking, and feet pounding along wood.

'They're coming.'

'Good. We can't hang around here.'

Mike knew how important it was to listen to every single sound so that later on he would be able to identify the escape route. But what was this? A boat?

'It's not possible.'

'What's that?' came the voice of the bearded man.

'To get away from the city by water. We've got barriers. You can't escape.'

Nobody answered him.

'Hey! Got room for David Drum and friends?' That was Gideon. He sounded some way off.

'Always got room for David Drum and friends!' said another voice, a voice that almost got lost against the sound of the lapping water and the boat's engine.

'OK. All aboard.'

Mike was ushered along wooden boards.

'David! Can you help Sunny? All right – watch out, Mike, big step in front of you.'

'Gideon? I thought you said David Drum was dead.'

'Another big step there. OK? Hey there! This one's injured.'

Silence.

'It's all right, it's all right,' Gideon was saying. 'Take him.'

'We've got him,' said a voice.

Mike was lifted onto what he perceived at once to be a deck. He was bundled down yet more steps, and was surprised to find himself seated on a very comfortable chair. Someone grabbed his chin.

'Open wide, my boy!'

'Not on your life!' Mike clenched his teeth but something was forced between his lips. Alcohol!

'All right, David, let's go.' A door slammed.

With a supreme effort, Mike grasped the blindfold and yanked it off. He blinked. He couldn't understand. He was in a well-lit, luxuriously decorated room, with deep red carpets and drawn curtains. There was a bar at one end.

'I can't believe this. It's a tourist boat.'

'Well, it used to be.'

Mike saw Gideon, resting one arm on the bar, and as his eyes got used to the light, he was able to get a better look at his companions.

Apart from Gideon, there was Sunny, sitting opposite him. She was white and looked sick. The woman he'd seen earlier was with her. The bearded man was not in the room.

As Mike focused more fully on Gideon, he could see the immediate likeness between the young man and Kurt Dane. Mike had only seen Gideon's father once, and that was a few years before. Tall and fair, startled, his hand resting on a door knob – then sinking against the door, still looking surprised, blood covering his chest.

'Let me have another look at your shoulder.'

'No.'

'Would you like more brandy?' Gideon brought a bottle over.

'Gideon, don't give that to him!' the woman told him.

'It's all right, he can't break it. This pseudo-glass is too tough even for him. Mike, is that strap tight enough?' Gideon's face reflected concern. 'We don't have any painkillers here, but the brandy will – '

'I know what the brandy will do.' Mike reached out with his left hand and twitched the curtains. All he could see was blackness.

'Mike!' Gideon closed the curtains. Then he stood between the Watcher and the window.

Sunny was crying, softly.

'It's just fear,' said Gideon. 'She'll be fine.'

Mike didn't care whether Sunny would be fine or not. He was trying to work out where they were going. He guessed they were heading up-river, inland. But why? Surely going 'over the water', now that he knew it involved real water and wasn't just some sort of code word for escape, meant getting to the estuary and then out to sea?

Mike cursed. If only he hadn't been injured! His mind raced: this sect was much more dangerous than he had ever imagined. They must be carrying out a massive operation – they were using a *tourist boat*! How many was he going to find 'over the water'? What was he going to do about it? And how?

'What're you thinking, Mike?' asked Gideon.

'He's thinking we aren't fit to live,' remarked the woman.

The craft began to slow down. They must be approaching a barrier. Mike didn't want to get caught in any crossfire, but he had to have help in getting these Illegals stopped. He couldn't move, but he could shout. Still, he reasoned, he wouldn't have to; these tourist vessels were always well checked. Any minute now the Ferrymen would be crawling all over this boat. He remembered his very short stint accompanying tourists, revellers, the privileged, along the river, protecting them with his Laserscan as they laughed at the old city from the safety of the water. Laughed, and pointed out the buildings and the inhabitants, and even watched them being picked off for their amusement, enjoying their safe trip into danger. How Mike despised tourists. He was glad he was out of that.

'Put the blindfold back on, Mike.'

'No way.'

'Sorry.' Gideon tied the blindfold around his eyes again. 'Are you ever going to let go of that brandy?'

Mike held on to the bottle as if it would save his life.

'Sorry . . . I have to do this.' Something was shoved into Mike's mouth.

'Gideon, open the door . . . just a bit . . . let's listen to what's happening on deck,' said the woman.

'I feel sick,' said Sunny.

'OK. I'll show you where the bathroom is.'

Mike guessed they left the room.

'Cut the engine!' That cry from up on deck made Mike sit up. He may not be able to do a thing, but this bunch of Unclean would soon be begging him for mercy.

'You're unauthorised. No pleasure trips listed for this time.'

'Special trip. Very important passengers.'

'Give the password.'

'Strangers and aliens in the world.'

'That's not –'

'Yes it is. Stand back.' Another voice! One that Mike instantly recognised. 'All right, I'll deal with this. Top level security.'

Footsteps. Someone new was coming into the room.

'James!' said Gideon.

'Gideon, bless you.'

There was an exclamation of shock.

'Gideon, what's this? Gideon! Do you know what you've done?'

'Picked up a Watcher.'

'Picked up Mike Merrick!'

There were plenty of things Mike would liked to have said to the Ferryman James Oakley if he hadn't had a lot of material stuffed in his mouth. His hand tightened on the bottle. He tried to get up, but someone forced him down.

'You're in trouble, Gideon,' said Oakley. 'Deep trouble.'

The woman was back in the room now, because she spoke.

'That's what I've been thinking right from the start! Can't we dump him here, with you?'

'He knows too much about us,' said Gideon.

'There is another way.' Oakley's voice was quiet now.

'No! You forget what we're doing this for – *who* we're doing it for. That's not our way, James.'

'I'm worried about this, Gideon. What does David think?'

'Just pass us through.'

'You've got clearance. I just hope you can handle this.' Oakley's voice was further away now. 'God speed, strangers and aliens in the world. May God be with you.'

They were moving again. Gideon removed the blind-fold and the wad from Mike's mouth.

'I don't believe this!' The miserable, surly, mostly mono-syllabic Ferryman, James Oakley, was helping Illegals escape!

'Believe it,' said Gideon.

The bearded man was there now, too. Sunny was missing, but Mike wasn't bothered about that.

'You're David Drum.'

'No.'

'They call you David.'

'I am David. A David. But not David Drum.'

Mike didn't believe him. He thought he was staring into the face of one of the leaders of that banned sect. And there, standing next to David Drum, was Gideon Dane, son of Kurt. Both of these would have to die; they had the mandatory death penalty, this sect. How had these people escaped justice for so long? What an oversight. What a mistake. Someone would have to pay. And James Oakley's name was added to a list Mike was keeping to the forefront of his mind.

'I wouldn't touch any more of that brandy, Mike,' said Gideon.

Mike hugged the bottle to his stomach. His warning glance made Gideon look uncomfortably at David.

Mike looked at David, too. David Drum! Yes, he was about the right age – mid-forties. He was burly, with red hair greying at the temples, and a beard flecked with white hairs. Who had claimed the execution of David Drum? Was it Rohan Adams? Mike couldn't remember. Was it James Oakley?

'You should be dead,' said Mike.

'So should you. You would have been, if we hadn't got you out. And it probably wouldn't have been quick. Do you know what they'd have done to you if they'd got you alive?'

'They wouldn't have got me alive.'

'Uh-huh.' David half-smiled at the others. 'We're not out of it yet, but you've done well tonight.'

Both Gideon and Shanna seemed doubtful about that.

'OK, Shanna,' said David, not needing an explanation. 'Want to say something, Gideon, my boy?'

'We're meant to save them, not hurt them,' replied Gideon, ruefully.

David sat down on one of the comfortable seats. 'Listen to me. If you hadn't *hurt* this one, you wouldn't be here talking to me now.'

'He's right,' affirmed Mike.

'We usually rescue people from your kind,' said David, rubbing his eyes. 'Not the other way around.'

'His "kind"?' Gideon apparently didn't like the word.

'Come on, Gideon. Does he want out, really, I wonder? I doubt it. Watchers don't want to be rescued.'

'James did,' said Gideon.

'That was different. And James isn't a Watcher.' David sat forward, and yawning, blinked blearily at the carpet. '*His* sort don't usually want out. That's what I'm saying.'

Mike thought of Jay.

'Some do.'

'Not you.'

'Never thought about it.'

David smiled a little.

'We couldn't leave him there. You said it yourself, he'd be dead,' said Gideon.

David raised his eyes. 'Would Mike have preferred that?'

Mike thought again of Jay. And when he had believed he was going to die – when Gideon stood over him with that Laserscan – would he have welcomed death?

'No. But I'd have liked better odds.'

'Better odds?' repeated Gideon.

'I'd have preferred to take out more of the Unclean city scum who killed my partner.'

Gideon didn't seem to know what to say to that.

'Don't try to understand him, my boy, you never will.' David got up. 'Looks like we're stuck with each other for a while, Mike. I don't think any of us are happy about that. We'll have to do some serious thinking pretty soon.'

'He's injured,' said Gideon. 'He can't hurt us right now.'

'But he won't always be injured,' Shanna said, 'what do you intend to do, keep breaking one of his bones every so often?'

'All right, we're nearly there. Shanna! You contacted Tris?'

'Yeah, I got him. He'll be waiting.'

'We're slowing down. Blindfold.'

'I'll get the girl. She's being sick in the bathroom.'

'All right. Blindfold her too. Let's go.'

Again Mike was plunged into darkness. He was levered out of his chair, and his head span so violently that he had to stop. He felt someone directing him up on to the deck, and then down on to more wooden planks, a jetty, and still he held on to the bottle.

Then he heard something else.

Armoured car! Mike felt triumphant . . . they're caught! But then he heard David's voice – and David didn't sound afraid.

'Tris! Tristram, back it up here.'

The vehicle came right up close. Mike was dumbstruck. Surely they didn't have access to an armoured car as well?

He heard the back of the vehicle being opened up. Inside, he reached out and found the familiar grille – only this time, he was on the wrong side of it.

'Get down!' A rough blanket was placed over his head. 'On the floor. I said, get *down*!' This was a new voice – tough, sharp, threatening.

'Mike!'

'Sunny . . .'

'I'm here! I'm under this horrible blanket and I've got a blindfold on. I am so scared, Mike. I am *so* scared! I've been really sick.'

'Yeah, well, don't try chucking your guts up under this blanket.'

The car started with a jolt, and the tough voice said, from the driver's seat, 'It's playing up again.'

'Tristram, come on!' David sounded worried now. 'Move it, it'll be light soon.'

Thoughts shot through Mike's mind in a jumble. He couldn't think straight. He tried to shake off the alcohol-fuelled muzziness. We've crossed the river. *This* is 'over the water'. North side of the city . . . or are we beyond the city? We've passed the north barrier . . . yes, we've passed it . . . James Oakley patrols the north . . . we're outside the city.

'Mike!' The girl tugged at his arm under the blanket. He shoved her away.

'They can't make it,' Mike muttered. 'They can't. They'll be stopped on the highway.'

The vehicle jolted again.

'Go, go, go!' shouted David.

Now the armoured car was shooting along. The smoothness of the road indicated they were on the highway, heading – where? Where could they possibly be going? They couldn't be going to the Towns. These people were Illegals! But there was nothing beyond the Towns. It didn't make sense. Nothing made sense. Nothing.

Mike felt the blanket being removed from his head. Before anyone could stop him, he'd taken the blindfold off and thrown it away. He could see the roof of the armoured car, and the shutters up at the sides. The single strip light above was bright but unflattering. Faces staring at him looked so, so tired.

'Come up here, Mike. On the bench.' Gideon helped him up. 'That must have been hard on your shoulder. I'm sorry.'

Mike's head had started to spin again. When he could focus, he could hardly believe his eyes. In the driver's seat was a figure, a helmeted figure, a figure dressed in black body armour.

'He's going to pass out,' said the woman.

Mike suddenly felt a tremendous wave of tiredness engulf him. He shut his eyes and drifted into unconsciousness. He felt someone take the brandy from him, and was too weak to protest.

He finally came to and found that the shutters had been opened. Disorientated for a moment, it took a little time for him to remember what had happened. The pain in his shoulder was worse. It had woken him. The numbing effect of the brandy had completely worn off and left its own mark in the shape of a crashing headache.

'Are you going to throw up?' asked Gideon.

'No.' Mike turned his head. The first light of dawn was visible through the open shutters; a silver thread, in the greyness, spread across the skies. They were speeding down a wide road; Mike didn't recognise it. Beyond the road there was water, and a vast expanse of – nothing. Just grey.

Sunny was asleep, her head resting against Shanna. The woman glanced at Mike, then away, her face a picture of disgust. Don't look at me like that, he thought. *You're* the Unclean. *You* should die. And you will, as soon as –

'Mike? How are you feeling?' Gideon persisted.

'Pretty bad,' admitted Mike.

'We can't do anything. Not right now. We can give you something for the pain when we get back.'

'Get back where?'

'Hah! Look at the state he's in, but he's not giving up.'

That was the driver. Mike took a good long look. He may be dressed as a Watcher but Mike was pretty sure it was no one he knew.

'Well, I'd like to know where I'm going. This is all new to me. I don't get rescued every day.'

'It *was* rather unexpected,' said David, from the front passenger seat.

'Yeah. Maybe I'll get used to it . . . who knows? Maybe you will too.' Mike peered out of the shutters again. 'I'd like to know where we are.'

David smiled, and watched the greyness go by.

No one spoke now. Mike eyed each one in turn. He wanted to remember their faces . . . just in case he ever needed to. But he got stuck on Shanna. There was something about her that struck him as unusual. Mike couldn't work out what it was, until he realised that the very fact that she was unremarkable to look at was the remarkable thing. Wavy brown hair skimmed her shoulders, and that was pretty enough; but the fact was that nothing about her seemed to have been enhanced, which was very unusual indeed for a woman over twenty. Her eyes weren't any standard colour. They weren't stunning. But they were full of lively expression, and that expression right now, as she realised he was watching her, was a mixture of contempt – and fear.

Mike looked away. He needed a plan. But what plan? What could he do but go along with them until he was fit enough to take them all out, or get help, feigning some sort of compliance? He didn't know what he was heading into. Perhaps the people who were living wherever they were going would feel even more worried about what

these rescuers had done. Maybe they'd be worried enough
to kill him.

Mike's eyes were drawn now to the rising sun. It
appeared out of the hazy distance, lighting small, fluffy
clouds in that new sky. The yellow clouds gave way to
brilliance and the greyness disappeared.

'Where are we?' Sunny was stirring.

'Another world,' said David. And to Mike, it did look
like another world.

'Where exactly are we going? Another Town? This isn't
the highway. This is the Deadlands. There's nothing out
here.'

'Yes, the Deadlands,' said David. 'But you're wrong
about it.'

'It's worthless. Wilderness. They can't even farm out
here. Pollution ruined it all years ago. Everyone knows that.'

'The government want the people under the very strict
control of the New Towns,' David told him. 'You know
nothing at all, Mike, my boy.'

'Have you *never* left the Towns before?' asked Gideon.
'I mean, apart from going into the city?'

'No one would want to come out here. It's not safe.'

This brought a sudden burst of scornful laughter from
the driver. 'What, and the city is? The New Towns are?
Hang around long enough and you wind up illegal. That's
safe, is it?'

Mike didn't like being laughed at. He sat back and
began to think of ways to despatch the driver first – as
soon as he could.

'It's going to be a beautiful day,' observed Gideon.

The waves of pain seemed to subside as Mike stared at
the perfect summer morning. There was such a lot of sky;
he'd never seen so much. The New Towns and the city
blocked so much of it. And what was this? Birds! Free
birds, birds flying in that golden morning!

'Geese,' said Gideon, pointing to the V formation.

Mike shook his head. 'This isn't right. There shouldn't be anything here. Nothing living. I don't get it. How did this happen? How did *you* happen, David Drum?'

'Ever tried to hold water in your hand, Mike?' David held a fist up at the grille, and then opened his hand. 'Slips through your fingers, doesn't it? You can't control everything. You can't control God.'

11

Another World

There were flowers – real flowers, simple flowers, patches of colour at the side of the road. This place wasn't dead, and brown, and yellow, as Mike had always supposed. It was green, lushly green, and wild, with tall grass everywhere. Vast tracts of flat land, dotted with derelict buildings in various stages of disrepair – no people, of course – still, Mike could hardly believe what he was seeing.

The road itself was getting bumpy now. The driver was skilful in negotiating large holes: as skilful as Jay had been in the city. A dark line appeared in the distance. Trees. So many of them – so dense! The darkness was running almost parallel with the road now. The car turned off, down a track into the forest. Mike hardly had time to think before they seemed airborne; they were crossing a bridge, a river was beneath them. Then straight, tall, black trees encompassed them, blocking out the sky. Nothing lived under those trees. It was like the city. Mike began to feel less threatened – because he *had* felt threatened, out there in that flat land full of sky.

'Praise God,' Gideon breathed.

Of course. They were hidden now. That dash in the open land had been dangerous . . . they could have been spotted from the air. Only government Heli-Jets ever came anywhere near the Deadlands.

The vehicle bounced over ruts in the track, jarring Mike's injury. And then at last the forest thinned out a little, and the trees were different. Light dappled in from above. David pushed open the passenger window, and Mike heard birdsong, real wild birdsong, for the first time. The driver turned the car further into the wood, and now there was a wider track to follow. And then they stopped.

For a moment, Mike thought he had been brought here to be killed. His eyes locked with those of the driver, who had turned to look at him, an arm languidly placed along the back of his seat.

'Bit of a novelty for you, isn't it, Watcher? Sitting back there . . .' The driver's words seemed to melt away. Mike thought it was due to the ferocity of his own stare – but the driver frowned, as if he was remembering something.

'We're here. Come on, Mike.' Gideon helped him out of the car. Mike wondered where 'here' was, and then saw they were on the edge of a large clearing in the middle of the wood. A track led through trees to some broken-down sheds, a wooden-slatted barn, and what looked like half a cottage.

It was quiet, except for the birdsong. Mike felt very uneasy. The smell – it wasn't anything he had ever experienced before. Earthy, woody, damp. Gideon's arm supported him, and Shanna brought Sunny along behind. The girl looked terrified.

A bird flapped overhead. Mike ducked, causing a searing pain to shoot through his shoulder.

'No one's going to harm you here, Mike,' said Gideon, 'I mean – not intentionally.' And they walked down the soft dirt track to the clearing.

A black dog, which had been lying outside the cottage, pulled itself to its feet and barked.

'Home, safe!' shouted David.

A grey-haired old woman appeared at the cottage doorway. David went to her, and slung his arms around her. The black dog raced to Tristram, the driver, its ears flat and its tail wagging madly. Mike waited for the rest of the Illegals to appear. It was a tense moment.

But there wasn't anyone else.

'Not so long next time, I promise,' said David. 'We'll never leave you alone so long again.'

'It's all right,' replied the old woman. 'I wasn't afraid. The Lord was right here with me.'

Mike felt a touch on his left arm. It was Sunny. She was far too frightened to speak.

'Meet Sunny,' said David.

'Oh, how wonderful! Welcome, my dear!' The old woman spotted Mike. 'But who's this?'

'This,' said David, 'is Mike.'

'Oh, how wonderful!'

'No it isn't,' said Shanna. 'It was all a complete mess.'

'It wasn't.' Gideon shook his head. 'It was meant to be. I don't believe it was a mistake.'

'We managed to rescue a Watcher, Constance,' Shanna hugged the old woman. 'A Watcher who doesn't want to be here.'

'Who said I didn't want to be here?' asked Mike, half expecting a lot more people to appear from one of the buildings. 'Get it into your head, city girl, I'm interested in this new world.'

'I'm not a city girl. I've lived all my life in the Deadlands. My parents were Illegals. I suppose I should never have been born – according to you.'

'But I'm a city boy.' Tristram bent down, patting his dog. 'City kid, rescued by David Drum. Number one enemy, eh, Watcher?'

The old woman was looking Mike up and down.

'What happened to him?'

'Gideon happened,' said David.

'I'm sorry,' Gideon said.

David ruffled Gideon's hair. 'So like Kurt.'

Tristram stood up, suddenly, and spoke quietly to Gideon.

'I knew I'd seen him before. It's him. The big guy from the other night.'

'You're kidding!'

'No, it's him ... and not only that, Gideon, I am absolutely sure I've seen him somewhere before and I can't place it, or him – but I will.'

'What's the matter with his arm?' asked Constance.

'Broken collarbone – and he's got a wound to the shoulder.'

The old woman came close to Mike, gazing into his face. She was lined, careworn, ancient. Older than anyone he had ever seen. She could have been over seventy! He shuddered. How he loathed the elderly. He was about to tell her to get away from him, but something in her eyes stopped him – they were a little faded, blue, but there was something in them he hadn't seen for a very long time. What was it? A sort of kindness, but more than that. He felt momentarily unnerved.

'You look dead on your feet. I think I should take a look at that shoulder.'

Mike moved as she touched him. 'I'm all right.'

'Well, that's not true, is it?' she said.

'Constance was a nurse, Mike. I think she should take a look,' Gideon told him.

'You said you were a doctor.'

'No, I didn't. I said, I wish. I only helped the doctor when he was here.'

'Oh, yeah? And where did he go?'

'Come on.' Constance put a hand on his sling.

'I'm all right! Didn't you hear me?'

Constance dropped her hand. Mike felt a growing anger. Here he was, a Watcher, surrounded by the Unclean, this filth, this rabble not fit to live, and he couldn't do anything about it. He was vulnerable. He hated that feeling.

'OK, Mike. Come with me.'

Mike let Gideon help him to the half-open door of the barn. Inside, straw bales, almost grey with age, were placed against a wooden partition, and Gideon helped Mike to sit down with his back resting against the wood. Dust particles danced in the sunlight streaming in from the doorway. Great black cobwebs hung about the struts and the rafters. Mike coughed. Dust and mould and dirt. He thought he would choke.

'Be back in a minute,' said Gideon, and left the barn.

For the first time since his 'rescue', Mike was alone. Were these few really the total number of Illegals here? It had to be a network of small groups. Yes, that would make sense, be safer. How could he find out where the rest were? He tried to imagine getting the information out of Tristram. That thought gave him quite a lift.

A sudden movement told him he wasn't alone after all. The dog was in the barn, sniffing at his feet.

'Get out of it.'

'I wouldn't let Tris see you kick his dog.'

David was sitting just outside the barn door. What was this – was Mike under some sort of guard? Gideon came back.

'I've got something for you.'

Mike saw the hypodermic syringe in his hand.

'What the – ' With a swift action of his left hand, Mike knocked the syringe from Gideon's grasp. The movement was agonising.

'It's a painkiller, Mike,' said Gideon, quietly.

'Do it, then. Do it.' Mike leaned back against the wooden slats, relief flooding him as the painkiller worked almost straight away.

'Sorry. I didn't mean to scare you.'

'*You*! Scare *me*!' Mike would have laughed – but somehow, he couldn't.

Constance was coming into the barn. She had a bowl in one hand, and a cloth in the other.

'Are you going to let me look at that shoulder now?'

'No.'

'Don't be shy, Mike.'

'Shy! You're not touching me.'

The old woman set her mouth in a firm line. 'Do you want me to have Gideon and Tristram hold you down while I do this? I'm going to take a look, Mike, and I'm going to give you a good wash.'

'Wash!'

'There's dried blood,' she said, softly, 'all over you.'

His blood? Yes, and Jay's blood too.

Mike glared at her. Never in all his life had he been threatened by an old woman! Still, he wasn't about to let anybody hold him down – and he knew they could . . . at the moment, anyway.

'You can look.'

Constance knelt beside him and carefully peeled away some of the clothing cut by Gideon's knife.

'Yes, that's a break . . . now, what's this wound? Needs cleaning. It's deep. You'll have quite a scar, Mike . . .' she trailed off as she looked at his back. Then she sounded brisk. 'You made a good job of this sling, Gideon, but we'll need a new one. Hold his arm.'

Gideon obliged as Constance knotted a new sling.

'Don't suppose you've got access to bone-knitting gear.'

'Sorry, Mike. We don't have all the things they have in the Towns.'

'No . . . don't suppose you do.'

'Have to be a natural healing. Take a few weeks. Lean forward.' He did, with difficulty, and she slipped the sling round his neck. 'Gideon, you're about the same height as Mike. He's bigger built, but I'm sure you must have some clothes that would fit him?'

'I don't want his clothes!' snapped Mike.

Constance was about to dip the cloth into the bowl, but Mike caught her wrist.

'You're having a wash, Mike. You should see yourself.' She spoke quietly but firmly and, unafraid, she held his gaze. He was *almost* ashamed at having grabbed her wrist so tightly.

The wet cloth touched his forehead and he flinched.

'Are you worried about the water, Mike? Don't be. We've got a stream nearby. It's not polluted. There are fish.'

'Fish?'

'Yes. We eat them.'

'That's revolting. Give the cloth to me.' He wiped his face and hair. 'That'll do.'

'OK, Mike, but I've got to clean that wound.'

He nodded. 'All right.' And she began to gently, very gently, clean it.

'So, Mike. Have you got family?'

'What?'

'Do you have a family, Mike?'

'Family! I'm a Watcher!'

'They're not allowed family, Constance,' came David's voice from the door. 'Illegal to have children by a Watcher, isn't it, Mike?'

'Do you have a girl?'

'What is this? Stop asking me questions.'

'I was married for thirty years until my husband . . . died.'

'Married! What – that commitment thing? No one gets married any more.'

'We did. We were in love.'

Gideon appeared with a clean shirt and trousers.

'In love. What trash.'

'Don't you believe in love, Mike?' Constance seemed surprised.

'This David Drum character has quite a hold on you, doesn't he? What does he offer you to follow him? Love?' Mike sneered. 'What else? What else would be worth risking your lives for in the city, getting the Unclean out, for what?'

'Mike, we're all Illegals here, but it isn't David Drum who ever had "a hold" on us,' said Gideon.

'Come on. Christian sect, yeah? Refused to take the Code. Didn't want to become part of the Free Church. Rather be the walking dead. That's some hold.'

'We *didn't* do anything and we *don't* do anything because of David Drum,' said Constance. 'David is dead. He died years ago. We refused to take the Code because we believed it to be wrong. We thought God didn't want us to take it. We couldn't compromise with what they call the Free Church.'

'God! Don't tell me you chose to be illegal for some god-figure.'

'He doesn't understand. How could he?' Gideon sat down opposite Mike, and looked at him with keen interest. Mike looked back, and saw instead Kurt Dane, hand on the doorknob. Kurt Dane, lying dead at his feet.

'Christianity is dead.'

'Does it look dead to you?' Constance smiled. 'We've got a living leader. How can it be dead?'

'So David Drum is alive after all. You just said – '

'I'm not talking about David Drum.'

Mike caught Constance by the wrist again, but not so tightly. 'That's enough.'

'All right, Mike.'

His eyes became heavy. He wanted to keep awake, to watch, to think, but he couldn't. When he woke up, it was with a start. It was twilight. He didn't know where he was. He tried to stand, but the pain in his shoulder reminded him with sharpness what had happened. He'd slept the whole day! The barn door was open; there was some sort of flickering light coming from outside . . . a fire . . . And what was that smell?

'You're awake!' Gideon was sitting at the barn door. 'Just in time for supper. Tris brought home some pheasants.'

Mike struggled to his feet and made it to the door. He could see the cobbled area in front of the cottage was filled with activity. Birds, skewered, were hanging above the fire. Mike thought he had never seen anything so barbaric in his life.

Gideon smiled. 'I guess you've only ever had Vermalyde. This is real meat.'

Mike leant his head against one of the doorposts. 'Real flesh. Ugh.'

'Funny the different things that disgust different people.' Shanna handed a plate full of flesh to Gideon. 'Does *he* want any, or not?'

'Shanna!' Gideon sounded reproachful. She sighed impatiently, took a deep breath, and looked at Mike.

'Do you want any food?'

If this was the only food on offer, Mike knew he had to have it. He had to get strong and fit to deal with these Unclean.

'She doesn't like me!' he observed, ironically.

'She's frightened of you,' replied Gideon.

'You're not afraid of me, Gideon. Or you don't seem to be. Why's that?'

'The pheasant's great. Try it, Mike. Tris is excellent with a slingshot.'

'City kid. He would be. How many Watchers has he brought down?'

Shanna shoved a plate at Mike.

'Enjoy it!' she said, in a tone which implied she'd rather he choked on it.

Mike realised he couldn't hold the plate and eat as well, so he sat down next to Gideon, put the plate on his knee, and tried some. It tasted surprisingly good. If he could just forget that he was eating real bird flesh, he might just about be able to stomach it. He had to.

The black dog was hanging round his feet again.

'*She* likes you,' said Gideon.

'Vermin. We shoot them in the city.'

'You shoot everything in the city,' said David, coming over, as Gideon got up and disappeared into the barn. Mike watched him go – and then he watched Shanna and Tristram. They were laughing together. Laughing at him? No – didn't seem to be. She was handing him a plate and he was joking with her. She slapped his shoulder playfully. Handsome boy, that city kid, thought Mike. Not such a kid, really – he looked in his mid-twenties, like the woman. And, in her ordinariness, she was handsome too, her face lit up with a wide smile. Handsome, but Unclean.

'Where's Sunny?' he asked, suddenly.

'She's with Constance, in the cottage.'

'Why did she want to get out?'

'I can't say.'

'I don't get it. She's not an Illegal. She's got no reason to want to escape . . . escape! Escape to what? To this? How many more of you are there? Why do you do it? Who wants to get out – to this? There's more to it, isn't there? Where do we go next? What's the next move?'

'You won't be getting answers to any of those questions tonight.'

'I want to know.'

'You'll have to keep wanting, my boy. Not used to that, are you?'

Mike felt a wave of frustration.

'The painkiller's wearing off.'

'That's a shame. We haven't got any more.'

'You want me to be in pain.'

'If we'd have wanted that, we'd have left you to the city people.'

Mike couldn't argue with that.

'Look, Mike. What do you see?'

'What?'

'What do you *see*?'

'A bunch of Illegals hiding out in an old farm.'

'Illegals. Haven't got the Code. Worse than that, Christians, banned, death penalty. And add to that Illegals helping other Illegals escape from the city.'

'You said it.'

'Verdict?'

'Death.'

'Executioner?'

'Me.'

'Got a problem, haven't we?'

'I'd say so.'

'And not long to come up with a solution.'

'Not long.'

'Shall I tell you what I see when I look at these people?'

'If you must.'

'I see people I care about. People I love. People to be protected.'

'OK. I get it.'

'I'm not sure you do.'

'Oh, I do. Tris is good with a slingshot? He's going to take me out, is he? He wants to. I can see that much. But who knows?' Mike handed his empty plate to David. 'A few days here, I might never want to leave.'

David silently took the plate.

'Makes me sick to my stomach,' said Mike. 'At the moment.'

'*You* make *me* sick to my stomach,' replied David. 'At the moment.'

Suddenly, a terrible cry split the still night air – a screeching, an eerie call, like death itself. Mike had heard some sounds in his life, but never anything like this. David half-smiled and said, 'It's an owl.'

'An owl?'

'A night bird. You'll hear some pretty strange noises out here in the Deadlands, Mike . . . just wait until you hear a rabbit screaming because it's been caught by a stoat.'

'What's a stoat?'

'A vicious killer.'

'Uh-huh.' Mike began to smile. 'Don't worry, David Drum. You won't hear any screaming . . . I promise.'

David seemed very disturbed by that remark.

Gideon came out of the barn, and slumped down beside the Watcher.

'Mike and I were just talking,' said David, 'about nature. Life and death. The hunter and the hunted.'

'Oh?' Gideon yawned.

David seemed concerned. 'Are you all right?'

'Yes . . . just tired.'

'You'd better take it easy.'

'I know.' Gideon yawned again. 'You tired, Mike?'

'No.' That was a lie. Mike was feeling quite drowsy now. He wondered if it was something to do with the food; maybe they'd put something in it – poison! He tried to fight the waves of fatigue . . . he had to fight it . . . but he couldn't. And he drifted off into a place of blackness disturbed only by the throbbing pain that was now his constant companion.

12

Perfectly Safe

'Look at him,' Shanna said to Tris.

'He's asleep.'

'He's not. He's plotting. Planning to kill us all. At least he hasn't got a Laserscan.'

'What, you think he needs a weapon?'

'Oh, Tris, stop it.'

'Stop what?'

'All *that* – just stop.'

'Well, it's true. I'd have felt better . . . well, this sounds bad, Shanna, but I wish Gideon had broken his leg not his collarbone.'

'I wish Gideon hadn't broken anything at all. I wish we'd left him in the city to get whatever was coming to him.'

'Do you really mean that?'

'Come on. Don't you think it?'

Tris wasn't sure how to answer.

'More struggling, Tristram? Better get used to it. We're all going to be struggling pretty soon.' Shanna sounded bitter. 'You know it's all over, don't you?'

'What's all over?'

'We can't go back to the city. Not ever. You know what Gideon said about what Lou told him. They'll kill us. We're their enemy now . . . because of *him*.'

'Not everyone will see it like that.'

'Oh, yeah? All those relationships we were trying to build – all that trust . . . it's all been for nothing. We should have left him. Gideon shouldn't have jumped on him. Tris, that Watcher should be dead.'

'No.'

She stared at him.

'No, I don't think he's meant to be dead. Look at what happened. They backed off . . . I think – I think – somehow God might have stopped them. Don't you?'

'Oh, *Tristram*! Don't give me that! Get real! Look – look at what he *is*!'

'Look at what I was.'

'That was different.'

'Was it?'

Shanna sighed, heavily. Everything was peaceful, so peaceful in the camp. Who would ever think they had a Watcher in the middle of it?

'Tris – do the Watchers . . . do you think they all know? If they've got the name it'll be far too dangerous to go back.'

'Suppose that's something we can thank him for.'

'Thank him!'

'Yeah. At least we've been warned. *Someone* knows. Maybe not all of them – I've heard no word. James would have told us, wouldn't he? Perhaps Mike got some information.'

'Well, they work in pairs. His partner would have known, at least.'

'His partner is dead.'

'And he should be, too.'

'I told you, I don't think so. And I'm uncomfortable with that.'

'Uncomfortable? Every time I look at him I feel like throwing up. I wish he was . . .'

'Shanna, I've got a good enough reason to whack him

right now. But that's not what it's all about. Not any more. Not for me. I can't go back to that. I *won't* go back to it.'

Shanna put a hand to her mouth. 'This is the biggest mistake we ever made. I think we should break camp and leave him here.'

'Shanna – '

She shrugged off the hand on her arm.

'Shanna, I know you're scared.'

'Scared!' She looked at him, with tears glistening in her eyes. 'Of course I'm scared! I haven't been so scared since we came back to the camp and found my parents and the others all gone! Watchers! I *hate* them!'

'You don't know that it was Watchers, Shanna.'

'Who else? Who else, Tristram?'

Shanna walked swiftly into the cottage, and stood at the door, looking out across the yard. There he was, the Watcher, like a great spider waiting to finish off the helpless flies in his web. She wiped away a few more angry tears, and then she felt a cool hand on her shoulder, and turned to face the old woman.

'Shanna, you're tired. Why don't you go to bed?'

Shanna tried to pull her emotions together. 'How's the girl?'

'Very troubled.'

'Are we going to move her on?'

'Yes, I think so. Not yet though. Come on . . . a good night's sleep is what you need.'

'Sleep! How can anyone get any sleep with – with – *that* out there?'

'David's taking first watch. And then Tristram. We'll be perfectly safe.'

'Perfectly safe! With a *Watcher* in the middle of the camp?'

'Mike won't try anything. Not yet.'

'How can you be so sure?'

'He's lost some blood. He's quite weak.'

'Constance, I am so afraid.'

'Let's pray.'

'Pray? Let's pray for protection. Don't ask me to pray for *him*.'

'We'll pray for him, we'll pray for you, we'll pray for us all.'

'You can't expect him to change! Constance, I'd believe it of anyone, but not – not *that*.'

'God changes them. We don't. Nothing's impossible to God. We have to focus on who God is, and not on what Mike is.'

'Constance, I wish I had your faith.'

'It's a hard situation. Hard for everyone.'

'But you don't understand. I can't do it!' said Shanna, helplessly. 'I just can't. I can't deal with it!'

There was a cry from the corner of the room. They'd made a bed up for Sunny by the only window in the cottage that wasn't broken. She was restless, squirming about on the straw.

'It's all right!' said Constance. 'We're here.'

The girl said something, and Shanna frowned at the old woman.

'Mike? No, he's not dead, my dear . . . no, you can't see him just now . . . you can see him in the morning – if you want to.' Constance murmured under her breath, 'Well, he might generate a lot of fear, but not for this one!'

And Shanna tried to puzzle out in her mind why the girl wasn't terrified of that – that *animal* – when the very thought of him made her sick.

* * *

Her footsteps sounded too loud as she walked slowly away from the altar. The aisle was still strewn with the battered blooms that had decorated the temple so beautifully during the Festival of Auran. She stepped over them, as if she could do them any more damage by treading on them.

'Juno!'

She was so deep in thought, she didn't hear her own name as it was called.

'Juno!'

Now she stopped, and looked round.

'It *is* Juno, isn't it?'

'Yes.'

James Oakley came towards her.

'Juno – I'm sorry about Jay.'

He sounded awkward – almost embarrassed. He obviously wasn't used to displaying any kind of sympathetic emotion. Juno smiled, faintly.

'Thank you.'

'He was a – a – good guy. I only met him once or twice but – I liked him.'

'I loved him.'

'Then he was lucky.'

'Not so lucky.'

'No – of course not. I mean – I'm sorry, Juno.'

'At least I know what happened to him. It's three days and Mike Merrick is still missing, you know?'

'Uh-huh. So I . . . hear.'

'Hello, James!'

Rohan Adams was standing behind him.

'Are you well?'

James Oakley looked uneasy. Top Watchers didn't usually make small-talk with Ferrymen.

'Umm . . . yes, very well.'

'Seen you here quite a bit, lately, James. I didn't realise you were – spiritual.'

'Er – yes – well, no . . . not really . . .'

'Did you enjoy the Festival?'

'I was on duty.'

'It was a wonderful Festival. Quite incredible. Everybody's exhausted. I didn't get to stay . . . that was a shame.'

'Yes . . . I'm sure it was . . .'

Rohan's arm slipped round the Ferryman's shoulders.

'We all have our spiritual paths to follow. Maybe you need some help. Perhaps you should make an appointment to see Father.'

'Oh no, I couldn't.'

'Why not?'

Oakley didn't seem able to think of an answer.

'Maybe I'll arrange something for you.'

'Oh – '

'And you.' Rohan Adams' attention switched to the girl. 'It's Juno, isn't it? Jay's girl.'

She glanced at him nervously, and nodded.

'It really was too bad about Jay.'

'Yes.'

'Mmm. We were close – once.'

'I know.'

She turned to leave, but felt a tight grip on her elbow.

'You were long-term.' Rohan raised his eyebrows. 'You must be a very special girl, Juno . . . are you finding religion helpful in getting over your sad loss?'

'I'll never get over it.'

'Well, that's – tragic.'

'I don't *want* to get over it.'

'No?'

'No. Not ever.'

'Then you need help.' Rohan glanced at James, dismissively. 'Go and pray, James. Write a request on some Sacred Paper. I guess that's what you're here for, isn't it?' He smiled at the girl and there was a glint in his pale eyes. 'Go write a prayer . . . write a prayer for Juno.'

James walked away, fast. Juno tried to release herself from the Watcher's grip but couldn't.

'Do you know James very well?'

'No.'

'Wondered if you were looking for a replacement for Jay . . . you could do better than a Ferryman, you know.'

'I'm not looking for a replacement. Let me go.'

'You want me to let you go?'

'Yes.'

'Say please.'

She looked at him with revulsion but forced herself to say the word.

'Please.'

He let her go and smiled again.

'Did Jay ever talk about me, Juno?'

'Yes.'

'I hope he was . . . *pleasant* about me.'

'I've got to leave now.'

'You know, I'm worried about you.'

'I have to go.'

'You seem eager to get away from me, Juno. Why would that be?'

'I'm not . . . I mean . . .'

'Gets lonely on your own, doesn't it? Are you lonely, Juno?'

'I'm – I'm all right.'

'Yes . . . you are.'

Juno turned away from the Watcher.

'I have to go. I have to be somewhere.'

'Wait. I haven't finished talking to you. Turn around.'

She did – reluctantly. He was looking at her, up and down. She tried to sound cool and keep her voice level as she attempted to turn the conversation into something a little less dangerously personal.

'They haven't found Mike Merrick yet.'

'No. They haven't found the Laserscan rifles either . . . we're hoping the city scum don't learn how to use them. And as for Merrick – I should think they had some fun with him. I only hope it didn't end too quickly. I would rather have liked to have watched . . . think I'd have enjoyed that.' He leaned forward and whispered. 'I'll come see you – soon.'

'No!'

His voice was low in her ear. 'No one says "no" to me. OK? No one who wants to stay legal. I don't think you'd last long in the city, Juno.'

'No, please!'

'Now, Juno, don't do anything stupid . . . I know where you live. I also know where your mother lives. And you have a sister. How old is she? Twelve? Or thirteen? Mmm . . . you think about your family, Juno. I'll think about them too.'

'Please . . .'

'You said you have to be somewhere. Well, off you go. And remember what I said: I look forward to our – meeting. It'll be interesting to find out just what Jay saw in you . . . Juno.'

The girl was too shocked to speak or even to cry as she left the temple. Rohan Adams kept smiling as he watched her go.

'You're not getting sidetracked, are you? You know what's at stake.'

Rohan spun round. The priest was glaring at him.

'How dare you speak to me like that? How dare you?'

'Just don't forget the importance of – '

'You tell me not to forget? *You* forget!'

'All right . . . all right, I'm sorry . . .'

'Don't speak to me again . . . unless I speak to you first.'

'But the time is almost here.'

'I know! You think I don't?'

'Father wants to see you.'

'Has he heard?'

'No. Not yet.'

Rohan Adams glanced at the altar. The Watchers Val and Rico were waiting for him.

'All right,' he said to them, 'now you get to know the whole deal.'

13

The Deadlands

'Do you know, I like it here.'

Mike ignored Sunny's remark.

'I was scared at first, but now it's like the best adventure ever. I mean, it's better than a holi-park. Ever been to a holi-park, Mike? It's not real, like this.' She looked up at him. 'I like your clothes, Mike. You look great in that shirt . . . you look great in anything.'

Mike dropped the few sticks he was carrying in his left hand. 'Yeah, you're back to normal.'

'Shanna gave me this dress. I've never worn a dress before. Do you like it?' She twirled round. It was a modest dress, floral, covering her knees. Her fair hair had a lustrous shine, and her face was glowing with the start of a tan. 'I feel great, Mike. This place is agreeing with me.'

'How did you come to be with them in the city?'

Sunny stooped, arranging the sticks on the fire. 'It's a good job I'm a quick learner. I'm getting good at making fires. I'm good at lots of things.'

'Answer the question.'

'Have you noticed how all the men sleep in the barn, and the women sleep in the cottage? It's only got two rooms. The rest is all fallen down.'

'Sunny!'

'I thought Tris and Shanna might sleep together, didn't you? They're always together. But they don't though . . .

126

sleep together, I mean.' Sunny stood up and tossed her hair. 'I quite like Tris.'

'Good morning!' David approached from the barn, blinking heavenward. 'Going to be hot again, I think.'

'Do you like my dress, Mike? You didn't say.'

'Morning!' Gideon's voice was as cheerful as ever. 'You're up and about early, Mike. Feeling a bit better today? You look better.'

'He does,' David muttered. 'That's why he's helping with those sticks . . . he wants to get as fit as he can, as quick as he can.'

Sunny glanced over to where Tris was talking to Shanna. Mike looked, too. There seemed to be quite a heated discussion going on. Tristram was shrugging his shoulders and calling to his dog.

David called to them. 'Morning prayers. Ten minutes, in the barn.'

'They do this all the time!' Sunny said to Mike. 'They're always disappearing to talk to their God.'

'I know. I noticed.' Yes, he'd noticed all right . . . times when they were all together, not expecting anything bad to happen . . .

'Tristram!' Sunny shouted. 'Tris, hi! Do you like my dress?'

Tris didn't answer her. He had his slingshot with him. Mike smiled to himself. Tris would love to use that on him, he was sure. But he wouldn't get the chance.

'Oh, I think he is *so* good looking. I think Gideon's good looking too, but he only ever talks to me about God. I think I'd better aim for Tris, don't you?'

'You're wasting your time, Sunny. You won't get anywhere with him.'

'Mike! Are you jealous?' she squeaked in delight.

'Don't be stupid.'

'Well, I'm sure I can get Tris. I'm years younger than Shanna. She's really old, she must be at least twenty-five. Why shouldn't I get him? I bet I can.'

'I've got a feeling these people aren't into what you're into.'

'What do you mean?'

'They're into marriage, for one thing. You know – one partner for life.'

'Oh yes, that's what Shanna told me. No *fun* at all. Still, maybe I can change that. You know, Tris is nice, but he's not so nice as you.' She ran her fingers down his arm. 'You really are looking good today.'

'Sunny! Shanna wants you,' said David. Mike didn't miss the deep frown of concern when the older man looked at Sunny. She was oblivious to it.

'I was just telling Mike that I really like it here.'

'It's a new thrill. Is that what it's all about, Sunny? Just a new thrill? You'll get tired of it – soon. She will,' Mike turned to David, 'and then you'll have even more trouble to deal with.'

'Mike! Need more sticks.' Constance was carrying a kettle to the fire.

'Mike thinks I look pretty in this dress,' Sunny was telling Shanna.

'Oh.' Shanna stared hard at the Watcher. '*Does* he?' She put a protective arm round the girl. 'Sunny, if he gets anywhere near you, you just tell Gideon or Tris.'

Mike laughed. 'And what will they do?'

'It's not what *they'll* do that worries me,' Shanna replied.

'Mike, the sticks!' said Constance.

'Three days. Three whole days,' he muttered.

'Three *long* days,' said Shanna. 'Just don't you touch this girl.'

'Which girl? Her? Or you? Wouldn't touch you – Unclean.'

'All right, that's enough,' said David.

'What's enough? You don't tell me when to speak.'

'Mike, my boy, while you're here, there are a whole new set of rules to play by. I'd have thought you realised that.'

'You're not going to make me play by your rules.'

'You'll live by them, while you're here.' That was Tristram's voice. He was standing behind the Watcher.

'You going to make me, city boy? I'd like to see you try.'

Tristram's gaze rested on Mike's shoulder. Mike, still in no position to carry out a threat, spat on the ground. 'You call this living?'

'What do you call what goes on in the Towns and city? *That's* not living,' said Tris.

'How did you ever escape the labour-force, city boy? A spell in the plant would have done you good.'

'How did I escape?' Tristram brandished his slingshot.

'You know what I'd like to do with that?' Mike asked him.

'I think I can guess.'

'Good . . . keep thinking about it.'

'I need those sticks, Mike,' said Constance.

'Get them yourself!' Mike's eyes met those of Constance and he saw emotion there. He immediately felt something he hadn't felt in a very, very long time. He was appalled and fought the feeling. Remorse! No. Never.

And yet this old woman had shown him nothing but kindness since he'd arrived. She washed and dressed his wound twice a day. In fact, she and Gideon were the only ones in this group of Unclean who hadn't shown him any vitriol, ill-concealed contempt or anger . . . and Constance had constantly displayed the sort of caring kindness that he hadn't known since – no, he didn't want to think about that.

He felt a sudden urge to apologise to her. He struggled with it. He couldn't do it. He was shocked to think he might even want to.

'Elderly filth!' For the first time in his life, he hated himself for saying it. He felt confused . . . and suddenly very worried.

'I'll help you get the sticks, Mike,' said Sunny.

'Shut up.' He went into the barn. Sunny rushed after him, but they heard him shouting at her to go away. David went to remove her unwanted presence before the Watcher did.

'Prayer meeting in the cottage, I guess,' said Tristram.

'I really can't handle this,' Shanna said, plaintively. 'I mean, I really can't.'

'He's lonely.' Constance got down on her knees beside the fire.

Shanna and Tristram exchanged glances.

'He's lonely,' repeated Constance. 'Can't you see it in his eyes? It breaks my heart. He's lonelier than anyone I ever knew before.'

'You can't get me to sympathise with him, Constance,' said Shanna. 'I'm sorry. I can't do it. I don't want to. It's impossible.'

'No. Nothing's impossible. Compassion. That's what we need.'

'You don't understand. I don't *want* to feel compassion for him!'

Constance was silent for a moment. Then she said, quietly, 'Shanna, when you think about the cross, the crucifixion, what do you see?'

'What?'

'What do you *see*?' insisted the old woman.

'What do you mean, what do I see?'

'Sin,' said Tris. 'All the wrong stuff we've done . . .'

'How much, Tristram? How much of the "wrong stuff"?' persisted Constance.

'All of it,' said Tristram.

'All of it? Are you sure?'

'Yes. All of mine.'

'And all of *his*?'

Tris shifted from foot to foot and said, 'Yes. I guess.'

'Shanna?'

'Con, don't you remember all those people in the city? What about Zach? Watchers killed him . . . they're inhuman. They are. How can you ask me to ever feel anything *good* for a Watcher?'

'Come on.' Constance ushered them both into the cottage. And there, joined by Gideon and, later on, David, they stayed – for a very long time.

Mike, in the barn, was furious with himself, with the camp, with everything. Three days here. Three terrible days. Day four was going to be just one more stretched-out period of frustration. How long would it be before he was fit enough to *do* anything? He had to push himself to pick up a few sticks. What if the wound got infected? What if he got a fever? He couldn't expect Constance to keep it clean now. He put the momentary feelings of remorse down to his unusual predicament. He wasn't fit. It was nothing to worry about. He had to work out a plan – he hadn't even begun to get a plan together in his head – what was *wrong* with him? He could just about stand the pain now, the dull ache, the fiery soreness. Get your head together, he thought. Get it together! He was hot. He had a fever. He was sure of it.

And where were they, these Illegals? It occurred to Mike that it had been a while since he'd seen any activity at all; there was no one else in the barn. He could see, just outside, Sunny sitting with Tristram's dog. She was stroking it, occasionally waving her hand in the air as the flies and other buzzing insects that seemed to be everywhere here, flew in her face. But now . . . here was movement from the cottage.

And what was this?

'What are you doing?'

Shanna looked as angry as he felt. She was carrying a bowl of water.

'Constance – she's – I've got the privilege of looking at your wound today.'

'No.' He'd got used to Constance touching him – so gently, too – but he didn't want this woman anywhere near him.

'Why?' Her lip curled. 'Elderly filth better than younger filth?'

'Get out.'

'Don't think I'm happy about this. But they don't want you to get an infection. And die.'

But you do, thought Mike.

'I think I've already got one. That should please you.'

She put the bowl down. Then she turned and walked out of the barn. Once outside, she leaned against the old brick wall of the cottage.

'It's no good. You're asking too much. I can't do it.'

'Yes, you can,' said Constance, softly.

'I can't bear it. I can't bear to touch him.'

'It's just fear. It'll be all right.'

'I know I shouldn't be frightened . . . I know it . . . deep inside. But I can't . . .'

'He's a man. He's injured. And he's weak.'

'Yes. Weak . . . like a vicious dog chained to a post!'

'Shanna! If he can't hurt you, and he can't right now, why not tend his wound?'

Shanna shook her head impatiently. 'I keep thinking about what he's done. And what he'd like to do.'

'You think someone is untouchable? That's not so, is it?'

'He *is* untouchable.'

'No. No one is untouchable.'

'I can do it,' said Tristram.

'Tristram, you go and get us a few rabbits. We'll need to eat tonight, remember.'

'I'll do it,' offered Gideon. 'No problem.'

'No. This is Shanna's task.'

Tristram took Shanna's hand. She nodded. And then she went back into the barn.

'All right,' she said. 'Let's do this.'

'Just can't keep away from me, huh?' replied Mike, with heavy sarcasm.

'If we're going to do this, let's get it over.'

She moved Mike's shirt. Then she uttered a small cry. She'd never seen anything like it in her entire life.

'Oh, God.'

This body had been the recipient of so much hatred. She stood away. Her stricken expression alarmed Mike.

'What's up? Bad infection, right?'

'I've – no, there's no infection.'

'What then?'

'Your back . . . I've never seen . . .'

For a moment, Mike didn't know what she meant. And then, he did.

'Oh, that. Happened when my partner – the one before Jay – got into some trouble with a Debtor who knew how to use a flame-torch. I kind of got in the way.'

He thought she was impressed. Women had been, in the past, after all; a certain *type* of woman – the only sort he'd ever really known.

'The Debtor paid . . . made sure of that . . . have a look at my chest. Got a big scar there, east to west – a city kid's revenge. He paid too. And on my leg – '

'Don't.'

'Don't? Don't what?'

She *wasn't* impressed. He could see it in her face. He
was irritated with himself for feeling disappointed. Why
should he feel disappointed that this Unclean woman
wasn't *impressed* with him? It was ridiculous. So he made
sure he sounded as if he really didn't care. And he didn't
. . . did he?

'Ah, I see. You don't want me to tell you that this is all
the result of the city scum, the Unclean, trying to do to
me what I do to them? Well, that's what it is, so too
bad. This is real life. This is how it is.' He fingered his
chin. 'Except for this one. That was Jay's doing. Total
accident. That kid wasn't much of a Watcher.' He
smiled a little at the sudden memory and spoke half to
himself. 'I don't know . . . it's crazy, the rest don't trouble
me at all. Not even the burn. But this little scar here still
hurts.'

'Jay . . . the Watcher who was killed?'

'Yeah, my partner. You should have rescued him, not
me. He wanted out.'

'The friend who wounds . . . the deepest cut of all,' said
Shanna, quietly.

'What?'

'Judas. Only that was no accident.'

'Judas? What's that?'

'Judas was a traitor. He betrayed his friend.'

'One of you?'

'Oh, no . . . long, long time ago.'

Mike frowned. The woman was pale, looking at him.
She was ill . . . no, not ill.

'You'd better not be feeling sorry for me . . . you are,
aren't you? Sorry for me!' New fury welled up in him.
'Don't pity me! I don't want your pity! Pity yourself!' He
grabbed the bowl with his left hand and with all the energy

he could muster, slung it across the barn. 'You're all as good as dead!'

Constance was waiting outside and Shanna ran up to her, feeling relief and comfort as Constance put her arms around her.

'Oh, Con. Such pain.'

'Such pain, Shanna, you're right. And most of it on the inside.'

'You knew what you were doing . . . you knew how I'd feel.'

They left Mike alone for a long time after that. Only he wasn't really alone; he was experiencing such a surge of conflict, he felt he was fighting an army of unseen enemies. That woman was Unclean. She pitied him. She did. He'd seen it. He'd have preferred her hatred. He'd have preferred her admiration. The pain was worse in his shoulder. He felt he was going crazy.

He was relieved when Gideon appeared and told him some of them were going fishing sometime soon; there was a big pond about a half a mile away, the stream fed into it: they'd catch plenty of fish. Would he like to go, if he felt up to it? Yes, yes he would like to go fishing, whatever that meant. Yes, he'd be up to it. He had to get out of this camp.

'Good!' said Gideon, and looked genuinely pleased. It struck Mike that Gideon always looked pleased and happy. He wondered, for the first time, if there was something seriously wrong with the boy. Was there something seriously wrong with the whole lot of them? Who ever would rescue a Watcher? He kept his eye on Tristram – Tristram who came back to the camp that evening with dead animals in his hand, looking tremendously proud of himself, his dog at his heels. They ate those animals . . . rabbits, they said – the ones that screamed when a stoat caught them – animals that ran free. They ate vegetables, too, dug up from the ground. After his initial revulsion at the thought of that *dirt* they'd grown in, he'd eaten some, and found they tasted better than anything he'd tasted before; but then, as they'd said, all he'd ever tasted before was Vermalyde in its various forms.

And all the time he was thinking, I have to get strong. I have to get fit. I have to have a plan. I have to work something out . . . but what? And when? And how?

14

Fishing

Mike wasn't sure if he was happy or not to see that Shanna was in the party going fishing. She didn't look at him. She hadn't tended his wound again; Constance had done that, smiling, caring, not saying anything about what he'd said to her. Why was this old woman so relentlessly *nice* to him? Why was Gideon always trying to talk to him, laugh with him? They *knew* he was the enemy. Here was Gideon now, walking alongside him, concerned that the half mile might be too much for Mike: after all, he was still in a weakened state.

'Take care, Gideon, my boy,' David had said, as they left the camp. Mike knew what *that* meant. And he noticed Tris was with them, taking his slingshot.

Mike was busy thinking about that slingshot as they walked to the pond. But when Tris grasped it, slapped a stone in it, and brought down a large bird, he wished he could see the whole event re-played. The city boy was good. A worthy opponent, thought Mike: probably the only one in this whole camp.

'Oh, Tris!' said Sunny – yes, she was there. 'Tris, that is so fantastic. You're a fantastic guy, you know.' And Mike had to smile to see the way Tristram was visibly embarrassed by her gushing flattery.

The first view of the pond – it was really a small lake – was an amazing one. It was shimmering, a silvery

137

brightness behind a row of trees; the beauty of it almost took his breath away. And it *was* beautiful. Perhaps the most beautiful thing he'd ever seen – he wasn't sure – he hadn't spent much of his life thinking about what was beautiful and what wasn't. Sunlight danced on the water, spangles of light like a shower. The shallow trickle running behind the farm was suddenly something far more mighty here, splashing into the deep water.

On the other side of the pond, the forest was thick and dense. Escape occurred to Mike, but it was impossible; Tris and that slingshot would stop him. And even if he got away, where would he go? How could he find the highway? How he hated this *trapped* feeling . . . the vulnerability which was so alien to him.

'Are you OK, Mike? You're sweating,' said Gideon.

'I'm all right.' That wasn't true. The walk had jarred the broken bone.

'You don't look all right.'

'I'm all *right*, I said.'

'Made of tough stuff, these Watchers,' commented Tris. Quietly, he said to Gideon, 'He's healing very quickly. Give him another couple of weeks and he'll be almost there.'

'Three weeks.'

'You think so? I don't. Got to do some serious talking when we get back.'

'Give it three weeks.'

'Two weeks, Gideon. Two weeks.'

They settled down on a grass bank beside the water. Mike sat down – carefully – with his back against a tree. And he watched the fishing. He watched every detail. After all, that was what he was trained to do . . . and take life, as quickly and cleanly as possible . . . yes, he knew how to watch; watch people, not fish, and he did that too. He watched Tris, smiling at Shanna. He watched genial

Gideon, patiently showing Sunny how to fish. He watched Sunny, giggling, enjoying herself, and found himself wondering again why she had wanted to get away from her life in the New Towns; a life of privilege – but no fishing. He was pretty convinced, actually, that she was just in it all for the adventure.

Mike watched Gideon's amicable expression break into soft whistling as he caught a silvery fish. Why, thought Mike again, why is Gideon always so affable? He remembered Kurt Dane, the hand on the doorknob, the blood . . .

Mike had never seen a real, live fish before. He didn't say so. He tried not to appear interested, but he was secretly enthralled by the scaly, flapping thing, the thing with a hook in its mouth, thrown into a basket. Mike watched, and by the time the sun was high in the sky, he was identifying with the silver captives, gasping for another chance of life. He felt as caught as they were.

But for all his sense of captivity, he couldn't help but respond to the quietness there by that water. He soon realised that he was experiencing something he never had before. It was an odd sensation, and one that worried him at first. He mustn't let go of his guard . . . he mustn't slip . . . but yes, he was relaxing. He couldn't help it. The softness of the breeze, the stream, the blue and red insects flying over the pond, insects that would have disgusted him just a few days before but now seemed fascinating in their four-winged, hovering beauty; it was peaceful. Really peaceful. Had he ever known such peace in his life?

A rustling in the bushes nearby made him jerk back into a state of alertness. Good job you were here and not in the city, thought Mike, suddenly annoyed with himself. You'd be dead.

'That dog again. Don't let her near the water!' said Shanna.

'She jumps in,' Gideon told Sunny. 'Scares the fish away.'

Tris called his dog.

'Let's give Mike a real treat,' said Gideon. 'You going to do it, Tris?'

Mike was on his guard. What did Gideon mean? It zapped into his mind that they'd brought him here to drown him. He tried to get up and his hand went down into some foliage.

'Ow! What's that?'

'What's wrong?' said Shanna.

'Pain . . . it's a rash . . . that plant . . .'

He noticed Shanna and Gideon exchange a fleeting smile. Had they deliberately engineered this trip so he could get infected by one of the poisonous plants in the Deadlands? This rash – what did it mean? How quickly would it spread? How long would it take to do its work? *What* was it going to do to him? How painful was it going to get? Was this what it was all about for them – they were going to get a kick out of seeing him in some kind of torment?

Shanna was shaking her head at Gideon. Why?

She got to her feet, picked a few large leaves from a plant nearby, and took them to the Watcher.

'It's a rash!' Mike repeated.

'Stop panicking. I thought Watchers could handle anything. Give me your hand.'

'No way.'

'Give me your *hand*!' She grabbed and held his hand firmly whilst she rubbed the leaves on the small white lumps. She could barely conceal a smile. Something about the incident had obviously amused her. Mike wasn't amused at all. It stunned him a little that these people who had rescued him were so sick as to bring him here and enjoy his agony when they'd said they were helping him . . . not that he wanted their help.

'Not everything here is your enemy. These are dock leaves. That pain will soon go.'

'What?'

'The pain . . . you should see your face. It's just a stinging nettle.'

The pain swiftly disappeared, and Mike was astounded. He almost thanked Shanna – but didn't. And he didn't hear Gideon say to the woman, 'He's becoming a bit more human to you, now, isn't he?'

Tristram was pulling up handfuls of long grass. He lit a fire, building a strange sort of primitive oven for the fish, covering it with grass. Some time later, Mike tasted the result; a fish called trout stuffed with something they called sorrel.

'Wow, this is just great!' Sunny enthused. 'Tris, you're so clever.'

'What does Mike think?' asked Gideon.

'About Tris or the food? The food's good,' admitted Mike.

He watched Gideon and Tristram exchange grins.

As Mike ate the fish, he thought about just what he was eating. How quickly he'd got used to eating stuff that had *lived*. He had to admit, this was something he'd miss back in the Towns.

'I always thought people who didn't have the Code were horrible,' Sunny was saying. 'But you're the nicest people I ever met.'

'Well, thank you, Sunny,' said Gideon, 'we like you too.'

Encouraging her – bad move! thought Mike, as Sunny smiled coyly at Gideon.

'Why don't you have the Code?' asked Sunny. 'Is it just because of your religion thing?'

'We don't want it. I was thinking,' said Tris, 'no one here has the Code, do they – except Sunny.'

All eyes switched to Mike.

'Don't be silly,' said Sunny, 'Mike's not an Illegal. He's a Watcher.'

'We know that, Sunny!' Tristram leaned back on his right elbow and looked at Mike. 'But you're not permanently Coded, are you?'

'Nobody is. Give me a Laserscan and I'll show you how easy it is to lose your legality.'

'Yes, but it's different with you. Government don't give Watchers a permanent Code, do they? Gets renewed, doesn't it, every six months? Why do you think that is, Mike? Do you think it's got something to do with control? Does the fear of losing the Code keep you under their control, Mike? Stops you getting too much power, doesn't it?'

'Does it? You tell me, city boy. You seem to know so much about Watchers.'

'Well, I know a bit. Shall I tell you what I think?'

'Guess you're going to anyway.'

'I think you're as much a prisoner as any of those city people.'

Mike laughed, scornfully. 'Yeah? How do you work that out?'

'Work it out yourself. You're not free to do anything or go anywhere or be anything other than a Watcher. Tell me that's not true.'

'I don't *want* to be anything other than a Watcher!'

'Don't you want to be free?'

'Free?' Mike stared blankly at Tris. 'No such word.'

Tris indicated everything with one arm. 'Yes there is.'

'Not in my world.'

'Then your world stinks.' Tristram sat up. 'They call this the Deadlands, but your whole world stinks of fear, fear, fear. And of course, that's what you want – isn't it? Only you're caught up in it, too . . . yeah?'

Mike said nothing.

'Do you know what it's like for those poor people in the city? Eh? Do you? Do you know what it's like for them every day knowing Watchers are just waiting for the opportunity to take them out – for no reason? Do you know what it's like living in that stinking place? The only hope they've got of getting out is to go and work in the processing plant. Do you know the conditions in those places? No one lasts more than five years because of the toxic – '

'City boy, you talk a lot.'

'Sometimes.' Tris lay back on the grass, his arms folded under his head. 'We never know what happens to the re-assessed but we've seen some of them come back from the plant. But they don't come back for long . . . they think they might recover but they don't. And yet, you know Mike, some of them think it's a better prospect than staying in the city; at least they get warm meals and a bed every night and probably best of all, no Watchers . . . and Med care every day if they need it – and they do.'

'All right, Tris,' said Gideon, 'it's late. We're all tired. Let's – '

'No. Don't stop me. I'm in the mood – and I've never had a captive Watcher before.' Tris glanced at Mike. 'I want to know what he thinks. Mike! Know what they all want, the city people, really? That New Town privilege. They'd give anything to go with those Aid workers, get reassessed. What do you think of Aid workers, Mike? I bet if you had your way there'd be no aid, no medicine, no food, no clean water or any help at all going into that place.'

Gideon, apparently increasingly uncomfortable with Tristram's heartfelt tirade against the Watcher, inter-vened.

'Come on, Tris. Not now, eh?'

But Tristram ignored him.

'Mike, what do you think of the Aid workers? Really? Think they're a waste of time? Don't you ever get sick of what you do? I mean, what kind of rewards do you get for it? Credit? Going to live long enough to use it? I suppose you get a hefty slice of that New Town privilege, don't you?' The Watcher didn't reply. 'Man, how can anyone think it's good in those places? You even spit or have a drink of alcohol and some Watcher is going to be on your tail ... and don't get anything wrong with your health! Anything too bad – you die; not so bad – you're dumped; and if you're born with anything wrong with you, or you're the result of one of those genetic – '

'Remind me to talk to you sometime,' said Mike, 'about this problem you have with your mouth.'

'Go on, Mike . . . tell me,' Tristram got up. 'Your world stinks. Tell me to my face that it doesn't. You can't, can you?'

Mike couldn't. He was angry. He felt as if Tristram had won some battle, a battle that he had lost and had hardly known how to fight.

'It's getting cooler – think there's going to be a storm,' said Shanna.

'Yeah,' said Tris, looking at the Watcher. 'I think that's about right.'

'Come on Sunny. Time to make a move,' said Shanna, nudging the girl, who was half asleep. 'You coming, boys?'

'In a minute.' Tris turned away, making an effort to calm down.

The girl and the woman headed for a small hut up the hill where they were going to spend the night. And Gideon talked quietly to Tristram about fishing: how many fish they'd caught, and whether they should spend time trying to catch more. Mike didn't take any notice of their conversation. He was feeling an unbearable blackness overwhelming him, a blackness springing from an unknown pit. The blackness flew over him and alighted on him like some foul bird. He hadn't been able to disagree with Tristram's statement about his world. He felt as if the city boy had made him admit something to himself that he would rather have forgotten. Yes, his world stank. It stank of death and corruption. He shut his eyes.

'I think this trip has been too much for him,' he heard Gideon say. 'I know that broken bone gives him a hard time but he's fighting it all the way. Still, I suppose he's trained to fight.'

'He's trained to kill.' That was Tris.

'You still don't hold out much hope for him then.'

'Far from it. I believe in miracles. Look what happened to me.'

'I believe too. Got to seek and save what was lost, like the Master.'

'Can't get much more lost than a Watcher.'

'And you wish I'd stayed lost,' said Mike, opening his eyes. 'Think I'm planning how to kill you tonight? Some things aren't possible, even for a Watcher.'

'I think you'd do it if you could,' said Tristram.

'Do you?'

'Yes.'

'OK. I'd have to.'

'Because you're a Watcher, or because you wanted to?' Gideon brought his knees up and rested his chin on them.

'What?'

'Would the Watcher kill us? Or would Mike?'

'You know, you don't make sense to me a lot of the time.'

'But this is easy. Would the Watcher kill us, or would Mike kill us? What do you think?'

'You're still not making any sense.'

'Then you can't separate the two.'

Mike felt as if he'd just been attacked and lost – again. He ran his left hand through his hair.

'At least I know what's happening in the city. I understand it. I don't understand anything about you or this place.'

'Do you still want to go back? I mean, really? What do you think you've got to go back to? Doesn't sound like you've got anything or anybody.'

Mike didn't need to hear that.

'You don't have to go back.'

'Right. This I understand. You mean, the city boy here is going to whack me with one of his stones. Or plant a knife between my ribs while I'm asleep.'

'You don't get it, do you!' exclaimed Tristram.

'I don't want to get it. You're thinking about it all the time, aren't you? How to do it. When to do it. You're transparent, city boy. Well, that's just fine by me; keep thinking. And when you're done, we'll sort it out between us.'

Tris shook his head. 'Watcher, you've got a lot to learn. You think I hate you because I was a city kid. It's true, I do hate everything about where you come from . . . where *I* come from . . . but it's not personal.'

'Yeah, right.'

'I hate what you *are* – what you *do*. I don't hate *you*. Do you understand that? Do you get the difference?'

Mike didn't.

'You can change,' said Tris. 'I did.'

'Mike, Tris is right. We don't hate you and we don't want to kill you! That's not why we rescued you,' said Gideon, earnestly. 'You don't have to go back – not because anyone is going to hurt you, but because you can stay with us.'

Mike laughed his sudden laugh. 'Stay with you! You don't want me here any more than I want to be here. I'm your worst nightmare.'

'But you don't have to be! You don't have to be our enemy. You don't have to threaten us. It doesn't have to be like that. Tris lived by violence in the city . . . it doesn't have to stay with you, control you.'

'It doesn't control me.'

'You're going to say, you're in control of it,' Tristram told him. 'But are you?'

'I don't speak your language, city boy. And you sure don't speak mine. All I know is, you don't want a Watcher with you.'

'No, but we want Mike Merrick,' said Gideon.

Tristram shook his head. 'Give it up, Gideon. He said it himself. He doesn't understand.'

'I'm sorry about that.'

You're always sorry, Gideon, thought Mike. Maybe one day I'll give you something to be really sorry about . . . maybe I already have.

15

Afterwards

Flames . . . shouting . . . a relentless howling, screaming mob . . . the lights went out . . . hammering, hammering, hammering –

'Jay!'

Mike woke up with the name on his lips. And everyone else woke up too.

'Mike! Mike, it's OK,' said Gideon.

'No, it's not. It's not OK. Nothing's OK.'

Mike felt a fool. He was in this tiny hut, an old shepherd's hut, they said. He was on the floor, furthest from the door. Shanna was next to him, then Sunny, then Gideon. Tristram was by the entrance. There'd been an intense discussion about the sleeping arrangements. It seemed to cause problems that men and women were all together. And then there was the problem of where to put the Watcher. The message had been clear to Mike as soon as the rain fell hard and they all took refuge in this claustrophobic place. He had to get over all of them before he could escape. And he wasn't even thinking of getting away.

They'd lit a small fire in the hearth. It cast weird shadows in the musty old building. A smoky smell mingled with damp and fish.

'What's wrong? Is Mike all right?' said Sunny.

'Nightmares,' said Gideon. 'He has nightmares. Bad dreams.'

'Why?'

'Well, we're trying to get to the bottom of it.'

'I should think his whole life is at the bottom of it,' Tris muttered, as Gideon stirred up the embers.

Mike felt too embarrassed to speak. He loathed them talking about him like this. He loathed them knowing his night-time vulnerability.

The hammering persisted. Rain slapped onto the flat roof and leaked down the walls.

'I'm really cold, Tris,' came Sunny's whining voice. 'Can't I sleep nearer to the fire . . . next to you?'

'I'm not near the fire.'

'This floor is so hard . . . it's all dirt. I'd like to sleep next to you, Tris.'

'Well, you can't. Shanna! You OK there, Shanna?'

'Of course she's OK,' Mike said. 'Why shouldn't she be OK?'

'Shanna, if you want to move – '

'Why should she want to move? What are you implying?'

'Nothing.'

'Yeah, right. Know how to push *your* button, city boy!'

'Don't try it!' warned Tristram.

'Let it go, Tris. Shanna's all right there,' Gideon told him.

'Yes, I am, Tris. I'm just fine,' said Shanna.

'Are you sure?'

'I'm sure.'

'Because if you're not – '

'*I'm* not!' complained Sunny.

They settled down again. Then Tristram's dog decided to move, and curled up at Mike's side.

'Look at that!' said Gideon.

'Get this vermin away from me!'

Tris called the dog and it went to him.

'That thing's a menace,' muttered Mike. 'It's always hanging around me.'

'She likes you,' said Shanna, quietly. And Mike was reminded of Jay talking about Sunny liking him – that night he was killed. Shanna was still speaking. 'You should be flattered.'

'Flattered?'

'Dogs are choosy. Tris rescued her from the city. Some Watcher had tried to finish her off. Not you though – she'd have remembered.'

Mike tried to ease his shoulder by sitting up straight against the wall. But it was running with water. He couldn't get comfortable.

'You all right?'

He didn't answer her.

'Mike! Are you all right?'

She'd used his name . . . why did that make him *feel* something?

'You care?' His voice was hard, but even the hint of her concern had touched him in a way he didn't want to be touched. Remember – this woman saw what the Debtor had done to you and from that minute has *pitied* you, he thought. She was looking at him, and for a moment he thought he didn't see any pity at all. She just seemed troubled . . . troubled that he wasn't comfortable. That pleased him. But he wasn't pleased that it pleased him.

'City boy likes you.'

'We're good friends.'

'Think he wants you . . . *close* to him tonight.'

'It's not like that.'

'What *is* it like?'

'We're friends.'

'Friends! Is that how it is for him?'

'What's the matter? You find it odd to think we might be friends?'

'Men and women aren't friends where I'm from.'

'That's sad.'

'Is it?' He shut his eyes, trying to block out any feelings of real attraction he had for this woman. He didn't want to be attracted to her. That wasn't in the plan. She was the Unclean.

But what was the plan? Well, he had time now to work it out. He'd more or less figured that they weren't likely to move him on to expose more of their network. So, what was going to happen to him? One thing was for sure, he couldn't let them decide that; he'd have to move first. He'd have to get fit enough, and not let them know, and then – then what? Nothing for it: he'd have to take them out, one by one. Tris would have to be the first; he was the biggest threat. Then David. Then Gideon – he'd make it quick for that naïve boy – and then Constance – and then Shanna –

He turned to look at her. She was asleep now. The firelight caught one side of her face. He found himself in the middle of a fantasy where he took Shanna back to the Towns. But she'd never go – at least, not willingly . . . she'd need some *persuading*. After all, she feared, hated Watchers – and she pitied him! Besides, she was an Illegal, she didn't have the Code, she was a *Christian*. And anyway – there was something else . . . something strange . . . something unlike any other woman he had known. But what *was* that elusive something?

There was a movement next to her – Sunny. What about Sunny?

Of course, killing them all wouldn't be enough. He needed one of them alive to find out where the others were. And there *were* others. David would be the best one, he must know it all; but no, perhaps Mike would spare Constance. He almost laughed out loud. Was he really thinking of sparing the elderly? It caught him in a wave of nausea: no, it couldn't be . . . did he *feel* for Constance? For Shanna? Why was he thinking he didn't want Gideon to suffer? Was it the result of some sentiment, some feeling? How had *that* crept up on him? No. This was all wrong. He didn't want to feel.

'You're losing your grip!' he said to himself. 'You're losing it. You've got to take them all out, and you've got to do it fast. As soon as you can. If there's more, let Cain sort it out.' He wanted to stamp right down on this bunch of Christians. Get rid of them. Erase them. Blot out any *feelings* for ever.

* * *

'He's not well.'

'His wound is healing. I think he's all right, just very tired. Better let him rest.'

'Gideon, we can't leave him on his own,' said Tris.

'The rain's eased off, we need more fish. An hour or so should do it.'

'Yes, but we can't leave him here for an hour.'

'I think we could. We can see the hut from the pond. I mean, where's he going to go?'

'What if he just upped and disappeared? I'd rather know where he was at all times, Gideon.'

'It's OK.' Shanna shrugged her shoulders. 'I'll stay with him.'

'No!' said Tristram.

'What's the problem? He looks pretty sick to me. The door will be open, you'll be just down the hill.'

'Shanna – '

'Tris – I've got to get over this. I'm beating it. I am. This will help.' Shanna smiled at him. 'Anyway, you two are good at fishing. I'm awful. Take Sunny with you.'

'Tris, will you show me how to do it today?' Sunny asked him, with her cutest smile. 'I want to get really good . . . you know, I pick things up really quickly.'

'What? Oh, OK. Shanna – if he gives you any trouble . . .'

'He won't. Look at him. He's sound asleep.'

'All right. Leave that door wide open.'

'I will!'

'Even if it rains.'

'Tristram, go!'

'In fact, stand there, right in the doorway, so we can see you. OK?'

'Tristram!'

'I'm not happy about leaving her with him!' Tris said to Gideon as they set off.

'It'll be all right. He's not going to do anything. Anyway, we aren't far away and we won't be long.'

Shanna watched them go. She stood at the open door, and saw them reach the pond. Tristram kept looking back at the hut – when he wasn't trying to get Sunny to leave him alone. She seemed to be edging closer and closer to him, talking, pointing, and her laughter drifted up the hill. Shanna looked up: the sky was relentlessly grey, with a few almost-black clouds not far off. It would rain again soon.

Suddenly, she felt uncomfortable. She turned – the Watcher was awake.

'Watching me?' she said, hiding her unease with an up-beat, confident manner. 'Well, I guess that's what you do.'

'Looks like you're doing the watching today, huh? Where did the others go?'

'Fishing.'

'They left you alone with me?'

Shanna glanced at the pond. Tris was looking at the hut again, and that dispelled the unease.

'How do you feel?' she asked. 'You're not looking so good this morning.'

'You scared?'

'What?'

'You heard me.'

Again she glanced at the pond. 'Scared? What of?'

'What do you think?'

'You?' She took a deep breath. 'No. I'm not scared.'

'You were.'

'I'm not now,' she replied, curtly.

'I think you are.'

'No.'

'Come away from the door, then. You keep looking at them.'

'I'm just seeing what they've caught.'

'That far off? You've got good eyesight.'

With some effort, he heaved himself to his feet.

'I'm not scared of you. All right?'

'You should be.'

'I don't think so.'

'I won't be like this forever.'

'Yes, Mike. We know that.' She purposely walked away from the door. 'Want some water?'

'A few scars . . . a few nightmares . . . a bit of pity for the Watcher. Poor judgement, Christian.'

'Perhaps. Do you want the water or not?'

'Feel sorry for me . . . like you'd feel sorry for that dog if it was injured. Right?'

Shanna hoped he didn't notice her hand tremble as she poured water from a large container into a small cup.

'I said, right?'

'No. Wrong. You're not an animal.' She felt her face flush as the significance of what she had just said hit home.

'Not an animal.' A hint of a smile made the Watcher's stern features a little softer for a moment. 'Yeah . . .' He'd moved to the remains of the fire. He steadied himself, his left hand on the shelf above the hearth. She handed him the cup, and he took it, drank, gave it back to her, and steadied himself again. 'Yeah, but you don't think I'm quite human though, do you?'

'I don't know what you mean,' said Shanna, a little too quickly.

'Yes you do.'

'Oh – you mean all that stuff they say about Watchers not having a soul.' Shanna spoke as casually as she could. 'I don't believe that.'

'Don't you?'

'Everybody's got a soul. Even – '

'Even me.'

There was a moment of silence. Shanna's uneasiness returned. The Watcher wasn't looking at her.

'It's raining again. The boys will be back in a minute. Better pack up – '

'You're scared now,' he observed, still not looking at her.

'I'm *not*!'

He looked at her then. Yes, he was injured, but he still had an imposing physical presence. He was over six feet – about six foot two – and powerfully built. Shanna began to feel very nervous. She wanted to go and stand right by the door, or even down the hill, but she also didn't want this Watcher to know that his intimidating manner rattled her. It was designed to do just that, of course; Mike was obviously very good at this sort of thing.

'Not many women want to be alone with a Watcher.'

'Yes, I know that.' Then, with a boldness she didn't feel, she said, cuttingly, 'Most of them have to be paid, don't they?'

Her words had an immediate effect. He seemed surprised. She'd thrown him off guard and she wasn't sure how or why. Anyway, it gave her confidence.

'Tris was talking about your world last night. But what I want to know is, what's it like, living in your world, Mike, a world where *nobody* cares? Where even the women are with you just because they can get a load of Credit, sleeping with a Watcher?'

He averted his gaze, resting his forehead on his arm. For a moment, she thought he was really ill. Then he spoke in a low, even voice, not raising his head, not meeting her eyes.

'Two types of women in my world. The scared type and the curious type. They pay the curious ones. Yeah, they rack up the Credit, and they get to have their questions answered.'

'What do you mean, their questions?' She immediately regretted asking. She was sure she didn't want to know the answer.

For a minute, she thought he wasn't going to say anything. And then he did.

'Well, you know . . . he's a Watcher . . . what's he going to be like? Give him some Stardust, let's find out . . . maybe even sell a few of the details to the kind of people who'd like to know.'

'That's – that's terrible.'

He looked at her. He had a very direct gaze. Shanna noticed for the first time how very brown his eyes were.

'It's just part of the deal.'

'It's a terrible deal.'

'You think so? Well, some of the guys don't mind what the girls do. Or care. Anyway . . . we can find the VidCams, it's getting the girls to keep quiet if they've been offered a fair amount of Credit that can be a bit more . . . difficult. Yeah, they like their entertainment in the New Towns; especially the government officials – the privileged.'

Shanna was sickened. 'I'm sorry, Mike.'

'Yeah, so are some of those officials.'

'Still, I'm sorry you've had that experience.'

'Experience? Oh, I've had experience.'

Shanna wondered for a brief moment ... did he feel vulnerable, talking to her like this? He'd made it clear he didn't want her pity.

'You say you're not scared ... maybe you want *your* questions answered, huh?' He put his head down again, and he sounded bitter. 'Better wait till I'm fit.'

'Shanna!'

Tristram's face was a mask of concern. There was an atmosphere in that hut; Shanna seemed distracted, and the Watcher, subdued.

'Shanna, you weren't at the door!'

'It's all right, Tris.'

Gideon was there now, too.

'Where's Sunny?' asked Shanna.

'She's coming,' said Gideon.

'OK.' Shanna went to the door, and called the girl's name. Mike watched her, closely.

'We'd better start back.' Tris addressed the Watcher. 'You well enough to walk?'

Mike said nothing. He was aware of Tristram's agitation; yes, the city boy really was keen on this woman. It occurred to Mike that he could use Tristram's feelings to his own advantage. After all, people got careless when they were on edge; they made mistakes. That could prove very useful.

'I said, are you well enough to walk?'

'Didn't catch that ... I was thinking about something else.' He was still watching Shanna, as she walked across the grass to meet Sunny.

'Don't get any ideas in that direction, Mike.'

'Told you I knew how to push your button.' A slow smile spread across Mike's face. 'Still, there's no denying it ... she does it for me.'

Tristram stepped forward, fists clenched. 'You ever touch her – '

'Tris, come on,' said Gideon, quietly. 'He's doing it on purpose. Mike isn't really going to harm Shanna.'

'Harm? Who said anything about harm?' There was a hint of real malevolence in Mike's low voice. 'What do you think, Tristram? Want me to warm her up for you?'

Gideon grabbed the furious Tristram.

'Tris! No!'

Mike kept smiling. 'Getting personal now, isn't it, city boy? Still want me to stay?'

'He's just trying to provoke you, that's all,' Gideon said, 'Tris, come on . . . he can see he's getting to you. Don't let him. Don't give in to this.'

'Watcher, you better never lay a hand on her!' Tris said, through gritted teeth.

'Or what?'

'I'm warning you!'

'Nobody warns me . . . OK?'

'Well I am, so get used to it!' Tris shook himself free from Gideon's restraint, and walked out into the cool air. And in that moment he knew that he would have to keep a much closer eye on Shanna . . .

16

Tensions

'David!' Constance spotted him standing at the edge of
the vegetable patch. He was leaning heavily on his shovel.
'David, are you all right?'

'No.'

'Are you ill?'

'Sick . . . sick in here.' David put a hand on his chest.
Mud splattered his shirt, but he didn't notice.

'It's going to rain again.'

'I keep thinking.' David turned his eyes on the old
woman, and they were moist.

'Oh, David.'

'I keep thinking about Kurt and the others.'

'We all do.'

'And I keep thinking about that time when we all came
back to the camp . . . it keeps playing in my head . . . it's
like a flashback . . . all the time.'

Constance was silent. She knew exactly what he was
seeing in his mind. That awful day when they – she, David,
Kurt, and one or two of the others – returned from their
city trip full of excitement; they'd met three people who
wanted to get out! But when they got to the camp (a lonely
spot, right by the sea . . . that gorgeous old house, half
ruined, but oh – so beautiful) all the others were gone.
Just gone . . . except for the children. The fire had been lit;
clothes just washed and hung on the makeshift line were

flapping in the evening breeze. Someone had started to cook dinner; vegetables were lying around waiting to be prepared. And there was Shanna and Gideon and the other children, hiding in the old shed, whimpering and crying.

'Con . . . your husband; my wife; Shanna's parents; Gideon's mother . . . Zoe, Vic . . .'

'I know . . .'

'Fifteen years. It's like yesterday.'

The children had been on the shoreline, fishing. They'd come back thrilled to have caught a crab. But everyone was gone. They'd hidden in the shed until the others came back.

'Watchers,' said David, fiercely. 'Watchers!'

'We aren't certain of that. We didn't find any evidence, not even a tyre track.' Constance rubbed his back and spoke in a soothing voice. 'Come on. The boys and Shanna will be home soon.'

'If that monster hasn't done something to them all.'

'David! He's not a monster. You know that.'

'I wish I could turn it off!' David put a hand to his head. 'But since he's been here, the tape runs and runs. It's getting worse. It's no good. We are going to have to have a big talk about everything . . . and then there's the matter of what to do next. I mean, we can't go back, can we? We'll have to move on – join up with one of the other cells.'

'Yes. Maybe.'

'Such a failure, Con. Such a total failure.'

'No. I don't think so. Wait and see.'

'Decisions. We've got to make decisions. Oh, Con! I just want the tape to stop playing! It's driving me crazy!'

Crazy! The word echoed around the clearing, and David and Con made their way slowly back to the camp.

* * *

'Any word?'

'Nothing.' Val was restless. 'Man, there's just no action tonight, is there?'

'Something's wrong,' said Rico. 'Thought the whole thing was sewn up. The way Rohan explained it, I thought the whole plan was foolproof. Do you think something's happened?'

His partner shrugged.

'I don't know,' said Rico, turning the car to avoid rubble in the road. 'Rohan's pretty smart. Maybe it's just a hold-up. Perhaps the timing's changed. But then, he'd have told us, wouldn't he? He told us everything else.'

'Maybe Rohan's not quite as smart as he thinks he is,' Val replied, coolly.

'Where *is* Rohan?'

'Off duty.'

'Doing what, Val? Do you know? He keeps disappearing. I wonder – '

'It's that girl.'

'What girl? Oh – *that* girl.' Rico pulled a face. 'She must be good.'

'He's enjoying it. Don't think she is.'

'Makes it a bit more exciting for him.'

'Yeah.'

Rico paused for a second. Then he said, 'Do you think it's true what they say about Rohan?'

'They say a lot of things about Rohan.'

'I mean, about his father.'

'Oh yeah . . . Debtor. He had to take a trip to the city.'

'And Rohan was the one who turned him in.'

Val pointed down a pockmarked street. 'That's where Jay got his.'

'And Merrick.'

'Still no information about that.'

'What a thought; wonder if they've got him alive somewhere.'

'Not a chance.'

'He was good.'

'He was old.' Val snatched up his rifle. 'There – on the corner. Look old and sick to you?'

'No.'

'What the hell.' Val jumped out of the car and fired.

* * *

The rain slapped against the loose slats of the barn, and the constant rattle of the tin and metal containers as the rain fell relentlessly through the many gaps in the roof almost drowned out the low voices of the people gathered in that place.

'Tris!'

The sound of his name being called didn't make Tris turn round. Arms folded, he was leaning against an ancient post, eyes fixed on the cottage across the yard.

'Tris!'

The Watcher was there. Sitting in the doorway. He was stroking Tris's dog. Yes he was. He was stroking it.

'Tristram, you haven't heard a word.'

'Yes I have.'

'Are you going to comment? Everyone else has.'

'The Watcher's petting my dog.'

'Tristram!' David slapped his hands onto his knees and got up. Tristram turned now, his dark eyes following David's worried pacing. Gideon was resting his arms on one of the stall partitions, uncharacteristically glum. He was also paler than usual. Constance and Shanna were perched together on one of the old straw bales.

'All right, you want me to comment. I don't like anything I've heard you say this morning. All right?'

'So you don't think it makes sense?'

'Of course I don't.'

'Not even in the light of recent events?'

'And there he is, petting my dog . . . the recent event.'

'We're *all* scared of what he'll do.'

'No,' said Constance, 'that's not quite true – '

'I'm not scared of him,' said Gideon.

'Neither am I.' No, thought Tristram; I'm ready for him. Anytime . . . if he gets anywhere near Shanna. And he pushed away any feelings of what might be right and wrong in that situation . . . he had to – he *had* to; it wasn't something he had the luxury of theorising about. He couldn't let anything happen to Shanna, could he? Still – that Watcher would never get her alone anywhere, anytime. It wouldn't happen.

'The Watcher isn't the only reason I want to move camp,' David continued. 'If you'd been listening to me, Tristram, you'd know that. Our time in the city is over. All right, we rescued him – it's done. And we've made enemies because of that. We can't turn the clock back. Look, we've given it our best shot, but it was only a matter of time. I'm surprised we've lasted there as long as we have . . . we've got to move on. This is it, the catalyst.'

'No. I want to go back. See if it's really over for myself.'

'Tristram! People don't want to know about escape as much as they did. They're more interested in fighting back, fighting the Watchers, trapping, killing them! Even if Mike is the only Watcher who knew about us – unlikely! – even if Edward and the rest find it in their *forgiving* hearts to give us another chance, there's a new spirit rising up in the city – and it doesn't want the Deadlands!'

'David's right,' said Gideon. 'There's a new aggression. People want what the privileged have got in the New Towns . . .'

'OK, it's getting worse,' admitted Tris, 'it's harder. But some still want to get out – look at Sunny. They still need us.'

David threw up his hands in despair.

'It's so easy for you! You're young. You've got energy, you've got life – '

'Life,' said Gideon, quietly. 'New life. Isn't that what it's all about?'

Tristram nodded. 'New, clean life. We've got it, haven't we? Isn't this what we're meant to offer others?'

'Like the Watcher? The Watcher who doesn't want it? You're not thinking rationally, my boy.'

'If I'd have thought rationally I'd never have left the city.'

'We can't afford to be reckless. We've got to protect ourselves!'

'Protect ourselves? We never could do that!' said Gideon.

'You're frightened, David!' Tris told him. 'I've seen real fear in your face, especially since we got back from the fishing trip. Fear I never thought I'd see.'

'Yes, I'm frightened! Yes, I feel more frightened every day! I'm frightened for you, for me, for Constance, for Gideon, for Shanna! We've got to get away.'

'I think we should,' Shanna said, slowly, 'it's sad. It's horrible. But there's no option. I knew it . . . knew it was over, as soon as we picked Mike up.'

Tristram put his hands on his hips. 'We're talking about two things here. OK, we've got to deal with the Watcher. But we can't abandon the city. All I can see here are people losing their faith. Well, I remember what it was like before I got mine. I still want to help people like me.'

'That's not fair, Tris,' said David. 'And besides, it isn't really two things at all. If we don't escape now, he will kill us. And I really think the whole lot of them – the Watchers – know about us. It's over. We've got to move before they come after us.'

'They won't do that!' exclaimed Shanna. 'Will they?'

'Oh, *Shanna*! Your memories are the same as mine! Or have you forgotten?'

'No, David. I never forget. Not for a second. How could I?' Shanna glanced at Gideon, and he bit his lip and looked at the ground.

'I'm going hunting.' Tristram walked out into the rain.

'We've got to think of our future!' David said to the others. 'We must face facts.' He put a hand to his eyes. 'We've got to admit defeat here. Our time is done. We've got to move.'

Gideon frowned. 'I don't know if I get what you mean about defeat.'

'Constance and I were talking when you were out of the camp. I told her and I'll tell you. I wonder whether we might have been wrong all those years ago to refuse the Code – and run.'

'What!' Shanna and Gideon said together.

'We haven't helped that many people get out, have we? Handfuls. Some of them have gone back to the city. A lot of work for what? So we can end our days waiting for *him* to break our necks in the middle of the night? Perhaps we should think of ourselves now, and just go, and make the best of it.'

'Christians refused the Code, because they believed. *We* believe. We can't have a Code that will yoke us with evil,' said Shanna, and she sounded shattered. 'I can't understand why I'm having to say this to you of all people, David.'

'We've got to be real! Some of the things involved in the prophecy just haven't happened.'

'What things? Do you need us to spell out to you what's happening all over the world? You know about the World Council and the leader of the – '

'All right, all right. But *he's* still not here, Shanna!'

'You can't say this. He's coming soon.'

David seemed suddenly deflated. 'I know. I'm sorry.'

'And you're saying that Kurt and David and the others died for nothing. And how could we ever have compromised with the so-called Church? And what about people like Tristram? Yes, there are too few . . . but if it wasn't for our – our obedience – Tris would be dead, or living without hope.'

'I know. I know!' David sat down and shook his head. 'I'm not saying good hasn't come from all this. I don't dispute that. It's what to do *now*.'

'It's Mike. He's at the heart of this problem. He *is* this problem,' Gideon said. 'But I do still hope. When I look at Mike I think of what happened to James.'

'James Oakley's a Ferryman. It just isn't the same! Watchers are a special breed . . . something quite unlike the rest of humanity. We all know what the city people say – Watchers haven't got a soul – and anyway, if we're running parallels with James, he'd been going to the temple. He was searching for the true God. When we found him that time, he was ready to hear what we had to tell him.'

'He never left the Towns though, did he?' Shanna stood up, and walked to the barn door. 'That's the one thing that's always bothered me about James Oakley . . . whenever I look at him I get this word "compromise" rolling around in my mind. He never really wanted to get out completely.'

'It's a good job he didn't,' said David, shortly. 'We need James where he is. Or we did.'

'Forgive me. Am I wrong?' Constance had been sitting so quietly, but now everyone looked at her. Her eyes were brimful of tears. 'But I *like* him.'

'Like who – James?' said David.

'I like *Mike*. I don't want him to leave us. I don't want us to leave him.'

'I think we'd better pray,' suggested Gideon. He grimaced suddenly, and shut his eyes.

'I'm prayed out, my boy – are you all right?'

'Tired. Very tired.'

'Well, rest. Look, it's decision time. Mike's getting stronger. We can't afford to keep waiting and waiting. We've got to do something.'

'But what, David?' Shanna whispered. 'What?'

* * *

Across the cobbled yard, Mike had a visitor. He saw Tris storming out of the barn; that interested him. He'd gone off into the woods. And now, here was Sunny, appearing from – where?

'You know those old sheds? There's a nice little place behind that one on the right.' She pointed. 'It's really quiet and private but you can hear everything that's going on in the barn if you listen very carefully.'

'And you did.'

'They're having a meeting.' She sat down at his feet. 'I heard what they were saying.'

'Let's have it.'

Sunny smoothed down her dress.

'What will you do for me if I tell you?'

'Sunny!'

'Oh, I'll tell you anyway. They're talking about you.'

'What a surprise.'

'And they talked about the city too. They said someone should be here but he hasn't come. He's coming
soon. I suppose that must be David Drum. And if they're
waiting for David Drum, then David with the beard
isn't – '

'I know that already.'

'Oh? How do you know?'

How could he say, he believed David was telling the
truth because he had a feeling David – and all of them –
always told the truth?

'What else, Sunny?'

'Oh, just religious stuff.'

'Getting bored? I said that would happen.'

'Well, they don't let you do much, do they? They don't
let you do anything really interesting.'

'I thought you liked it.'

Sunny screwed up her nose. 'I like Tris. I could have
fun with him but they don't let you.'

'I told you. They don't agree with your sort of fun.'

'They're all really nice though, in a weird sort of way.
They keep talking about this man who lived thousands
of years ago as if he were still alive.'

'You never did answer my question about how you came
to be with them in the city. I think it's about time you did.'

Sunny shrugged her shoulders. 'Just a buzz.'

'A buzz?'

'Yeah. I told them I was having a baby so they'd get me
out. An illegal one, you know.'

Mike sat back. 'And are you?'

'What? No. Get real.' She sighed. 'I really do like you,
Mike.' She moved and put her head on his left shoulder.
He shook her off.

'Cut it out. It's just another buzz.'

'I'll wear down your resistance sooner or later. You see
if I don't.'

She got up and stood in front of him.

'I am pretty, though. Admit it.'

'Go away.'

'I'll get you to admit it one day soon. I know you think I'm pretty really.' She flashed a beaming smile at him, and wandered off to meet Constance, who was hurrying out of the barn. It was a few minutes before Mike realised that there was some sort of problem.

Sunny rushed back to him, her vivid face a picture of concern.

'It's Gideon!'

'What about him?'

'He's collapsed, Mike! He's sick. He looked dead to me. Oh, Mike! Do you think all these Illegals have got some sort of terrible illness and I might catch it?'

Illness! That was something Mike hadn't thought of before . . . were these Unclean all sick? Was Mike already infected? And what could he do about it now?

17

A Sick Man

It was afternoon before they let Mike go into the barn.

'What's wrong?'

'He's sick.'

Gideon was lying on his straw bed, arms folded across his head and eyes. Shanna was kneeling beside him, dipping a cloth into the same bowl they used to treat Mike.

'They said he's had it before.'

'Keep your voice down, Mike.'

'What?'

'Too much noise hurts.' She put a finger to her lips. 'Lower your voice. Please.'

Mike tried to. 'What's the matter with him?'

'Headaches. Blinding headaches. Affects his vision. He has to lie down till it's over.'

'Nothing they can do for me, Mike.' Gideon was still trying to sound upbeat. 'It's genetic. My mother had the same thing.'

'Then your mother – '

'Was an Illegal. Of course. Became illegal when she was sixteen and had her first attack. She met my father in the city. So you see before you the result of a very illegal union.'

'Lie quietly,' said Shanna, 'getting uptight will make it worse.'

'So, Mike,' said Gideon, 'what's the verdict? Do you think I deserve to die? I'm not useful to anyone like this

. . . but I'm not like it all the time. What a dilemma, eh? Not the death penalty, is it, debilitating illness . . . they'd have to assess me, like they assessed my mother . . . might be of some use to society, so off you go to the city. Unclean. Eh, Mike? Unclean.'

'You said it.'

'Oh yes, I'm Unclean!' Gideon tried to laugh. 'But you see, I'm not. I'm Clean because someone else made me Clean. Clean on the inside. Do you know what it's like to be Clean on the inside, Mike? I wish you did.'

'He's rambling. Can't you give him something?'

'Like what? Painkiller? All gone. You had the last of it.'

'So you don't think I should die, then, Mike?'

'Gideon, try to sleep,' said Shanna.

'But he hasn't answered my question.'

'You people are full of questions . . . well, some of you are,' said Mike, with a brief glance at the woman.

'What's going on in your heart makes you Unclean, Mike, not getting sick or spitting on the pavement!' said Gideon, too brightly. 'They get upset in the Towns, don't they, when someone spits? Gets them worked up. They like everything to be Clean. Clean! Unreal.'

Shanna stood up and spoke to the Watcher.

'He gets upset when he's sick. He feels so useless. He gets angry sometimes.'

Mike couldn't imagine good-natured Gideon angry.

'He just feels so helpless, Mike. It's a horrible thing to feel helpless.'

'Yeah.' Mike ran his free hand through his hair. 'Is there nothing you can do?' Surely he didn't *care* whether this boy was sick or not . . . care in the respect of wanting him to be well? He hardly listened as Shanna talked about a plant called feverfew that grew in the yard and how that was meant to ease this sort of headache. He only snapped out of his own thoughts when he heard a noise behind him – Tris was standing in the doorway.

'Tris, get me some feverfew, will you?' asked Shanna.

Tristram bent down, silently, and picked some of the green foliage that was growing by the barn door. His eyes never left the Watcher. He gave the plant to Shanna.

'Is the car OK?' she asked. 'It sounds rough.'

They'd just cleared some debris from the track which led right into the camp, and had attempted to bring the car into the yard. First the car wouldn't start; then it did, but cut out just as Tris brought it onto the cobbles.

'I'm going to be working on it,' Tris said. 'Right outside, here in the yard.'

Shanna shot a brief smile in his direction. 'I don't think it'll rain again for a bit.'

Mike sat down on one of the straw bales. He wasn't going to move and he made sure Tris realised that.

'Right here. Right outside.'

Mike felt a real kick. He had Tristram really worried. He watched Tris start work on the old armoured car and wondered where these Illegals had found it . . . or stolen it. What had happened to the original occupants? Had the city boy taken them out with that slingshot? Then his attention was taken by something else. Shanna was preparing the feverfew leaves for Gideon. She broke them up so carefully – she had beautiful hands, long fingers . . . he watched the way her hair fell over her face and she brushed it back. He liked that movement. There was something so different about this woman – but apart from the naturalness of her appearance, he still couldn't think what it was . . .

'He'll be OK in a day or two.' Shanna leaned against the partition right beside the Watcher. 'He's sleeping now. That's the best medicine.'

'What makes you care?'

'What do you mean?'

'What makes you care so much?'

'Do you like seeing Gideon in pain? Really? I'm not sure you do. You wanted me to help him just now. Remember?'

Mike did, and he was embarrassed about it.

'Well, *I* don't like to see him in pain. And I *want* to help him. I care about him. He's like . . . he's like my brother.'

Mike couldn't get that. 'Brothers, friends . . . you've got a funny way of treating guys.'

'I don't think so. We're all people, Mike. Got to help each other.'

'And the people in the city?'

'Well . . . *that's* good!'

'What is?'

'You called them "people".'

'No I didn't.'

'You did.' She smiled at him. For a moment he thought it was worth a slip of the tongue, calling that scum 'people', just to get her to look at him like that.

'You want to help them. Why?'

'Because I believe it's the right thing to do. We can offer them something.'

'Offer them what? This?'

'Yes, this. But more. Offer them something better, something real, something true. Something beyond what they've got.'

'There's nothing beyond.'

'Yes there is. Hope.'

'Hope for what? Living in the Deadlands?'

'It's not so bad, is it?'

He decided not to answer that.

'Anyway, much more.' She rested her head against the partition. 'A hope beyond this life. Beyond time itself. No more sickness, crying, or pain. No more darkness. No more fear. Unconditional – love.'

'Shanna!'

'What's up, Tris?' she called.

'Can you come over here?'

Gideon seemed all right for now; he was still asleep. So Shanna wandered out into the sunshine.

'What's the problem?'

'Just start it up, will you?'

Shanna climbed into the driving seat and tried to start the car. It spluttered and that was all.

Tristram slammed the bonnet down.

'It's just about had it. Maybe we should ask Mike to get us a new one.'

'Mike!' Shanna slapped her hand on the steering wheel and laughed a little. 'That's what this is about.'

'What?'

'You're worried ... whenever you see me talking to him! That's why you're hanging around me so much.'

'Hanging around? I'm not.'

'Yes, you are. Every time I turn round – ever since we went fishing ... the only time you aren't right behind me is when you really *have* to do something else.'

'Yeah, well ... I've got good reason.'

'What reason?'

'You didn't hear some of the stuff he was saying.'

'What stuff?'

Tris didn't seem to want to tell her. He grabbed a rag and wiped his hands. 'Look, Shanna, I just don't think it's wise for you to be anywhere with him on your own. All right?'

'On my own? Tris, we're in the middle of the camp. I'm never on my own with anyone ... not even you.'

'No, that's true.'

She got out of the car.

'You don't need my help here.'

'Just looking out for you.'

'I know. I appreciate it. But it's interesting, you know . . . he's opening up a bit more. Talking. Asking questions.'

'Oh yeah?'

'Mmm.'

'I wouldn't encourage that, Shanna. Let David talk to him. Or Gideon.'

'Tristram! You all wanted me to be nice to him, didn't you? Yet when I am, you don't like it!'

'Don't be naïve.'

'I am not naïve. Don't call me that.'

'I think it was better when you were scared to death of him.'

'Make up your mind, Tristram. Just tell me how to act, what to think, what to say, and I'll do it. That's what you want, isn't it?'

'No, of course not.'

'Well, stop treating me like a child!'

'I'm not.'

'Yes, you are.'

'Shanna! This could be the way he operates! Starts to ask you questions – '

'Or it could be for real.'

'Five minutes ago, you wanted him dead! Now he's some sort of fascinating project!' Tristram threw the rag down and tried to reign in his sudden burst of emotion.

'Tris,' said Shanna, quietly, 'I'm not a kid, you know?'

'I *know* that! But – he knows it too.'

'Let's not fall out. Not over *him*.' Shanna put her hand forward. 'Friends?'

Tristram seemed hesitant. Then he took her hand.

'Yeah. Friends.'

'He seems to have stirred us all up,' she said, 'in one way or another. Doesn't he?'

Tris nodded. 'Shanna, I've – I've been having some pretty bad thoughts about him . . . I mean, *pretty* bad . . . thoughts I haven't had about anyone in a very long time. Thoughts I'd hoped were part of my past.'

'Oh, Tris. I'm sorry – come on, they're only thoughts though, aren't they?'

'For now.'

Shanna looked troubled, and then her face brightened. '*I* know. What if he felt a bit more *involved* with us? He might loosen up a bit with you and – '

'I don't want him to "loosen up" with me!'

'Come on, think about it! If he were involved with us, he'd feel more part of us. Surely that would be good?'

'Involved?' Tris sounded wary. 'How involved?'

'Don't sound so worried! Look, if anyone would know about the car, he would, right?'

'You mean, you want me to ask him?'

'Why not?'

'He could mess with it.'

'Could he really make it worse than it already is, Tris?'

'Well . . .'

'And you can keep your eye on him.'

'I'm not sure . . .'

'Mike!' Shanna waved towards the barn. The Watcher had been standing in the doorway, observing them. 'Mike – can you come and give us a hand here? We've got a problem with the car.'

'He won't help.' Tris turned his back, bending to pick up the rag. He was startled when he heard the Watcher approach.

'Open it up, then.'

Tris stared at him.

'Open the bonnet.' Mike indicated his broken clavicle. 'Can't do it with one arm.'

If Tris was surprised to see Mike helping, Mike was even more surprised to be doing it. He shouldn't help them, of course. When Shanna had asked for his assistance, he should have said no. But he'd figured three things: firstly, he might be able to permanently disable their car; secondly, it might unsettle Tristram further if Mike was seen to be near to Shanna; and then there was the other thing . . . the woman might be appreciative if he looked as if he was doing what she asked. And he really wanted her to be appreciative. But it didn't take long for him to realise he didn't have to think about doing anything at all to the vehicle.

'Nothing I can do, city boy. Your engine's shot.'

'Oh, great.'

'Will we ever get it going again?' asked Shanna.

'Maybe. But you won't get far. One trip to the city. One way. That's it – my guess.'

'Oh, well. Thanks, Mike,' said Shanna.

'He didn't actually *do* anything!' Tristram pointed out.

'Thanks for offering, anyway.'

'Yeah.' Mike eyed Tris.

'Thanks,' muttered Tris. 'Man,' he said, after the Watcher had disappeared back into the barn, 'I wonder if they're all like that.'

'He's never known love, you know. Never. Not real love.'

'How do you know?'

Shanna shrugged. 'Just a guess . . . something he said.'

'I should think he's been with so many women who look the same he must feel as if he's been faithful to one woman all his life,' Tris remarked caustically. 'No – actually, I take that back; I don't think he could even imagine "faithful". What a way to live.'

They missed Gideon at supper, but Sunny very kindly said she'd keep him company. She took her plate into the barn and promptly lay down next to him, whispering. David wasn't happy with it. He asked her if she'd sit up and talk to Gideon properly. But she said he was ill and she was trying to be *nice*.

The rain kept off, so the rest sat as usual round the fire, voices low. David, having given up trying to persuade Sunny to move, seemed gloomy; the others, pensive. Mike, however, was feeling stronger, and enjoying the food more and more. He was half-listening to a conversation between Shanna and Tris. They were talking about people he didn't know. Tristram was saying – in a sarcastic tone of voice – how he hoped someone called Mole was having a good time now that he was reassessed. And then they started talking about the Aid workers and saying that at least the people in the city could rely on some measure of care . . .

That was too much for Mike. He laughed. And his laughter seemed to split the clear night air.

'All right. We know what you think about the Aid workers,' said Tris, dismissively.

'No, you don't. You have no idea.'

'Yes we have. We all know what your solution is, Mike, and it isn't bandages and food.'

Mike caught Shanna's eye in the firelight.

'I could tell you something about the Aid workers.'

'Tell us,' she said.

'Something nobody knows but Watchers and government . . . and the MedCent.'

'I know what it is. A friend of ours called Mole got taken for reassessment,' Tris said. 'You Watchers use the Aid workers for cover . . . you get a bit of information, eh? You know, I feel sorry for those doctors . . . they try their best.'

Mike laughed again.

'I saw you talking to Mole the night he was taken. You were with them.'

Mike put his empty plate down.

'You going to deny it? You were roughing him up.'

'You think so?'

'Yes. I saw you. You were trying to get information, weren't you?'

'Poor Mole,' Shanna sighed. 'All he wanted in the world was to be re-Coded.'

'No one gets re-Coded,' said Mike.

'What!' The Christians looked at each other.

'They do, though,' said Shanna. 'The Aid workers take them back to the Towns for reassessment. It's when there's a space in society . . .'

'No one,' repeated Mike, 'gets re-Coded.'

'That's not true,' said David. 'Come on, my boy. Why are you saying this? We know a lot of people who've been reassessed.'

'Ever wondered why you never see them back in the city? You think they all live such good and legal lives, huh?'

'We thought . . . we thought they were just really careful . . .' Shanna's voice trailed off into the darkness. Right then, she saw with astonishing clarity how very ingenuous that thought appeared. 'Oh, no . . .'

'Tell us,' said Tristram. 'Tell us what happens to them.'

'Tell you some other time, city boy. When you're not eating.'

'Tell us *now*.'

'Yes, now Mike, please,' Constance was sitting next to the Watcher. 'Please – we've got to know.'

Mike looked at the group of now-familiar faces in the flickering light. You think Watchers are your biggest enemy, and you're right. But the doctors are hardly on your side, David Drum! If you only knew . . . feel sorry for them, huh? Well, get this! He was about to speak but stopped. Why did he want to divulge the information to this group of Unclean? Well, he figured, why not? They were never going to get the chance to tell anyone else, were they? And if he was honest with himself, it might even give him some satisfaction to shed some light on this particular hypocrisy. He'd had a bellyful of this deception over the years.

'You want it, here it is. They get assessed all right. You see, people don't much like *age* in the Towns . . . a lot of people pay well to provide for their future. I mean, new Codes aren't cheap and neither are new faces, new – you name it – whatever you want to enhance or prolong your life. Oh, and there's plenty of scope for all sorts of experimentation when you have the raw material.'

Tris stood up and took a few steps away from the rest.

'My God.'

'Yeah, I kind of thought it might turn your gut over.'

'We didn't know!' Constance cried, helplessly.

'We should have done!' David covered his face. 'We shouldn't have believed anything good would come out of those Towns.'

'We've got to warn them!' said Tris. 'We've got to go back . . . tell them.'

'They won't believe us.' Shanna's voice was faint. 'The Aid workers are their biggest hope . . . they think they're wonderful.'

'Mike!' Tristram addressed the Watcher, urgently. 'What about the priests? Sometimes they smuggle people out. Usually children.'

'Yeah.'

'Mike?'

'Festival times.'

'Festival? You mean . . .'

'Auran's a hungry god, you know.'

Now Tristram really was sick. He walked away into the night, followed only by his dog.

'My God!' murmured David. 'We knew Festival times were bad, but . . .'

Mike felt a hand on his arm. It was Shanna.

'Mike, do they know? The people in the Towns? Do they know?'

'Special sacrifice, Festival days, strictly clergy. Anyone who has knowledge they aren't entitled to becomes immediately illegal. Death penalty.' Mike was going to add, 'Hey, that makes you all illegal! May have to do something about that!' but he couldn't quite say it. The satisfaction he'd expected to feel wasn't there; an uncomfortable sick kind of feeling was rising up, instead. He thought maybe tonight the food had disagreed with him.

Shanna was right in front of him, the total anguish clearly etched on her face.

'Look,' he said, 'people in the Towns don't like to ask too many questions. They don't want to know. Makes them nervous.'

Constance, visibly upset, got up and went to the cottage.

'But if they did know,' persisted Shanna, 'they'd stop it. Wouldn't they?'

Mike couldn't answer that.

'*Watchers* know!' said David, suddenly. '*You* know. *You* let them do it!' He got up, and stared with utter contempt at the Watcher. 'You tell us all this for the thrill of watching us throw up?'

Mike's tone was very even and measured. 'I *did* say I'd tell you some other time.'

'Of course, it wouldn't mean anything to you, would it?' David let loose all the pent-up feeling that had been slowly leaking out of his every pore since Mike had been rescued. 'You're killing kids all the time.'

'No.' Mike looked up at the man. 'Not children.'

'Oh, of course – just the sick and the elderly. And you stick so rigidly to that, don't you!'

'No, I don't. But I don't kill children.'

'What, you check their ages before you shoot them? What's the cut-off point, then, Mike? Ten? Twelve? Fourteen? What about when they're stoning Watchers? Do you ask them how old they are before you fire? Well – *do* you?'

Mike's eyes locked with David's.

'Anyway, you dump them in that place! They're as good as dead, as soon as you do that.' David put an arm round Shanna. 'You really are a sick man, Mike.' And they silently made their way to the cottage.

Mike sat alone, staring into the fire as the first drops of rain began to fall. David's venom had hit home.

18

Feelings

Rohan Adams didn't like being laughed at.

Oh, he knew they were laughing at him ... the way they stopped abruptly when he walked into one of the plushest Guest Rooms the Relaxation Centre had to offer.

'Hey, Rohan.' Val sounded relaxed. He smiled at the girl who was lying in the bed beside him. 'Want to join in?'

Rico was in the corner, on a couch; at least, Rohan thought it was probably Rico. The girl with him was obliterating the view.

'Get up.'

'What?'

'I said, get *up*!'

Val pushed his girl away and frowned up at Adams. 'Since when did you start giving the orders?'

'Since you began to work for me.'

'Oh.' Val laughed a little, and his girl joined in. 'That's what we're doing, is it? Working for you?'

Rohan Adams was quick with a knife. It ripped into the headboard beside Val's ear and he got up very fast indeed.

'Get some clothes on, both of you!' snapped Rohan. 'And get rid of those – girls.'

They did, and in a few minutes both Watchers were standing in front of Rohan Adams, fully dressed and more than a little tense.

'What happened to your face?' asked Rico.

'Merrick. A long time ago. Are you trying to be funny?'

'No, I meant, there are scratch marks – '

'He likes scratch marks!' observed Val.

'Shut up!' said Rohan.

'OK, what's going on?' Val demanded. 'You walk in here calling the shots. What *are* the shots, Rohan? Thought we were clear . . . but nothing's happened.'

'It will. There's been a delay.'

'How long?'

'Not your business. Just be ready. *All* the time.' Rohan fixed him with his cold glare. 'Remember, you're being well paid for this.' And he muttered, under his breath: 'When I get my hands on the one who is *causing* this delay, they'll be well paid too. In full.' He took his knife out of the headboard. 'And remember this, as well. Nobody laughs at me. Nobody.'

* * *

'I'm really annoyed.'

'So am I. So leave me alone.'

Sunny sat down next to Mike.

'You should have heard what David said to me. It was awful.'

'Sunny – '

'I was only keeping Gideon company.' The girl tossed her hair. 'I wasn't doing anything wrong. The way David stormed in and – and – shoved me out of the barn the other night was – well, it was – ' She sniffed. 'I've never been spoken to like that before in my whole life. Did you notice I didn't eat anything today? No, not today or yesterday. I'm really upset, Mike.'

It was raining again. The freshness of the air cleared the stuffiness of the barn.

'I can't forget it. I haven't spoken to him since. I really hate that David. And Gideon got up this afternoon and he came into the cottage to talk to Constance and he walked right by me and I said was he feeling better and he wouldn't even look at me. Mike! I only kissed him!'

'You probably frightened the life out of him.'

She leaned against the Watcher. 'I didn't enjoy it much – kissing him. I'd much rather – '

'Forget it.'

'Sunny! Come and help me prepare the meal.' Shanna walked in, shaking the rain out of her hair.

'I don't want to help. I want to sit here with Mike.'

'Perhaps Mike would rather be alone.'

Mike looked at her. She hadn't spoken much to him since the revelation about the reassessments and the priests of Auran; in fact, hardly anyone had spoken for nearly two days. There was an almost tangible heaviness on the whole lot of them, and it wasn't just due to the persistent rain and the thunderstorms that had kept them awake at night. Mike was struggling to get his head round why they would be so affected by what he'd said; and yet, when he looked into himself, he knew. That choking revulsion was in him too. Always had been; he just hadn't acknowledged it. The words, 'You're a sick man,' revolved relentlessly around his mind and wouldn't stop.

Shanna looked very good that evening. Mike couldn't help admiring the view; his attraction to her was growing stronger and he wasn't bothering to fight it. Sunny knew something about *attraction*, and immediately recognised the expression on his face. Her pretty features were clouded with sudden intense jealousy.

'Come on Sunny,' said Shanna.

'I said, I'm staying here with Mike.'

'Well, I don't want you,' Mike told her.

'That's not what you used to say.'

'What?'

'Mike, the baby. My baby. Remember?'

He remembered.

'Why would a baby be illegal, Mike? Something wrong with it, maybe? Why else?'

He frowned.

'Watcher's child,' she said.

Mike stared at her. She smiled at him.

'Oh you're joking! You didn't tell them that.'

'I didn't tell them which Watcher.' She stretched her arms out in front of her, lazily. 'I didn't tell them it was yours . . . but it *is* his, you know, Shanna. He was always *pestering* me . . . and you can't say "no" to them. They won't let you.'

Mike was dumbstruck. Shanna's mouth was slightly open.

Mike stood up. 'You can't believe her. She's not even pregnant!'

'Go to the cottage, Sunny.'

'OK.' Sunny's words had done the damage. She was happy to leave now.

'She's lying!' Mike laughed; then he stopped. 'She's *lying*!' He could hardly stand it – the old expression of disgust was back on Shanna's face.

'Answered a few of *her* questions, did you? Poor kid.'

'Oh, that's it!' he said, turning away. 'Fantastic.' It wasn't fantastic. But why did he care?

* * *

'No, Shanna. Definitely not.'

'She said it.'

'And you believe her over him?'

Shanna didn't answer. She just watched the raindrops dancing between the cobbles in the yard.

'Well, I believe *him*.'

'She said – she was saying he forced her.'

'Oh, I shouldn't think that was true!'

Shanna turned and faced the old woman. 'Why?'

'She's not afraid of him.'

'No – I noticed that right from the start.'

'And I've watched them together. I've seen the way he behaves towards her. He's got his own moral code, you know. Haven't you noticed?'

'No.'

'Oh yes, he has. It's not the same as ours. But it's there. Yes, he's rather puritanical when it comes to Sunny!'

'But not very puritanical when it comes to sanctioning child sacrifice.'

'I hardly think he was in a position to stop that . . . even if . . .'

'Even if he wanted to?'

'Well . . .'

'He could have done something. David was right . . . Mike kills children.'

'You told me Mike said he didn't.'

Shanna's voice was barely audible. 'He's a *Watcher*, Con.'

Constance put down the shirt she was trying to repair. Her finger was bleeding.

'Come on, Con. The light's too bad. Think of your eyes.'

'I've been thinking a lot, but not about my eyes.'

'Where's the girl now? I sent her over here.'

'She didn't come. I saw her playing with the dog in the rain. She was hanging around Tris again. She really is keen on the boys. Too keen.'

'He said – he said – she wasn't even expecting a child.'

'Interesting.' The old woman's face creased into a puzzled frown.

'You believe him?'

'Mmm . . . I think I might, at that. She acts very strangely for someone who initially told us she was a frightened, pregnant young girl.'

'So you're saying you think Mike . . .'

'He's very straight talking you know. Very direct. If he says something like that, I should think it was true.' Constance, sitting on the ledge by the window, patted the space beside her, and Shanna sat down. The rain sprinkled through one of the broken panes.

'You're saying he's not all bad. But he is.'

'And yet you're beginning to like him, aren't you?'

'No! That's not – no, not *like* him.'

'You do . . . a little.' Constance smiled.

'I don't know. I feel – *compassion*, maybe, now . . . compassion.'

'Well, that's what we prayed for.'

'Yes. It's a miracle I feel anything at all for a Watcher.'

'Hmm. He's an attractive man, too, isn't he? Or haven't you noticed that?'

'Attractive? No! I haven't – I haven't noticed that.' And Shanna's face reddened slightly.

Constance chuckled. Then she sat back thoughtfully. 'So Sunny isn't having this illegal child? Then what's she up to, I wonder?'

'I accused him.'

'Sorry?'

'I told him – well, no, I didn't tell him – but he thinks I believe Sunny.'

'Do you, now?'

'No. I don't think I do.'

'What are you going to do about it?'

'I don't know. Have to say something to him, I suppose.'

'That's only fair. Do it when we have our meal.'

But Mike wasn't there for the meal. David told the others that Mike didn't feel like eating with them in the cottage that night – or eating at all. Sunny said she didn't feel like it either – but managed to force down a fair helping of the cold duck that was served with some of the crisp lettuce grown behind the barn.

* * *

Mike felt so tired. So very, very tired. Two days, three nights of rain. Thunder and lightning were a good accompaniment to his nightmares. He'd never slept very well, even before he'd come to this place, but now it seemed as if sleep was deliberately eluding him. He kept seeing Shanna's look of disgust . . . it was a new facet to old dreams.

'Constance says you should have the sling off soon.'

'Trying to cheer me up, Gideon?'

'Cheer you up? You know how I feel about injuries, sickness.'

'Yeah. And I'm sick, right.' Mike wearily turned his head and looked at the young man. 'You're looking better, anyway.'

'Oh yes. It never lasts long. It's just . . . well, I'm great now.' And Gideon smiled at the Watcher. 'Makes you appreciate being well, doesn't it, when you've been ill. And you'll be fine soon.'

'Tell me, are you really like this, or is it an act?'

'Like what?'

'This naïve – cheerful – whatever it is. You can't really be glad to think I'll soon be fit. How can you be?'

'Mike, you know me. I hate to think I've caused anyone pain.'

'And yet you know this injury is the only thing between you and death?'

Gideon looked startled. The expression reminded Mike of Kurt Dane, up against the door, slumped in a pool of blood.

'No, it's not an act. You really are that naïve. That's why you got me out of the city.'

'Mike, come on. You know us now.'

'Yeah. I know you now.'

Gideon hung around for a bit, but David called him; there was a high wind and one of the fences that kept wild animals away from the vegetables had come down. He wanted help in putting it back up. So Mike was left on his own.

* * *

When Shanna approached the barn, she was sure she was doing the right thing. She ran across the yard, the wind whipping her hair. Pausing for a moment, she stood outside the barn. Then she took a step inside.

The rain drummed down on the old roof, showering in through the broken slats and making her shoulders wet.

'Mike?'

He was in the shadows.

'Oh, there you are . . . I came to talk to you.'

'Oh yeah?'

'Mmm. About Sunny.'

'Uh-huh.'

'I think you ought to know . . . I believe you.'

He repeated it slowly: 'You believe me.'

'Yes. I don't think you . . . I mean . . .' Her hands were like ice. She was wet – but that wasn't what was making her suddenly feel cold. Fleetingly, she thought of what Tris had said – or not said – and his protective shadowing of her. Maybe she hadn't been too wise, coming here when the Watcher was alone, and David, Gideon and Tristram weren't about. 'Well, I believe you. That's it.'

'And that's meant to make me feel good?'

'Well, it's meant to make you feel better.'

She had no way of knowing what had flashed into Mike's mind. He'd seen himself reaching for her in the night . . . seen her responding to his touch, calling his name . . .

'I know what would make me feel better.'

Shanna noticed that the wind had caught the barn door and it had swung shut. Mike had moved towards her as he'd been speaking. Unnerved, she tried to sound brusque.

'Look, I only came to say I don't believe you ever touched the girl, OK? I mean, I think she's making it up and I don't know why and I'm sorry I said what I did.' She fixed her eyes on the door.

'You're sorry, huh? Well, that makes everything all right, then, doesn't it?'

He was mocking her. She felt a stab of real annoyance. 'Well, obviously not. Still, I don't suppose it matters to you what I believe. Who cares, eh, Mike?' She turned to go. 'My mistake.'

Mike leaned forward quickly and blocked her way, his left hand resting on the doorpost.

'You think I have no feelings at all?'

She felt her face burning. She was angry with him, confused, and frightened.

'Well, that's what you've been trying to tell us all the time you've been with us, isn't it?'

'Maybe I should show you something about my feelings. Would you like that, Shanna, huh?'

'Get away from her.'

Tristram was standing in the doorway.

Mike was silent for a moment. Then he said, 'You know, city boy, your timing is just terrible. Someone should adjust your clock.'

'Shanna, step away from him.'

Mike spoke to the woman. 'We'll do this some other time, when we won't be interrupted.'

'That time is never going to come, Watcher. Shanna –
move!'

As she did, Mike stood up straight. 'You know, I'm
beginning to feel like my old self. Fitter and fitter.'

'Yeah. So I see.'

Shanna quickly left the barn.

'Got to keep one of you alive. I've decided. Definitely
going to be her, Tristram.'

'Over my dead body.'

'Sounds good to me.'

Tristram opened his mouth to say something else – but
he stopped. He looked for a moment as if something had
triggered a switch in his brain: in fact, he looked as if he
remembered something – something that hit him with
such power that he seemed to be struck dumb.

Outside, the rain cooled Shanna's hot face. She could
hardly gather her thoughts together – how could she have
been so foolish? Tris had said she was naïve. He was right.
She'd put herself in the kind of danger she had most
dreaded, and why? Because she'd let down her guard. Mike
wasn't just a rescued man – he was what he was. How could
she have allowed herself to forget that, even for a moment?
He'd been weak . . . that was the point; now, he was getting
stronger. *This* was who he was. Going to apologise to a
Watcher – *alone*! She was furious with herself.

'Shanna! I'm so sorry. I should've been here.' Tristram
was behind her. 'You're shaken up. Let's get you to the
cottage.'

'I'm all right . . . no, don't touch me. I'm all *right*!'

'Shanna! He didn't *do* anything, did he?'

'No!'

'Thank God. I was just in time.' Thunder was rumbling
around, and Tris had to raise his voice to be heard. 'What
were you doing in there with him? You know what I said!'

'Talking!' Shanna yelled back, over the rain.

'Talking! This close up!' Tris held his hand a few inches from his face.

'He didn't touch me. I'm all right!'

'What did he do, to get you in there with him?'

'He didn't do anything! I went to apologise!'

'You went to *what*!'

'I thought I'd hurt his feelings.'

'What!'

It sounded as ridiculous to her now as it apparently seemed to Tris. He grasped her arms. 'You wouldn't be so *stupid*!'

'Don't talk to me like that!'

'You're crazy!'

'I'm not answerable to you!'

'Do I have to spell it out? He's – '

'He's a human being with feelings! Isn't that what we've been working on? We were praying, hoping he'd change!'

'*Feelings*? I hope you're telling me you just care about his soul – if he's got one!'

'He's got one.'

'Oh, Shanna . . . don't do this to me!'

'Don't do what?'

'No, I can't take this – you keep away from him, you hear? If something happened to you . . .' And then he bent forward – and kissed her.

Shanna felt dazed. 'What was that for?'

'What do you think?'

'You never kissed me before!'

'You know I wanted to. Come on, I thought my feelings for you were obvious.'

'Yes – no – I don't know.'

'Shanna, I didn't want to offend you, I didn't want to get it wrong. You're so important to me.' Tris pushed the wet hair off her face. 'Should I have made myself clearer? How clear do you want?'

'But – we're friends!'

'Yeah . . . well, I can't be friends, not any more. I want more than that. I *love* you!'

Shanna felt as if someone had taken her calm inner world, turned it upside down and shaken it. Her feelings were scattered, splashing to the ground like so many random raindrops. She broke away from Tristram, and stumbled to the cottage.

Constance and Sunny were there.

'Shanna! Look at you . . . you're soaked to the skin! What's the matter?'

'Nothing.' That wasn't true. And there was no fooling Constance.

'Are you all right, Shanna?' asked Sunny. 'You look a bit funny.'

'Sunny,' said Constance, coolly, 'please will you just fetch me some of those potatoes David pulled up? They're in the old shed . . . you know which shelf.'

'But it's raining.'

'Please.'

Sunny's face darkened with petulance, but she went.

'All right, Shanna. Now tell me – what's wrong?'

'Nothing's wrong.'

'You're crying.'

'I'm not . . . it's the rain.' Shanna tried to sound calm and in control but failed. 'Oh, Con! I did something stupid.'

'You went to the barn. I saw you.'

'And –' Shanna grabbed some of the old material they were using for towels and held it to her face. 'Tristram . . . Tristram says he loves me!'

Constance just smiled.

'You don't look surprised, Constance.'

'I'm not! Are *you* – really? I'm just amazed he didn't tell you sooner.'

Shanna blinked at the old woman. 'Con, Tris and I have been such good friends.'

'Things change.'

'I know. But – '

'Friendship is good. But between men and women . . . well, you've usually got to make a decision somewhere along the line . . . unless you're my age, or very, very young.'

'Yes . . . I know that.'

'And you're not my age. And you and Tristram – you're not children.'

'Con – I'm afraid. I am. I'm afraid.'

'What of? Tristram?'

'I don't want to lose what we've got.'

'You won't lose. You'll gain. If that's what you want – if *he's* what you want.'

'Oh, Con.' Shanna shut her eyes. 'Why am I so scared?'

'Why did you go to the barn?'

'I was stupid.'

'You went to apologise to Mike, didn't you?'

'Stupid.'

'He likes you.'

'Likes me?' A shudder ripped through Shanna's body. 'I'm the only young woman here apart from Sunny. That's what he likes.'

'Shanna, I think you're wrong about that. I think he likes *you*.'

'No. I can't . . . no.' Shanna stood back. 'I'm going to change these wet things and go find Tris.'

Constance's voice was very calm. 'Shanna, you're making a very big decision: a decision involving someone else's deep feelings. Be completely sure of what you're doing and why you're doing it.'

Shanna knew why she was doing it. She didn't need any more advice from Constance. She wanted Tris. Yes.

She felt so *safe* with him. It was right. The realisation exploded on her. She had to tell him, and tell him fast.

But by the time she had changed and dried off, he had gone.

And so, apparently, had the Watcher.

19

Darkness

'Where's Tristram?'

Nobody seemed to know. Then Gideon said he'd seen Tris in the yard when they'd come back from fixing the fence – just when that thunderstorm broke and there was all that heavy rain – and he'd mentioned seeing a deer in the woods. Tris had gone to check it out.

'Where's Mike?' David's gaze fixed each person in turn.

'I saw him,' offered Sunny. 'He was walking out of the camp. He didn't look very happy.'

'Oh, God. It's begun.'

David leapt up. His plate fell to the floor and he strode to the cottage door.

'How long ago did you see the Watcher, Sunny?'

'Well . . .'

'Sunny!'

'I don't know. Just after I finished washing and scraping all those horrible dirty potatoes.'

'Late morning,' said Constance.

'And now it's what – half past one.' David spoke half to himself. 'I'd have thought he'd have started at night. How wrong can you be? How lax! How ridiculously casual . . . we've got this Watcher in the middle of our camp and we should've been watching, waiting, on our guard, all the time.'

'Calm down, David, dear!' Constance said. 'He's still got a broken bone, you know. I shouldn't think – '

'Neither would I,' said Gideon.

'Broken bone! I wonder if it was ever *that* bad? How could we think that he wouldn't try something like this, as soon as he was . . .' David shook his head. 'We've been so . . . oh, God! We've been so stupid.'

'We got used to him,' murmured Shanna. 'Started treating him like a normal . . . man.'

'Probably part of his plan. Catch us off guard. Well, he's done it.'

Shanna listened to David's increasingly anxiety-laden voice with a feeling of sharp terror. Had the Watcher gone after Tris – because of her? She put her plate down.

'Shanna! Come back!'

'We've got to find them!' she shouted.

'She's right. Gideon – Mike may be heading along the track, trying to find the road.'

'David, I don't think – '

'Gideon! Just *do* it, boy!'

'OK, I'm gone!'

'Be careful!' David called after him. 'Remember – '

'I remember!'

'Con. Stay here with Sunny.'

'What's all the fuss?' asked the girl, plaintively. 'You don't like Mike very much, do you? Don't like me, either. I hope he hasn't gone. I don't want to be here if he's gone.'

Shanna was running across the cobbles, and looking into the barn. Nothing – just the drip, drip of water dropping from the roof through broken slats. Real fear gripped her. She raced to the edge of the clearing. No sign of anyone.

'Tristram!'

Nothing.

She went to the sheds. There was this little place . . . Tris often sat there when he wanted to be on his own but not too far away. How many times had she seen him sitting on that old broken stump, his dog at his feet? He wasn't there.

But someone else was.

She turned, fast. But Mike was on his feet and his hand swiftly tightened round her arm, spinning her round to face him.

'Looking for me again, Shanna? You know, this is getting to be a habit. I'm going to start asking myself what it is you want from me.'

'I don't want anything from you!'

'You keep on coming to me. What's on your mind?'

'Nothing! And I don't – '

'You came to me in the barn.'

'I came to apologise!'

'Oh yeah? If a woman comes to a Watcher in the Towns . . .'

'We're not in the Towns, thank God!'

'You know what I think?'

'I don't *care* what you think! What have you done with Tristram?'

'You don't want Tristram.'

He pulled her towards him.

'I think you like being alone with me.'

'No!'

He pulled her closer.

'You want to lie down with me, Shanna?'

'No! Mike! *No!*'

Then something happened. It was instantaneous. He saw – really saw – the fear in her eyes. And words came into his mind.

'Shanna – '

He stopped. He couldn't say what was in his head. And what was in his head stunned him. 'Shanna . . . don't be afraid of me. I don't want you to be afraid of me.' He was shocked; he hadn't wanted to say that to anyone – *anyone* – not for a very long time, not since the day he'd switched off his emotions for good.

He had no choice. Still reeling from the impact of his own feelings, he let her go.

Shanna was feeling something, too: a sudden, intense rage.

'What do you think I am?' she spat. 'I'm not one of your "curious types" from the Towns! You think every woman should be available to you? Not here! I bet you never get refusals in the Towns, but they don't get a lot of choice, do they? We're different! I'm different! Or haven't you noticed?'

Of course he had! He knew the Christians didn't do what people did in the Towns. He'd been telling Sunny, right from the outset!

'Force and fear are the only things you understand, aren't they? You sicken me!'

'Shanna, no – not force . . .'

She was silent for a moment, and then she spoke with total distaste. 'You can't really think I'd ever *want* you! That's too *ridiculous* for words! Do you honestly think just because a woman shows you some measure of care, of concern, of respect, that she wants to sleep with you? I don't want you anywhere near me! Get it? Hasn't it ever occurred to you that a – a – *decent* woman might not see anything in you that she would want – ever? Look at you! Look at what you are! Credit doesn't mean *that* much in the Deadlands, Mike!'

Mike turned about, abruptly. For a split second Shanna thought she'd said far too much – did she imagine it? Had those brown eyes momentarily expressed some sort of distress? Maybe so – but she wasn't going to try apologising again. There was no room here for regret. She made her escape whilst she could, and thanked God that she had the chance. She could hardly believe it when she ran straight into Tristram.

'Tris! Thank God! Thank God you're all right!' She threw her arms round his neck.

'Hey, that's nice!'

'Hold me, Tris. Just hold me.'

'For ever, if you want.'

The dog jumped around them both, barking and yapping with excitement. They both laughed; Tris with sheer happiness, and Shanna with relief.

Mike saw it all. And he wasn't laughing.

It hit him with force: he knew what it was about Shanna that was so different. She was Clean. That was absurd, of course; she wasn't Clean at all, she was the Unclean. But he knew with absolute certainty right then that he could never legitimately lay a hand on her.

The crushing realisation came down on him like a heavy weight. Even if she wanted him – and she'd made it devastatingly clear that she didn't – he'd have to become a Christian and actually make some sort of commitment to this woman! The shockingly ridiculous thought would have made him laugh if dark, overwhelming depression hadn't got in the way.

He went to the barn, accompanied only by the awful, aching alone-ness, that feeling of complete alienation, of not connecting with anyone. It had always been there, *always*, but now the gaping void seemed like a real force, a living being, right inside him. He was too wrapped up in his own darkness to notice the sheer relief on David's face, and the knowing smiles exchanged by Gideon and Constance. Nobody tried to talk to him; the shut-down expression on his face warned them all to stay away.

Shanna: there was a new scene playing in his brain.
Shanna, with Tristram. As the day turned to night he tried
to reason himself out of the unwanted emotions that were
drowning him. She was with Tristram, her friend; she was
decent, really decent, not decent like the so-called nice
people in the Towns; she was Clean. No *decent* woman
would want Mike; he had *nothing* to offer. How did you
win a woman like that? In the Towns, you didn't have to
think: it was there, you took what you wanted, even if a
little persuasion was occasionally needed, it happened;
for Mike, it hadn't happened for a long time. He was sated;
he just didn't *want* any more. Until now; until her. But
how could he ever hope to gain respect, even affection,
from someone like Shanna? Because yes, respect and
affection were what this woman would give – and need.
And Mike was just not equipped to be with someone like
that. He didn't know how to behave. It was nearly dawn
before he saw plainly that he'd only ever related to women
in one way – physically – and it wasn't good enough. He
knew nothing about women. Nothing at all.

It was midday when Gideon and Tristram came into
the barn. The dog ran in, too, soaking wet.

'Man, there's nothing out there. We're going to starve
to death before Mike can finish us off. Wish I could have
caught that deer.'

Yes, Tristram was buoyant today. Well, thought Mike,
dully, he would be; Tris was so full of sheer high spirits
he couldn't stop smiling. Glancing at him, Mike could feel
no jealousy; he simply knew that Tris would be far, far
better for Shanna than he could ever be. She'd be happy
with this ex-city boy Christian *friend*. But then, they were
all going to die . . . weren't they?

'Finish us off? We thought you were already victim
number one yesterday,' Gideon told Tris. 'David was
going crazy.'

You're mad, thought Mike. Mad to joke like that.

'But you know what, Tris? I've been thinking.'

'Really?'

'Yes. About Mike.'

'Uh-huh?'

'I just don't think you want to harm us now, do you, Mike? You've lived with us. You know us. You know we'd never harm you. Well . . . I mean . . .'

'Nice touch, Gideon. Remember the shoulder.'

Mike, sitting on a straw bale, fixed his eyes to the ground and spoke in a low voice.

'Better do it soon, Tris.'

'Do what?'

'You know what. You're never going to let me go, and I can't let you go. You know in the end it's going to be between you and me, city boy.'

'You're fond of that expression.' Tris came and sat down in the straw near to Mike. He rubbed at his wet dark hair with a piece of material. Thunder rumbled around and crashed. 'But I'm not a city boy any more. Come on, Mike. Listen to Gideon. You must be as sick of this as we are.'

'You know what I'm all about.'

'Yeah, but we keep hoping.'

'Well, don't,' said Mike, flatly. 'You're wasting your time.'

'My parents were Debtors, Mike. I didn't want to be brought up in the city. I had no choice. But I got out. I let it go. That life is behind me.'

'Whacked a few Watchers, city boy? I never did find out how many I've got to repay you for.'

'If I hadn't defended myself, I'd be dead.'

'I've seen you with the slingshot. You're good.'

Tristram's face registered surprise; he hadn't expected the Watcher to compliment his skills. 'Well, I had to be.'

'You'd be good with a Laserscan.'

'Hah! No skill in that. Anyway, I'm hardly qualified to be a Watcher.'

'I didn't say that. You're no Watcher.' Mike muttered, 'Too much emotion.'

'Yeah, that'd be right. Can't have any emotions, can you – Watcher?'

'Can't afford to.' The words tasted like death. He thought of Jay. 'It'll cost you your life.'

'If it was a choice, I'd choose the emotion. You may as well be dead without it. You know, you've got to feel something, Mike. You've got to. How do you feel, for instance, when you can't take out the old who buy new faces, a new Code, eh? Doesn't that make you feel something? The one thing you're not is a hypocrite. That's something we *have* got in common.'

There was no response from the Watcher.

'Anyway, thanks for the compliment . . . I guess.'

'I don't compliment. I tell it as it is.'

'OK, let me tell you how it is. You know if you go back to the city you'll go back to death.'

'You'd be glad of that. Huh?'

'No.'

Mike made a disbelieving noise.

'Man, you could make it so much easier on yourself. And on us. I wish you could see it.'

'Mike,' said Gideon, 'Tristram is right. You'll go back and die. You know it.'

'Got to avenge Jay.'

'That's a lame excuse,' said Tris.

'Know much about revenge, city boy?'

'Plenty.'

'And you let it go, do you? That's your way, part of the religious thing, as well, is it?'

'Yes. And I struggle with it every day. I mean, *really* struggle.'

The quiet reply was laced with meaning. Mike felt he was missing something – but he didn't know what; he just figured Tris was still hung up about what Mike might do to Shanna. 'Well,' he said, eventually. 'It's not my way. I've got to check out.'

'You mean, you've got to check *us* out.'

'Not interrupting, am I?' Constance was in the doorway. 'Stop crowding Mike, boys. I want to have a look at that wound . . . Well, that's doing nicely. Mike, you're a quick healer.'

'You're a good nurse.'

It slipped out. He didn't mean to say it.

'Get that dog away from me or I'll wring its neck!'

Gideon glanced at Tris, and a smile began to form on Tristram's lips.

'What are you smiling at?'

'You like my dog.'

'I *don't* like your dog!' Mike retorted, furiously. But he did. He liked the way it followed Tristram so loyally on hunting trips. He liked the way it wagged its tail when it came up to him, with big soft eyes reflecting a hope that it might receive some kindness.

'I think David wants a word with you, Tristram,' said Constance.

'Another meeting? Decided what to do with me yet? Better do it fast!' Mike called as Tris and Gideon left the barn together. Constance sat next to him.

'Oh Mike. If only you would just decide to stay with us!'

'I'm tired.'

'We want you to stay. I want you to. Gideon wants you to. Tristram and Shanna – '

'Shut up!' Mike ran a hand through his hair, and then he said, 'I'm sorry. There – you've got my apology. That doesn't happen often. But I can't stand it. Just stop saying that stuff.'

'What stuff?'

'Stop being so nice to me! I can't deal with it!'

'I don't think you want to kill us all – not any more.'

'Don't I?'

'No. I don't think you could kill Shanna.'

He stood up, and turned his back on her.

'Or Gideon. Or me. Or Sunny. Or even David and Tris.'

'Huh! Don't push it.'

'Mike, I think you tell the truth. If you say to me now that you want to kill me and Shanna and Gideon, say it. I'll believe it.'

'All right! All right! I don't *want* to!' He slammed his fist into the nearby wall. There, it was out. He'd said it. 'But I don't have a choice! All right? Are you happy now?'

'No. I won't be happy till you say you'll stay and you won't go back to being a Watcher.'

'I am a Watcher. I can't stop! I've been a Watcher since I was seventeen years old. What do you want me to do? It's what I am!'

'Seventeen? Oh Mike. That's so young.'

'I wasn't much older than Sunny when I first took a life. Yeah, it's young. But it's not a tragedy, is it? That's why they liked me. That's why they trained me. Saw the potential.' But even as he said what he'd long been proud of, he felt dead inside ... a total deadness. Where had that deadness come from? Had it been there all along, like that ache of loneliness? Was it all part of the same thing?

'Who did you kill,' asked Constance, softly, 'when you were Sunny's age?'

'My mother's man. Old man. Disgusting old man. Got tired of her and she couldn't get Credit and she couldn't cope with the idea of ...' He shook his head, trying to shake the memory out of his brain. 'I *hated* him. I still hate him.' The words seemed to turn to ashes in his mouth. 'I see his face on them all.'

'All the elderly?'

'I *never* want to be old.'

'Well, that's not likely to happen, Mike, is it? You're going to see his face in your reflection long before then.'

He turned then, and saw her face was wet. He felt a sudden rush of emotion, emotion he didn't want, emotion he couldn't name, but whatever it was, emotion he couldn't deal with.

He was trembling as he ran his hand through his hair again – trembling! Mike, the Watcher!

'I've got to get out. It's killing me here. I've got to see David. Now.'

20

Compromise

'Sorry, Mike. David's busy.'

'Well, I've got to see him! Gideon, tell David it's urgent.'

Mike paced about the barn. It was too much. All too much. This emotion – no. He couldn't have it. He didn't want it. It had been buried too long and he didn't want it surfacing.

'Oh, help me!'

He was appalled to have said that, even to himself. And it *was* to himself – he couldn't be talking to their God. What had happened to him? He was *feeling* . . . yes, all sorts of emotive thoughts were leaking into – or out of – him; he wasn't sure which. He was enjoying their food. He was so totally drawn to Shanna. He liked Constance. He'd felt concerned for Gideon – Gideon Dane! He was complimenting that city boy. He liked the dog. He liked the *dog*!

This was terrible. He should have been more objective right from the outset. He should have been constantly thinking of ways to kill them all. He'd got lazy. He'd got careless. He'd given way to feeling . . . she'd rejected him but that ache for Shanna was still there.

'I've *got* to get out of here.'

He ought to be thinking about escape. The collarbone was healing. The shoulder wound wouldn't stop him.

You're all illegal, he wanted to shout: you've got to die. I may not want to do it, but you've *got* to die!

But could he do it? If it came to it – could he?

That thing, that reason to live, that motivation, that which had given such a focus and vision and a reason to be – that which had given him life itself – it was slipping through his fingers and he couldn't hold it. How had he let it happen?

David appeared at the barn door.

'David!'

Steady, Mike.

'David.'

David raised his eyebrows, scrutinising the Watcher with wary eyes.

'I want to talk to you.'

'All right, my boy, talk.'

Gideon was hovering behind David.

'Alone.'

Was David nervous? He was licking his lips.

'Well . . .'

'David! I'm not going to do anything.'

David hesitated, and then nodded. Gideon disappeared.

'Are you going back to the city?'

David just stared at him, blankly.

'Are you?'

'I don't know. Tris wants to warn them about what you told us . . . but I can hardly think we'll ever be able – '

'Take me back, David. You don't want me here. You never have. Here's the deal. Take me back – and I won't tell them about you.'

'What?'

'They don't know about you. It was just me. I got the name . . . David Drum.'

'Are you telling me that the Watchers *definitely* don't know about us?'

Mike wrestled with what to say next. If he said yes, they might take him back. If he told them the truth – that he was sure someone knew something but he didn't know what – they wouldn't take him back. They'd never return to the city and he'd never get away.

It slapped into his brain, unwanted: Constance telling him she thought he told the truth. He spat, and cursed.

'I don't know. *I* didn't tell them anything. I didn't know anything. I was on your case . . . I don't know if anyone else was. They might have been. It's possible. OK – likely. Very likely. All right?'

'You didn't tell *anyone* anything?' David looked disbelieving.

'We're meant to. Doesn't always happen.'

David bit his lip. Mike cursed again. He *had* to tell him.

'OK, I'm pretty sure someone else was – is – active on your case. All right?'

'Well, that's your answer, then, my boy. We can't go back . . . anyway, the city people would probably string us up because of you.'

Mike felt a mounting desperation. He slipped his arm out of the sling and tried to hide the pain. 'Look at me! What have I got to do? Give me another week here and you're in trouble, you know it. Take me back – dump me on the outskirts of the Town – you can get away, and I can go back. Come on, this is the best way out! Get rid of me now, while I still can't do you any damage!'

David stroked his beard thoughtfully.

'I won't say anything about you! Even if they know about David Drum, I can keep my mouth shut – give them no help!'

'That's a rash promise, my boy, and one you know you won't keep.'

'You could break camp, go anywhere, I don't know where this is – I could never lead them to you. David! Listen to me.'

'You know about James. A lot of people might die if we let you go.'

'If you let me go! Will you be able to stop me soon? Look, I don't care about James. Think about it. Just do that.'

'All right, Mike. I'll think.'

* * *

'Well,' said Gideon, 'At last. We're getting to him.'

'If anyone's getting to him, it isn't us,' replied Tristram.

'Look at his face. He's getting really desperate.'

'He's getting really dangerous.'

* * *

It was hot. Mike stared up into the sky. He was calmer now. The unwanted emotion had drained away leaving the black cloud of depression that had been his companion for longer than he liked to admit.

Mike's gaze didn't stray from the sky. It was a clear night. The rain and storms were past. There were thousands of piercing white dots caught up in the dark blue blanket above: stars. Why were there so many? Why had he never seen them before? Of course he had seen them. Seen them but not looked at them.

'Mike!' Sunny was creeping away from the fireside, glancing furtively over her shoulder. Shanna was deep in conversation with Constance.

'Get lost,' said Mike.

'Mike!' She crouched in front of him. 'Mike, if you go, take me with you.'

'Go? What are you talking about?'

'You're going to leave.'

'Don't think they want that, Sunny.'

'Mike – I won't let them do anything to you.'

'*You* won't let them?'

'I'll kill them myself.'

'Sunny, they aren't going to hurt me.' Not even the hot-shot, Tris. No, not even him. That realisation had zipped into reality only a few hours before. The only reason Tris would ever have challenged Mike would be if Mike had touched Shanna. And of course, that was what Mike had been threatening, winding the city boy up to see how much he could take. Without that – no, Tris wouldn't harm the Watcher. He wasn't a killer. If he had been, once, he certainly wasn't now. Something had changed him . . . living in the Deadlands maybe. Mike turned his face towards Sunny.

'They won't do anything to me. They *rescued* me. Remember?' Yes, and at some cost. They were undoubtedly hated for it in the city. All their work was probably finished – because they rescued him.

'But you're still going to go. When you do, take me with you. That's all. Please.'

She seemed younger than ever in the firelight.

'Don't feel tempted to stay?'

'I want to be with you.'

'You mean you're fed up and want to go back. Can't get anywhere with Gideon, or Tris, so the game's over, huh?'

'I want to be where you are.'

'You want to get away before they realise what a liar you are.' Mike removed her hand, which was tending to wander up and down his side.

'Do you think Shanna's pretty? Do you think she's prettier than me? She's old. And she's Tris's girl, anyway.'

Tris's girl. She's Tris's girl.

'Tris is in love with her. Do you think anyone will ever be in love with me, Mike?'

'No.'

'You haven't got anyone to love, have you?'

Mike felt a tight knot in his stomach. 'I'm warning you.'

'Other men think I'm attractive. Why don't you?' Sunny searched his face for some response. 'I'd do anything for you. What can I do to make you want me, Mike?'

'Nothing. Believe it.'

'These Illegals should all die, shouldn't they?'

Mike frowned, surprised at the turn in conversation.

'I mean, they're Christians. They should die. Isn't that the law?'

'Yes. It's the law.'

'Would it make you happy, Mike?'

Mike laughed suddenly. 'Oh, I see. You're going to wipe out the camp, are you, just for me?'

'If I did, you'd like me.'

'Run away and play, little girl.'

She got up and left him. And he was glad.

* * *

'I'm not happy with this. Not happy at all. How dare you do this? How dare you keep this information from me?'

James Oakley hesitated when he heard that voice. He stopped outside the half-open door and listened.

'No, don't smile about it. Didn't you hear me? It's diabolical, using my own – my own daughter!'

'Yes, your own daughter. I really must have a little word in her ear when we catch up with her. I don't like the way she's always *late*. It can cause a few problems, you know . . . waiting for Sunny. People start asking awkward questions. They start doubting my word. Losing respect.

I really don't *like* that. I must ask her why she feels the need to be so – late. And cure her of it, maybe.'

Oakley could see Stirling Cain rising to his feet. Who else was in the room? Whoever it was had invoked a rage so violent that Cain was visibly shaking as he walked round the desk, pointing a bejewelled finger at someone just out of view.

'Don't you threaten my daughter.'

'Threaten her? There's an idea. I must mention it to Father.'

'Father! Take that insolent smirk off your face. You'll suffer for this.'

Now came the smooth reply.

'I don't think so.'

'You don't *think* so!'

Oakley froze. He had recognised the other speaker.

'You're finished, Adams,' Cain was promising.

'No – o. I don't think so.'

'What the – '

'On the contrary, I'm just starting.'

Footsteps echoed on the tiled floor and Adams came into view.

'Come on in, James.'

James Oakley took a deep breath and entered the office.

Cain was apparently making an effort to compose himself. He returned to his desk, sat down, slapped a palm down onto a red button, and the door shut behind Oakley.

'Never seen you nervous before, James!' remarked Rohan Adams.

Oakley clenched and unclenched his fists, his gaze locked on the Watcher Adams. Adams didn't look at him. He smiled, and strolled with exaggerated ease to a small marble bust of Auran, placed in a corner.

Oakley was becoming increasingly agitated. His usual lugubrious features showed animation. Cain didn't seem about to speak.

'Sir, you wanted to see me?'

Adams uttered a small laugh. Cain leaned back in his chair and raised his eyes to meet those of the burly Ferryman. He brought his hands together on the desk in front of him. Every move appeared to take a hundred years. James thought the white-walled, high-ceilinged office was getting whiter. The brightness was beginning to hurt his eyes. He felt the floor move and gripped the edge of Cain's desk.

'Get your hands away from that!' Cain glowered at the white fingers on his desk. James fought the feeling of unsteadiness that had overtaken him.

'How are things on the north barrier?' asked Rohan Adams.

'Shut up, Adams. I'm dealing with this. Oakley! Going to be sensible?'

'Sensible?' Beads of sweat were appearing on Oakley's brow.

'Somebody's helping Illegals escape from the city,' said Rohan Adams, still not looking at him.

'Your name has come up in connection with that!' Cain glared at Adams. 'And here's another name. David Drum. What do you make of that, Oakley, eh? David Drum!'

'I – don't know that name,' stuttered Oakley.

'You *do* know,' said Adams.

'David Drum! What do you know about that name?' Cain asked, his voice rising. 'Oh, come on James! Don't let's have to make this difficult.'

'David Drum. Christian preacher,' said Rohan Adams. 'Are you a Christian, James?'

'No.'

'No?' Rohan Adams' smile broadened as he looked at the marble bust. 'Do you know who this is, James? But of course you do! This is Auran. It has been said – and yes, I can see it – that I resemble him. Or he resembles me. What do you think?'

'I – I – don't know.'

'Do you think if you write a prayer on a slip of Sacred Paper and give it to me, maybe I would answer it?'

James Oakley went as white as the walls.

'You see James, you have to think . . . who answers prayers? Who reads the Sacred Paper?'

'Adams!' shouted Cain, 'I will deal with this!'

Adams turned and laughed aloud. Oakley was holding a knife.

'Oh, this is too easy. Are you really that stupid? Well, you must be.'

Oakley lunged towards him, and Adams grabbed the hand that held the knife.

'You complete failure,' sneered Adams. 'You're the cause of the deaths of David Drum and all the friends of David Drum. What was it you told the gods? Or the one God? Or whatever it is you think you were praying to, Ferryman? Careless. You'd never make a Watcher.'

Oakley was larger in stature than the Watcher but Adams easily backed him to the wall. Effortlessly, he turned the blade towards the Ferryman. The smile didn't leave his lips.

'Now look what you've done!' Cain roared.

'No matter.' Adams stared at the ever-increasing pool of blood on the tiled floor. 'We knew . . . and he was expendable once the transmissions started.'

'You're expendable too. Don't you forget that.'

'No, you see, Cain, that's just not true.'

'We're all expendable, Rohan! You're no exception.'

'Oh, but I am. Nothing's going to stop me.'

'Stop you? What are you talking about?'

Adams stepped over the body of James Oakley.

'Destiny. Surely you believe in destiny?'

'You're out of your mind. I've always thought you were.'

'I'll come back when I've achieved my goal. Then we'll see who's out of their mind.'

'Adams! I haven't given you the authority to do anything.'

'I've got all the authority I need. Ask Father.'

* * *

'I brought you some soup. You didn't eat anything for breakfast, or at midday. You didn't eat anything yesterday, and not much the day before. You must have some supper.'

'Not hungry.'

Constance sat down. She looked very warm and very weary.

'It's so humid. We need more storms.'

'No,' said Mike. 'No more storms.'

'It's all right for you young ones,' she chided. 'But when you're my age, you feel the heat.'

It struck Mike suddenly that he hadn't thought about age lately . . . only when he'd had that – that *discussion* with Constance. But age hadn't been much on his mind, nor anyone else's, it would seem. Their lack of concern about such things must have rubbed off on him, he thought. And more than that. Here was Constance: her fair, wrinkled skin, the crown of grey hair. But he didn't see age; it simply wasn't true to say that he hated all the elderly any more. The thought made him feel totally defeated. He was seeing things differently and he didn't want to. But he couldn't deny, when he looked at

Constance, kind Constance, Constance who had something about her that he hadn't experienced since – yes,
since his mother died – he had none of the urge a Watcher
should have.

'I've got to get away.'

'I heard you spoke to David.'

'I've *got* to get away.' He'd been thinking: If only he
could get back to the life he'd known before, everything
would be all right, back to normal. As soon as he left this
strange environment, this peace, this . . . whatever it was,
whatever he couldn't discern, the much-needed cold
hardness would return. It was lying dormant, even now.
It wasn't gone. It couldn't be gone.

'Mike, what do you know about Sunny?'

'I know she isn't pregnant.'

'Are you sure?'

'Of course I'm sure. She's playing a game. She's a
privileged kid and she likes some danger. But she's bored
now, and she wants out. I'll take her with me. And don't
worry, she won't say anything about any of you. I'll make
sure of that. She'll do as I say.'

'She's a sad girl. She's looking for love, you know that,
don't you?'

'Love?'

'She's going about it in the wrong way, of course. All
this chasing after men . . . she'll get attention, but . . .'

But she'll get used, used up, dumped, lonely. Mike
imagined an older Sunny with a different body-shape and
a different face but the same desperation about the eyes.
Sunny, herself the Watcher's child, the daughter of death,
allowed to live only because her father had become a
member of the government.

'We were hoping she'd stay with us. But yes, if you go
back she'll go with you, because she won't want to stay
here if you go. She's very fond of you. It's a shame, because

if she goes back to the Towns, she'll lead a very unhappy life, for all her privilege.'

'Don't lay that one on me.'

Constance smiled and offered him the bowl of soup.

'You're good to me. You have been from the start.' Mike took the bowl. 'I'd like to know why. I'm your enemy, after all.'

'I don't believe that. And I don't think you do any more.'

'Maybe not now, not here. But back there – '

'Not even back there.'

Mike noticed his hand suddenly tremble as he held the bowl. No! No more trembling. He shoved the bowl back at her.

He walked across the cobbles, taking the sling off, although no way was he fully fit. He threw the sling down in front of David.

'OK, you going to take me back?'

David didn't look up. He stared into the fire.

'We can't go back. It's too dangerous.'

'Give me the car then. I'll go alone.'

'We can't do that, Mike. The car – '

'It'll make the one-way trip. Come on.'

'We haven't made a decision yet.'

'Well, what are you waiting for?'

'We're waiting for you,' said Gideon.

'What? Waiting for me to be fit enough to do what I have to?'

'Waiting for you to change.'

'Change? I don't change! I don't *want* to change!'

They were all silent. Even Sunny, who seemed unusually subdued.

Mike cursed. 'All right, that's it. You've been waiting – waiting too long. I'm fit, Christians, fit enough to take you all, and I will. This is the time. Let's do it – now!'

Nobody moved. No one looked at him.

'Who's first?'

Then Shanna looked. Did he see something in her eyes
– some measure of warmth? No. He was imagining it; this
woman didn't want him.

Sickness twisted his gut. 'I said, who's *first*?'

Constance was behind him, her voice low and caring.
'Have some soup, Mike.'

'Come on. Sit down. You look tired,' said Gideon,
kindly.

Mike was still trembling. What's happened to me?
Where's the anger? Where's the hard-edged single-
mindedness? This weakness must be a reaction, an
aftershock, a blip on the scanner of my life . . . I've given
them a chance. Why have I given them a chance? I kidded
myself it was a choice and I was making it but it isn't. It's
not a choice. I'm fit enough now . . . I have *got* to do it.
And I can't. And I know I can't. I can't do it here, I can't
do it anywhere. Worse: I can't go back. I've lost it. It's
gone. I'm dead.

And now Shanna was standing up; Tris put a hand out
to her but she ignored it. She was gazing steadily at the
Watcher, shaking back her hair and walking right up to
him. She was close – too close. 'You want someone to be
first?' she whispered. 'Me. Do it. Go on.'

When he spoke, his voice was heavy with all the feeling
he had for her. He just couldn't hide it and didn't try.
'You know – you know I can't.'

Now his eyes were on the rest of them. Congratulations,
David Drum. You've completely destroyed me.

'You should have left me to die with Jay. I wish you
had. You've stripped me naked here and I don't know
how you've done it. I don't know myself any more.'

Sudden, terrifying fear swept over him. More fear than
he'd ever felt. He had to get out of that camp. He turned,
and walked. And walked. No one tried to stop him.

Perhaps this was what they wanted, after all – that he would just disappear. He *wanted* to disappear.

He wasn't a Watcher any more. He wasn't anything. He was lost. Weakness, emotion, feeling, and fear: all the stuff of his nightmares.

Somehow, Mike had reached water – where the stream met with the river. How did he get here? The twilight was shrouded in mist. Was the river deep enough to drown him? That was the way out. Maybe that was why he was here. A voice seemed to whisper to him, 'Check out, Mike. Check out – like your mother.'

21

Hunted

'Mike!'

Gideon was behind him, swinging a lamp.

'Go away, Gideon!'

'Mike!'

'Go *away*!' Mike, staring into the water, clenched his fists.

'Don't do it.'

The lamp hit the ground as Mike turned and grabbed and then shook Gideon. The old feeling started to come back. This was it. It surged through him. The power of life and death. But Gideon wasn't afraid. He didn't resist or shout. Gideon: trusting, innocent, idealistic, good-hearted Gideon, who was everything Mike wasn't!

'You don't want to hurt me.'

Mike shook him again. 'No?'

'No.'

What made him so calm?

'Hate me, Gideon! Can't you just hate me!'

'Stay with us. Join us.'

'Stay with you! Stay with you! Shut up!'

'I'm sorry.'

'Sorry?' Anger welled up to fresh levels in Mike. 'Why are you sorry, Christian? You've got nothing to be sorry for, have you? You've got a straight pass to Paradise and a God who loves you!' Mike laughed, contemptuously.

'See, Gideon, I don't just watch, I listen pretty good too! I've heard you praying, I've heard you talking about the man on the tree, Jesus, the sacrifice, the man you give your lives for, the man who is God and who rescued you. Rescued you! Like you "rescued" me, huh?'

'Yes, Mike. But his is the bigger rescue. Let him do it – for you.'

'What, your God wants me, does he? Wants a Watcher? Do you know what I've *done*, Gideon?'

'No – but *he* does. And yes, he wants you. Let us help you, Mike.'

'I don't *want* your help! Do you know what your help has done to me? Taken away everything I am! Left me with nothing!' Mike pulled Gideon very close to him. 'Do you know what they teach you to do as a Watcher, Gideon? If for one second you doubt, you have to look at your hands, and you have to remember that you are an executioner for the government. And when you look at your hands you feel a kick, pride, call it what you will. Why is it that I just feel sick to my stomach now? Sick! I can't join you, I'm not part of you, and I can't kill you, Gideon! What does that make me? Why can't I kill you? I kill the Unclean!' He was shouting now. 'I execute the Illegals! I do it, I've always done it, it's what I am! But I can't touch you, none of you! You're all too – CLEAN – for me!' He pushed Gideon away, hard.

Gideon attempted to pick up the lamp but Mike stopped him.

'You're always sorry. You're always saying it,' he said, through gritted teeth. 'Do you understand what sorry really is? Well, let me tell you, sorry is everything I've got. See? Sorry is being so full of the city that you can't ever wash it clean. If I washed in that river every day for the rest of my life I couldn't get the stinking filth of the city off me!'

'It's not the city, Mike! It's you!'

'Do you think I don't know that!'

Mike's anguished roar came from the depths of his being. Something snapped within him, and he stood back from Gideon. His strength left him, suddenly, and with it, all the anger. The confession had done something to him. And he knew it was true.

It was him. He was the Unclean. It was he who wasn't fit to live. It wasn't these Illegals, these Christians, who were the filth. He felt broken.

'Why didn't Jay go free that night? Why didn't I die then?'

'Mike.' Gideon's voice was hoarse. 'We're all the Unclean until we let Jesus wash us. He was the Clean for the Unclean. You're beginning to see. You've got to stay with us now, Mike, *please.*'

'I can't. I've done too much.' Mike felt a new and repugnant sense of filth clinging to him. 'I am the city. I brought it here. I've got to leave.'

'No, Mike. Let it leave you.'

Could it be possible – to be free of all that clinging evil? That companion of darkness that had always – *always* – been there, and which had only now revealed itself in clarity?

'What's that noise?'

Mike had difficulty gathering his thoughts.

'Armoured car . . . Tristram's come to your rescue.' Mike listened. 'No. Wrong direction. What's beyond the river?'

'The road.'

'Watchers.'

'What!'

'Watchers.'

* * *

'Dead slow. This isn't the city.'

Rico cursed.

'What's the matter? You look as if you're afraid to breathe.'

'It's the pollution,' said Rico. 'It's the air.'

'There's nothing wrong with the air!' snapped Rohan Adams.

'Rohan, we weren't expecting to have to come out here.'

'You're on a priority government mission. You don't expect. You see nothing. You hear nothing. Just obey me.'

'But the Deadlands – man, you didn't say anything about that.'

'Well, where did you *think* we'd be going?'

'I don't know, Rohan, the city I guess. Another Town maybe. But not here.'

'Rico, you are *really* beginning to annoy me.' Rohan made a point of checking his Laserscan. 'I can do this job with just Val . . .'

'No, it's all right!' said Rico, quickly.

'Is it? You sure?'

'Yes – yes! I've never let you down, Rohan. Never disappointed you.'

'I know . . . that's why I picked you.'

Rohan turned and glared at Val, who was sitting on the ledge behind the seats.

'You got any problems with the Deadlands? Problems we can sort out right here, right now?'

'No.' Val sat back and started to check his rifle.

Rohan Adams tapped the scanner. 'There. We're nearly on top of them. Stop the vehicle. We'll go in on foot.'

'On *foot!*'

'Rico!' Rohan Adams slapped his hand against the dashboard. 'Don't question me!' He looked at the driver. 'Don't you trust me?'

'Yeah, Rohan. With my life.'

'Good. That's what I like to hear.'

* * *

'Gideon! There you are. Gideon, Tristram's spotted something on the road.'

'I know. Watchers.'

'Oh!' Constance put a hand to her mouth.

'They've found the bridge. They've stopped the vehicle,' said Tris. 'It's a good thing I was tracking you, Gideon. I'd never have seen them. Come on, we've got to move.'

Shanna's face was a picture of shock. 'They can't be looking for us! How would they know? And – and we're right in the middle of a wood!'

All eyes, but David's, were fixed on the Watcher as he walked into the barn.

'Scanners. They've got scanners,' said David.

'But I don't understand!'

'Don't you, Shanna?' David cast a brief, scathing look in the Watcher's direction. 'Are you all so surprised?'

Constance began packing things away. Gideon knelt, and helped her.

Shanna stared at the Watcher. 'You know, I was beginning to believe – '

Tristram caught her arm. 'No time for that.'

'This isn't down to me,' Mike told Shanna.

David laughed – it was a hollow, disbelieving laugh.

'Do you know,' said Tristram, 'I should've whacked you right at the start instead of struggling with it.'

'You can get as steamed up as you like. It wasn't me.'

'I believe him,' said Gideon. 'Anyone could have told the Watchers about us. There are people – city people – who know.'

'Not our exact location.' Tris pushed Shanna behind him and stood between her and Mike.

'You've got a traitor in your camp,' said Mike. 'A Judas – isn't that it, Shanna?'

'I think Mike – '

'That's enough, Gideon, my boy. No more waiting. This is where your gullibility has brought us. I knew this would happen.'

'David! I'm sorry – '

'You brought him here! What a fool I was to go along with it. How totally stupid I've been. He was never going to take us all out – he was going to lead them to us. Stupid!'

'David – '

'Gideon! Shut *up!*'

'Why don't you stop arguing,' said Mike, 'and look for the transmitter?'

'What transmitter?' asked Gideon.

'The transmitter that's giving your position away to the Watchers. There's got to be one. They couldn't track you long-range with Laserscans.'

'We don't need your advice!' David shouted. 'I ought to let Tristram take you outside, right now! You know, I feel like doing it myself!'

Mike turned and left the barn. Tris darted after him.

The tall figure of the Watcher strode past the smouldering remains of the camp fire, into the cottage. They saw him outlined in lamplight. Someone screamed.

By the time Tristram reached the cottage, it was quiet. Mike was standing there. The slender, fair-haired girl was on her knees, crying. The Watcher held his left hand out, palm up. In that palm was something very small indeed.

'In her shoe,' said Mike.

The others were there now.

'Sunny! Oh, my darling, do you hate us all so much?' asked Constance.

Sunny shook her head, still sobbing.

'Did he get you to do this? Eh? The Watcher?' asked David.

'Nothing to do with me,' said Mike.

'You knew she had the transmitter.'

'No,' said Mike, 'I didn't know she had any agenda at all.'

'Was it her agenda – or yours?' sneered David. 'Are you trying to shift the blame to this poor child? Is *that* what you really are, Mike?'

'You can think what you like, but this is how it is. I figured if it wasn't me, it had to be her – this *poor* child. I was looking for a transmitter. So I *asked* her. You know, she can be incredibly frank – when you ask the right questions in the right way.'

'Mike, I did it for you! I did it for you. I thought you'd be pleased!' Sunny scrambled to her feet and put her arms round him. 'I wanted you to like me. I thought you'd want me if I pleased you. Aren't you pleased, Mike? Aren't you?'

No, he wasn't pleased.

'I thought you'd be glad, Mike. Why aren't you glad?'

No victory. No triumph. No joy in their imminent cleansing. No gladness that these Illegals – these that had caused him so much pain – were about to die. Mike looked down at the girl, clinging to him. She *was* just a child; a poor child.

'You better get that car moving, Tristram. I've de-activated this transmitter but it won't be long before they're here. And if they get within Laserscan range, you've had it.'

'As if you care,' said Tristram, sarcastically.

'Do what I say or don't do it. Your choice.'

They left the Watcher there with Sunny.

'Why did you do it?'

'I told you. I told you.'

'No. Let's have it all.'

'It was Father.'

'Cain?' Mike held her at arm's length. 'Tell me.'

'No, *Father*.'

'Father?'

'He found out about David Drum. He said someone wrote something on the Sacred Paper. He just wanted to get them all. All the Christians. He hates them.'

'But why didn't the Watchers know about this?'

'Rohan does!' she sobbed, and clung to him again.

'Rohan. Yeah.' He held her away. 'So Father sent you into the city, with some tale that would mean they'd get you out. The illegal baby! And you'd have the transmitter. You'd lead them to the base.'

'I had to target a Watcher. That's what Father said. I liked Jay. But he had this girl, Juno, so . . . I mean, if David Drum had spies, they had to believe that I was with a Watcher, it had to be realistic . . . that's why I got into your apartment, Mike . . . I wanted people to see I was with you.'

Mike was stunned. He was her second choice!

'Sunny, you sure know how to make a guy feel good about himself.'

'I'd do anything for you, Mike. Anything. When I saw you that night in the city it was Jay I was after, but then I met you and I really did like you.'

'But why did Father use *you*?'

'He told me I'm special. He says the gods say I'm special.'

'You could have been killed, risking your life for him.'

'I wanted to help him. He made me feel . . . important. He was always saying I was *precious*. And he said it was all a secret . . . a really important secret and I was a crucial part of it. I wasn't even to tell my own father about it. But

Mike, I like you better than I ever liked Father. I didn't
activate the transmitter right away, you know, because
you got rescued too. I thought we could have some fun. I
didn't want to go back straight away. I liked it here! Oh
Mike – please say you like me. Please say you don't hate
me. You look so angry.'

Gideon was at the cottage door. 'The car won't start.
We've got to go on foot. We've got to leave everything
and go – now. Mike! Have we really got a chance of
escaping them?'

Mike thought about Constance, trying to run to get
away from the Watchers. He dropped the transmitter into
Gideon's hand.

'You want to put them off your trail? Reactivate this.
Make Tristram's dog swallow it and send it in the opposite
direction to wherever it is you're going. It'll buy you some
time.'

Now Shanna was there. 'Come on, Sunny. We've got
to go!'

'You don't want me. You don't want me now.'

'Yes, we do. We love you. We all do.'

'No. You'll never forgive me.' Sunny burst into fresh
tears, and slung her arms round Shanna. 'I'm sorry. I'm
sorry. I don't want you to die. I don't. I don't.'

'Come on, Sunny. Got to be quick.'

'What about Mike?'

'What *about* Mike? Are you going to help them, Mike?
Help them find us?'

Mike took a long, silent look at Shanna. Then he glanced
at Sunny. 'Go with Shanna. If you want to please me, if
you really want to make me happy, stay with her. Stay
with these people.'

'Mike – ' A trace of a smile flickered round Shanna's
mouth. Then she was gone, taking the girl with her.
Gideon was looking at the transmitter.

'How do you reactivate it?'

Mike showed him.

'OK.' Gideon was pale, but looked far more determined than Mike had ever seen him.

'Not thinking of doing something stupid, are you?'

Gideon's smile was faint. He seemed suddenly older.

'Don't be a fool. Do you know what they'll do to you if they catch you? Gideon? *I* know. And you don't want to be there.'

'I'm not the first to lay down my life for my friends. My father did. And someone greater than that did it many years ago.'

'Gideon!'

'It was my fault. All my fault. I've got to do this.'

'Gideon, if you hadn't rescued me you'd all be dead. Sunny – look, I can't explain now – but you got a little extra time.'

'Mike, tell them I'm right behind them.'

Mike was seeing Gideon lying on the straw, suffering with that sickness he had; and he was seeing much greater suffering . . .

'And you, Mike . . . what are you going to do?'

'What am *I* going to do?'

'Come on. We didn't rescue you for you to throw it all away by going back.'

'OK, Gideon.' Mike smiled, slowly. 'Let me show you . . . show you what I'm going to do.'

22

Decoy

'Right behind us? I'm worried.'

'Mike said he was there,' said Shanna, 'Mike said he was coming.'

'Mike said, Mike said!' David spat. 'Where is Mike?'

'I'm going back,' said Tris.

'You can't.'

But Tris was gone.

He knew those woods. They held no surprises. He raced into the camp. The full moon lit the once-safe yard. There was no sign of life.

He went to the cottage.

Nothing.

Out again ... and his dog was whining in the bushes.

There, rolled into the ditch where they'd thrown their rubbish.

A body.

Was it the Watcher?

'Gideon!'

* * *

Mike picked his way along the track. It was still slippery after all that rain. The lamp was swinging madly as he moved, and in its light the mud looked black, so black.

His mind was firmly fixed on the task. He thought of nothing else. Something told him it was hopeless, it was stupid, it was an idea born of desperation that would never work. But still he gripped that little transmitter, gripped it tightly in his right hand.

Faster, Mike, faster . . . he urged himself on. Branches slapped at him. He didn't know where he was headed; he only knew he had to get away from the camp, away from the Christians.

He tripped. He was down. He got up . . . his shoulder was burning. He blocked that out. But something he couldn't block was the growing feeling that he was leaving behind everything that was *good*. He was heading away from that . . . to what? Death, darkness, emptiness . . . but at least he could buy those people some time.

'Watcher!'

'Tristram?'

'Surprised? I bet you are!'

There was Tristram, running along the track in the moonlight.

'You're not so fast, Watcher. No way am I letting you go.' Tris stood right in front of him. 'Not so fit after all, are you? You said in the end it was going to be between you and me. Well, let's finish it here and now.'

Mike shook his head, breathing deeply.

'Look at you! I always thought Watchers were the fittest of the fit. You look like a worn out old man!'

'Tris – '

'You killed Gideon.'

Mike put his head down, his chest heaving.

'You've killed your last man, Watcher.'

'Didn't kill Gideon.'

'Liar.'

'Had to stop him.'

'You killed Gideon, just like you killed – '

'Tris, not now. Haven't got time for this.' With one springing move, he put all his weight behind his left arm, and Tristram fell under the full power of the back of Mike's hand.

Mike checked Tris's body, and with a supreme effort, dragged it into the bushes. And then Mike went on his way.

*   *   *

'Rohan!'

'What is it?'

'Strong signal.'

'Close enough for Laserscan?'

'Yes.'

'Do it . . . what's the matter with you? *Do* it! Rico!'

'Still feeling uneasy?' asked Val – and he sounded pretty uneasy, now, too.

Rohan snapped at them. 'You afraid? Eh? Are you? I'm going to give you something to be afraid of, right now! You think I can't do this job alone if I have to?'

'I don't know, Rohan. I guess you need us,' said Val, 'or else you'd – '

Rohan's voice was tight and menacing. 'Don't guess! There's only one thing you have to do . . . obey! If you can't get that right, we'll have to *address* the problem. Understand? You want to fear something, fear *me*!'

'OK, Rohan! Relax!'

Rico frowned. 'There's something wrong . . .'

'What?'

'There's only one of them. Coming this way.'

Bushes, lit up by the Watcher's search-beacons, rustled and moved.

Then Val shouted: 'Watchers! Stand still for scan check! Stand *still*!'

* * *

Mike hit the ground. The pain in his shoulder was sharp again. There was a Laserscan in his back.

'What the – '

'It's Mike. Mike Merrick. Scan check complete. It *is* him.'

'What! Check it again!'

Someone's foot connected with his side. 'Turn over.'

Mike obliged, shielding his eyes from the hand-held beacon.

'Mike!'

A strong hand lifted him up.

'We thought you were dead!'

'Hey, Rico! You sound almost pleased to see me.'

Rico slapped him on the back.

'Man, you're injured – what happened to you?'

'Mike!' That was Val. 'Unreal! You're full of surprises. What are you doing out here?'

'Now *that* would be interesting to hear.'

The others stood back as Rohan Adams stepped forward.

'Rohan! What a *pleasant* surprise. You in charge?'

'Oh yes,' said Rohan Adams. 'I'm in charge.' He looked at the Watchers. 'Did I tell you to lower your Laserscans?'

'Rohan, it's Mike,' said Rico.

'I can see who it is. And he has the transmitter.'

'What, this?' said Mike. 'Here, catch.'

Rohan caught it, deftly.

'I found this. They must have planted it on me while I was asleep . . . When I woke up, they'd gone – '

'It didn't occur to you to deactivate it?'

'No. I wanted you to find me! I wanted to get out of this place. Anyone here got anything to drink? I've been running all night . . . with a broken shoulder, too.'

'Here, Mike. Pure water from the Towns.'

'Oh, that's good. *Pure* water.'

'We thought they'd taken you . . . but we thought you were dead. Mike, we found Jay.'

Rico and Val were full of questions but Rohan Adams said nothing. He deactivated the device and threw it into the bushes.

'You've been tracking *me*, Rohan. Can't say I'm sorry about that. I just want to get back to the Towns. This is a weird place.'

'Yeah,' said Rico. 'This place gives me the – '

'Michael,' said Rohan, carefully, 'care to explain just what you're doing here?'

'Well, you're after the Illegals, aren't you?'

'Yeah, Mike. They're getting people out of the city,' said Val.

'They might try, but no one wants to go . . . who wants to live in the Deadlands? Not me, that's for sure. Do you know what's in the water? There are these – '

'David Drum,' interrupted Rohan.

'David Drum?' Mike nodded. 'Yeah, that's them. A bunch of pretty sick Unclean who want to live in this – this *place*.'

'What!'

'Get this – they "rescued" me from the city! Can you believe it?' He grinned at the men. Rico whistled, and Val laughed.

'Go on,' said Rohan.

'They got me out. Wanted to ask a Watcher a few *questions*. Held me captive, then they left me for dead. It's a miracle I got away . . . blindfolded . . . they broke my – '

'And Sunny Cain?'

'Sunny Cain?'

Rohan Adams spoke very slowly. 'The transmitter.'

'Oh! That explains where they got it.' Mike drank some more of the metallic-tasting water and tried to hide his revulsion. Sunny . . . he thought swiftly. They'd go after her; they'd find the others. 'And why they killed her.'

Rohan seemed genuinely surprised. 'What! They *killed* her?'

'No point in trying to get the girl back, guys. She's dead.'

'I thought these Christians didn't believe in violence.'

Mike laughed. 'Where did you get your information? It's trash. They use that name but they aren't Christians . . . unless they all lost their faith. They can get pretty tough when they're pushed.' Mike opened his shirt. 'See? I wouldn't answer their questions so they broke my collarbone. Stabbed me there, too . . . had to do that to stop me doing any *damage* to them. Did I put them in a spin!'

'Yeah, I bet!' Rico chuckled.

Rohan Adams put his finger to his lips. 'No. Something's not right.'

'I only saw three guys . . . briefly, when I wasn't blind-folded. I'd have taken them all, but with the broken – '

'Three! You mean we're out here after *three* people?' said Val.

'Yeah – all looking ill. Think they'd been out here too long . . .'

'Obviously not ill enough to be unable to break your collarbone, Michael.'

'. . . and then they moved – well, I guess when the transmitting started. Oh!' Mike gripped his stomach. 'This place is full of poison. Let's get out of here.'

'Yeah . . . it's the pollution, Mike,' said Rico. 'It's the pollution.'

'Oh yeah, you could never survive . . .'

'But *you* did,' said Rohan.

'They fed me . . . I guess they had to go back to the city for supplies.'

'Back to the city?'

'Uh-huh. Heard them talking. You want to find them, that's where they'll be. You know, we ought to make a move. You don't want to be here when it gets light. The sun –'

'That's enough.' Rohan Adams turned to the others. 'All right. Get back to the car.'

'Very wise move, Rohan,' said Mike.

'Not you.' The Watcher Adams gripped Mike's arm and looked at Val and Rico. 'Go on, back to the vehicle. Take the beacons with you. Leave me one light. Oh – and leave me a Laserscan. I've got something to sort out with Michael.'

'Rohan –'

'Go!'

'Come on, man – it's Mike!'

'Go back to the car.'

Suddenly, there was a noise in the bushes.

'It's an animal!' said Val.

'Shoot it!'

Val took aim. 'Missed. It was too fast. Looked like a dog.'

'Man! Are there wild dogs out here?' Rico asked.

'Yeah,' said Mike. 'Loads. Fierce, too. Killers. And big. Teeth? Never seen dogs like it.'

'What's that?' Val went to the bushes, and then exclaimed in surprise. 'Something else here!' He levelled his rifle. 'Out! And slowly.'

'Oh, *Tristram*!' Mike shut his eyes.

'Well, look what we've found now!' Rohan turned to Mike. 'An explanation, please, Michael. I rather think you know more than you've said.'

'Let him go. He's not one of them.'

'Michael, what aren't you telling us?'

'He attacked me in the woods. I hit him. I don't know who he is. He's no one.'

Rohan's Laserscan was in his chest. 'No one, eh?'

An owl screeched. Rohan, Val and Rico were startled; Mike tried to grab Rohan's Laserscan, but he wasn't quick enough, and the rifle was pressing hard against him again.

'What was that? Merrick, I said, what was that noise?'

'Rohan, I tell you, you don't want to be out here at night.' Mike looked at the other Watchers. 'He's going to kill me. He's always wanted to. He could never do it in the Towns, but out here, like this, with me injured, no weapon – oh yeah, he can do it now.'

'Shut up!' snapped Adams.

'Val, Rico, you better get him to do it fast because if you stay here much longer you're going to get really sick . . . like this guy is sick . . . don't *touch* him! Can't you see the rash?'

'He hasn't got a rash!' Adams barked, 'Merrick, shut up, before I *make* you shut up!'

Rico stepped forward, hesitantly. 'Rohan, what if there are lots of them – sick?'

'Read the Laserscan!'

'Maybe they don't register . . . perhaps the pollution . . .'

'Don't be stupid!'

'This one didn't register . . .'

'Of course he did, you just weren't looking!'

'It only registered Mike . . .'

'You weren't *looking*!'

'Mike, are you sick?'

'No, he isn't! Rico, you're losing it!'

'Can't we do this,' said Val, 'back in the Towns?'

'Back in the Towns? And lose them all?'

'They aren't here, Rohan! There's no one . . . no one else.'

Rohan wiped sweat from his brow. Then he turned to Tristram. 'David Drum – heard of him?'

'Never.'

'Shall I kill him?' asked Val.

'Yes!' Rohan changed his mind. 'No! No.' The Laserscan dug deep into Mike's ribs. 'You say they questioned you? Well, Michael, I've got a few questions of my own. And I am going to *enjoy* asking them. And what I can't get from you, I'll certainly get from him.' He glanced at the others. 'All right. Back to the Towns.'

Val and Rico didn't seem to want to move.

'Now what?' Adams demanded.

Val nodded towards Tris. 'Rohan, if he's sick, and he's in the car – '

'He *isn't* sick! There's no sickness in the Deadlands. You're just told that!'

'What was that noise?'

'There isn't any noise! Get them in the car! Now!'

'What's the matter with you?' Mike muttered to Tristram, as they were shoved towards the armoured car. 'If someone hits you, can't you just stay down?'

'Didn't hit me hard enough, Watcher.' Tris put a hand to his painful jaw. 'And when I came to, I followed. I was listening . . .'

'Next time I hit you, stay *down*.'

'Shut up!' Rohan's rifle stabbed into Mike's back. 'And, Michael, you'd better start thinking about what's going to happen to you back in the Towns. I want everything. Everything you know.'

'Told you everything. Location won't make any difference.'

'Oh, it will, Michael. Believe me – it will.'

23

Captive

'What's going to happen to us?'

'We're going to die.'

Tris sat down on the hard bed. 'That's what I like about you: so positive.'

'We're in the MedCent. No point in being positive, city boy.' Mike paced to the door, and stood with his back to Tris. 'They don't usually put two in together. Guess they've just been to the city . . . got some reassessing going on.'

'You mean, this is where – '

'Oh yeah. This is where.'

'Is the room bugged?'

'It's not a room, it's a cell. Cell five. I knew one of the last occupants . . . so did you. Your friend Mole. And no, it isn't bugged. Lots of things happen in these *rooms* they don't want any record of. So if you've got anything to say to me, you better talk fast, because we aren't going to be talking for much longer.'

'I haven't got anything to say. Not to you, not to them. Well . . .' Tris shrugged. 'There is something.'

Mike turned to him.

'You were trying to save us, weren't you? I heard some of what you were saying to them.'

'I tried. It was a long shot. Anyway, it's given the others some time.'

'Yeah . . .' Tristram's eyes were on the floor. 'You tried to save me, too.' He went quiet for a moment, and then he said: 'I don't understand. If you did all that, why did you kill Gideon?'

'I didn't kill Gideon.'

'He looked dead to me.'

'Then you didn't look too closely. I didn't hit him as hard as I hit you . . .'

Tris touched his jaw, which was showing some heavy bruising.

'. . . but then, you're pretty tough, aren't you, city boy? Going to have to be in a minute.'

'Why did you hit him?'

'He was going to be the decoy. He was going to run with that transmitter, and I couldn't let him do it . . . If they'd caught him – '

'They'd do what they're going to do to us.'

'Yeah.' Mike was thinking about Gideon: he was mulling over in his mind the fact that he'd felt protective . . . Gideon, tall and fair, looking like Kurt Dane; Gideon, good-hearted and open; and *sick* . . . well, his life was saved; Mike had repaid a debt there.

'You think Gideon's not strong. But he's stronger than you think, Mike.'

'Hope you're feeling strong today, city boy.'

'Let's not give up hope. We're still alive.'

'You'll wish you weren't when Rohan Adams gets his hands on you.' Mike walked over to him and spoke in a low voice. 'Look, do you want me to – sort you out?'

'What?'

'You know . . . swift and clean. No chance of you telling them anything you don't want them to know. Huh?'

Tris was shocked. 'You're serious, aren't you!'

'Of course I'm serious. It'll be fast, you won't feel a thing.'

Tristram got up and walked to the other side of the room. 'Thanks – but no thanks!'

'You're going to wish you'd taken me up on that offer.'

'Maybe. Maybe not.'

'Maybe?' Mike shook his head. 'You better start praying, Christian.'

'What do you mean, start? I haven't stopped.'

'OK.' Mike added, awkwardly, 'Guess you could include me . . .'

'Can't you get it into your head? We've been including you from the very first moment you set foot in our camp. Yeah, even when you were being . . .' Tris licked his lips. 'Mike, can I ask you something?'

'That's polite . . . don't think Rohan's going to be quite so polite.'

'Do you have feelings for Shanna?'

'What?'

'Shanna. You know what I'm saying.'

'Watchers don't have *feelings* for Illegals, Tristram.'

'You do. It's the way you looked at her when you said, who's first?'

'I don't have feelings for Shanna.'

'You do, don't you?'

'Remind me to *talk* to you sometime about your tendency to argue with me.'

'Yeah . . . you have feelings for her all right.'

'She's your girl. I was just – like I said – pushing your button. That's it.' Mike faced the door again. 'Come on, Rohan. I know this is part of the game.'

Something suddenly slipped into Mike's mind. It was a name: Stirling Cain. Did Cain know he was there? If he did, would he get Mike out? Or not?

Mike glanced over his shoulder at Tristram.

If he found out the details of where the Christians were – and Tris obviously knew – then he could do a little bit of bargaining. He'd told Rohan that Sunny was dead, but what if Cain found out his daughter was alive and Mike was the only one who knew where she was?

Tris would never tell, of course; not without a little persuasion. But it was the one way Mike could save his own neck. Was it worth a try?

But even if he extracted the information and got word to Cain, and he didn't know how he'd do that, he'd be signing the execution order for everyone else: Constance, David, Gideon – and Shanna. And Sunny would return to the life she'd had in the Towns.

He rested his forehead against the cold wall. No. He couldn't do it.

The door slapped open.

'At last!'

'So sorry to disappoint you,' said the doctor, coming in, but making sure the orderly stayed in the doorway, 'but it isn't Rohan Adams. Not yet, anyway.'

'Oh, great.' Mike looked at him. 'How's the nose?'

Doctor Fabian Stone instinctively put a hand to his nose.

'I'd like to say it's good to see you, Merrick, but that's not strictly true. I suppose I could say it's good to see you *in here.*'

'Yeah, I'll bet.'

'I've always been intrigued by you.'

'Feeling sentimental? That's a first.'

'It's your sense of self-preservation. You're older than most Watchers . . . but still, prime age.'

'What does he mean, prime age?' asked Tristram.

The doctor's face broke into a sinister smile. 'Do you believe in the soul, Mike Merrick?'

'Well, there's a surprise! This must be a spiritual retreat and all the time I just thought you tortured Illegals.'

'They say Watchers don't have a soul. I'd like to find out if they do. Do you think it's real? Do you think it's a physical thing . . . a thing you can find? I do. What makes it switch off, do you think, in death? What if it never switched off? Would we all be eternal? The soul! Where do you think it lives, Merrick? Whereabouts in your body?'

'You come anywhere near me and you'll find out about eternity pretty quick.'

'You're in no position to threaten me, Merrick. Not any more.' The doctor smirked, and then instructed the orderly. 'Bind him! Take him to – let me see, what happened to that Illegal in room three . . . oh yes . . . cleaned it up, have you? Well, put him in there.'

Mike eyed the orderly. 'Like the doctor's nose, huh? You want a new one, too?'

The orderly looked worried. The doctor raised his voice. 'Do it! I've got the hypo *right* here. If he tries anything – Merrick! You know what this stuff will do.'

The orderly snapped some binders on Mike's arms.

'Still got the bad attitude I see,' said Mike.

The orderly spat at him.

'Stop that! Don't contaminate him! I want him in peak condition!' The doctor muttered, 'Let's get these questions over with. Then we'll begin.' He shut the door, leaving Tristram alone.

The orderly gave Mike a shove in the back. Just as he did so, someone came round the corner and began to walk down the corridor. She had her head down and seemed totally immersed in her own world. She didn't look well. Juno! Mike didn't recognise her at first – she was much thinner, looked older, haggard; almost as if she were haunted by something monstrous.

The doctor spoke to her.

'Where's Adams? Is he here?'

'Oh yes. He's here,' she said, in a dead voice.

'Get him. I want to speak to him before he does anything.'

'*Does* anything?' She seemed to find that faintly amusing. She raised her eyes – and met Mike's. She breathed in, sharply. The orderly gave Mike another vicious shove. And Juno watched the Watcher being locked into room three.

* * *

'No!'

'What do you mean, no!'

'They're prime specimens. I want them!'

'I don't care what you want!'

'You'll ruin them!'

'Father wants them dead!'

'No!'

Rohan put his hands down on the desk and leaned across.

'You don't disobey the direct order of a member of the government . . . or do your really want to live with the consequences?'

'Do you know what rubbish I picked up last night? This is a god-send!'

'Unfortunate choice of words, Doctor Stone! This is Auran's doing. And they're both going to die!'

'Auran! Auran!' the doctor exclaimed. 'I can't believe you really – well, let me examine Merrick at least!'

'No way. Your examinations are so often terminal, doctor. I can't allow that.'

'All I ask is that you let me look at him – then do what you have to, but do it carefully so that the – '

'Don't tell me how to do this!' Rohan reached across the desk and yanked the doctor to his feet. 'You think those two have been brought here for your ridiculous experiments?'

'You think prolonging youth, active life, is ridiculous?

I might just remember that when I've got you under the laser!'

Rohan let the doctor go – with some force. The doctor fell back into his chair.

'Father laughs at you. You're trying to find the secret of eternal life . . . as if it can be done by medical examinations or bought with Credit!'

'It can be!' The doctor glowered at him. 'It's a cell, it's a gene, it's somewhere in the body. It's a switch. I've just got to find it. That's more plausible to me than any of that trash Father feeds you.'

'Father's the one with all the power. He's the one who has the secret. The gods have given it to him . . . and he is going to give it to me.'

'The gods!' Now the doctor threw his head back and laughed. 'The gods!'

Rohan narrowed his eyes and fingered his Laserscan rifle.

'I am really not happy,' he said, 'with people who mock the gods.'

'Adams, Father is only a man!'

'More than that.'

'Oh, he's powerful; he's a member of the government, answerable to the World Council, as we all are – but he's just a man under authority – to hear you speak, you'd think he was superhuman! He's had surgery, you know!'

'He is *more* than a man!'

'No, he isn't!'

'The gods speak to him!'

'The gods, the gods! There are no gods! It's just another means of control. I cannot believe you entertain such puerile thoughts! I don't think much of you, Adams, but I thought at least you were intelligent!'

'You have no idea of the power Father has! They live in him. He is their spokesman. He hears their voices!'

'I expect he does – when it suits him.' The doctor stood up. 'You crave power, Adams, but you won't get it from "the gods". I don't know what game Father is playing with you, but he's certainly not about to share any of his elevated position and power with a Watcher.'

'I will be more than a Watcher. I *am* more.'

The doctor laughed again, but made sure he stood out of Rohan's reach. 'Oh, he's told you that, has he?'

'I really do wish,' said Rohan, malevolently, 'that you wouldn't laugh like that. I find it deeply – *irritating*.'

'Let me tell you something, Adams: I knew Father, years ago, when he was a young priest. He didn't hear from the gods then, although he would have done anything for status and power. He got some information – oh, it must be fifteen or sixteen years ago; still not sure how he got it, but he was sleeping with one of the girls who was hanging around the Relaxation Centre. Maybe some Watcher had been a bit talkative with her. Next thing we knew, he was heading off to some god-forsaken part of the Deadlands – near the sea, they said – got there before the Watchers had even left the Towns and captured a whole community of Illegal people single-handed – some renegade religious sect. Yep, loaded them into the back of an Aid truck, brought them back, and was given the privilege of executing the lot . . . right there in the temple. For that, he was given swift elevation in the priesthood. No gods involved – just a girl's information and a ritual dagger.' The doctor stroked his chin. 'Maybe I should see Father and discuss some kind of compromise regarding the patients.'

Rohan's rifle was in his stomach.

'Who are you? Who are you to talk about Father like this?'

'Come on, Adams!' The doctor glanced down, nervously. 'Let's reach some sort of agreement. What information are you looking for from Merrick and this Illegal? Is it really worth killing them for?'

'What are you? What are any of this Town scum but city scum in disguise?'

'I will go to Father.'

'You will not. He has given me a mission and I will carry it out.'

'Mission! Father has you where he wants you – his own pet Watcher.'

The rifle stopped the doctor from moving.

'One step out of this room, Doctor Stone, and you're illegal. Or dead. I'm just thinking about which one I would prefer. Could you last in the city? Mmm . . . probably. The people worship you, don't they? You're – why, doctor, you're almost a god!'

'Don't you threaten me!'

'Why not? I rather enjoy it.'

'The government need me. You know it. I'm skilled. Really skilled. I'm very valuable . . . you ought to remember that. And I can report you for this.'

'Oh yes. Always assuming you get out of the room alive! Laserscans are quiet, you know . . . so, so quiet. A silent death. Do you witness many silent deaths, doctor? Where the life just leaves the body – like a whisper?'

'OK!' The doctor raised his hands slightly, and sat down very carefully. 'I get the message. No need to overdo it.'

'Overdo it? There's a thought.' Rohan's words were brimful of menace. 'I am going to talk to Michael Merrick. And if you don't like that, too bad. You can have whatever's left of him, but I don't think it's going to be saying much. And after him, I want the Illegal. Don't get in my way. Or I might just forget how very valuable you are. *Get* it?'

'All right, all right!'

'I really don't like your laugh, you know.'

'All right! I'm sorry.'

The doctor looked relieved as Rohan Adams lowered his Laserscan.

'You win, Adams, you win.'

'Oh, doctor. I always do.' Rohan quickly raised his rifle again and fired. And the plaque that read 'You shall not die' fell to the floor as the body of Doctor Fabian Stone crashed across his desk. 'No more laughing now, Doctor Stone. No more laughing now.'

24

Questions

Rohan left the doctor's office and walked swiftly down the corridor towards room three.

'Juno! What are you doing?'

'Nothing.'

'Come away from that door.'

'Mike Merrick's in there.'

'I know that!'

'I thought he was dead.'

'He will be, shortly.'

Rohan Adams eyes wandered from Juno's face to her feet and back up again.

'Well, you may as well make yourself useful. Prepare a hypo ... you know what I want. Well, go on! What's wrong with you?'

'I'm not feeling very good.'

'You're not *looking* very good.' Rohan's expression registered disapproval. '*Do* something with yourself, and make sure it's done by the time I *visit* you.'

Juno shut her eyes, and looked as if she felt like vomiting. Rohan noticed.

'You know, I'm beginning to find you rather tiresome ... oh, don't look so hopeful. Not *that* tiresome. Yet.'

Rohan nodded to the orderly, who began to unlock the door to room three.

'Juno, go to number five and give that Illegal a shot. No, don't bother preparing one for Merrick. I want him to be as alert as possible when we – talk.'

Rohan walked into the room, and the door banged behind him. Mike, seated on the bed, looked up.

'All right, Michael. Let's get this done.'

'Does Cain know I'm here?'

'I'll be asking the questions. I'm sure you realise that.'

'Does he know?'

Rohan rolled his eyes in mock exasperation. 'No. Why?'

Mike half-smiled. 'No reason.'

'What do you know about this Illegal we picked up?'

'What Illegal?'

'Oh, Michael! Don't start getting clever with me!'

Mike stood up.

'Still afraid of me, Rohan?'

'Afraid? I'm not afraid of *you*, Merrick!'

Mike showed him the binders.

'Oh . . . I think we'll leave you as you are for now, Michael. Now, let's think how we're going to do this. Are you thinking about it, Michael? Good. After all, you know how it works.'

'Oh yeah. I know how it works, Rohan.'

* * *

Tris opened his eyes as they unlocked the door.

It was a nurse, a whey-faced girl with a hypodermic syringe. She was very young.

Tristram got up. He'd been kneeling.

'Are you ill?'

Tris wondered if things would get any easier for him if he pretended he had some Deadlands sickness. No; nothing would convince that Watcher Rohan Adams that he was suffering from something that the Watcher knew didn't exist. Besides – he hadn't been ill, he'd been praying.

'Are you sick?' the nurse repeated.

'No. I was – ' Tristram hesitated. He wasn't sure the medical staff knew why he'd been brought in. Adams knew; would it make things worse if the medics knew he was a Christian? Tris shut his eyes again. He *wouldn't* deny it. 'I was praying.'

'I pray,' said the nurse, quietly. 'I pray hard.'

'They're going to kill us.'

The nurse glanced at the hypo in her hand.

'Oh – excuse me,' said Tris, bitterly, '*you're* going to kill us.'

'No.'

'Huh . . . is that going to be good for my health, then, nurse?'

The girl seemed to go even more grey about the face. 'No.'

'That Watcher . . . Adams . . . has he got Mike? Mike Merrick? The guy I came in with?'

Her voice was barely audible. 'I know Mike Merrick.'

'What's happening?'

The nurse shook her head.

'What's your name, nurse? I guess you'll be the last girl I see.'

'Juno. It's Juno.'

'OK.' Tris eyed the half-open door. 'All right, Juno. One question before you do what you have to . . .'

'No questions.' She took a step towards him.

'Have you ever been in love? I'm in love. I've got this girl. I'm never going to see her again, Juno.'

'Stop it.'

'Stop what?'

'You're trying to make me feel . . .'

'I don't think you want to hurt me. But that Watcher Adams does. And he's hurting Mike right now.'

There was a shadow at the door. The orderly was there.

'Come on!' he snapped. 'You're taking your time.'

Juno moved to Tris. 'Got to find a vein.'

'How can you do this?' asked Tris.

'Be quiet.'

'But how can you?'

'Juno! Hurry up!' said the orderly.

She took Tris's hand.

'I can't find a vein. Help me here. Help me.'

* * *

'Do you think they're still alive?' asked Shanna.

'I don't know.'

'You don't think so.'

Constance shook her head. 'I see what happened. Mike took the transmitter from Gideon . . . then Tris found Gideon . . . and then the Watchers . . .'

'When Mike hits you,' said Gideon, grimacing, 'you know it.'

'Good thing David went back to look for you. I'm surprised we ever got away.' Shanna turned, and looked out across the valley.

It was early morning. Mist lay in deep pockets as far as the eye could see. Here and there, hills and trees rose above the greyness.

'But we're safe,' said Constance.

'I don't suppose there's any point in going to search for them,' ventured Shanna.

No one answered.

'I'd better go and see to Sunny. She's asleep at last,' said Constance. 'I wonder if she'll ever get over this. She keeps saying . . .'

'She keeps saying she's killed them,' murmured Shanna.

'She's been very badly treated, that poor girl.'

'But not by Mike.'

'No,' said Constance. 'Not by him. But everyone else seems to have treated her like . . .' Her voice trailed away.

'Mike acted to save us,' said Gideon.

'I hope Tristram knew that,' said Shanna. 'I hope . . .' She felt something pawing at her leg and, bending down, made a fuss of Tristram's dog. 'You got away. You'd never have left him . . . if he was alive.'

'Don't give up hope, Shanna,' said Gideon. 'Tris knows where we're heading. He'll meet us there . . .' But he didn't sound as if he believed what he was saying. 'Rest now. We've still got some way to go. Try to get some sleep while you can.'

'I'm never going to see him again.' And the thought came to Shanna's mind: *I'm never going to see the Watcher again either.* Mixed emotions welled up from the pit of her stomach. And now she was trying to think of Tris, but she couldn't get Mike out of her head . . .

* * *

'OK,' said Rohan. 'Let's begin. Do you feel up to it, Michael? You really are looking your age, you know. Thirty-three, aren't you? Mmm. Too old, Michael. Too old.'

Mike was thinking of any way he could overpower his adversary, but he also knew Rohan very well. Rohan was fast, he was strong, he was good – Mike was injured, in binders, and was staring at a Laserscan. Rohan had a knife, too. Mike decided to talk for a while – maybe relax Adams a little, get him off guard. It was worth a try, at least.

'How far are Rico and Val involved?'

'What?'

'Do they know what you're doing?'

'What did I tell you about asking questions?' Rohan raised an eyebrow. 'If you think they might come to your assistance, forget it. Won't happen, Michael. They know exactly what I'm doing, right now, and they'll be well paid for their *support*. You see, they work for me.'

'You mean, they work for Cain.'

'Oh no, Michael. They work for *me*.'

'What's this? A new subsection within the government?'

'More of a special task force . . . a special mission . . .'

'So let me guess. This is something to do with Father.'

'Now, then, Michael, how did you work that one out?'

'Your religious leanings are hardly a secret.'

'I'm not convinced, Michael.'

'That's tough.'

'You're going to tell me everything you know . . . and don't give me that *stuff* you gave us earlier.'

'I've told you everything I'm going to.'

'No. I don't think you have.'

'Put the Laserscan down. You know you aren't going to use it. Far too quick.'

'Well, that's true . . . but you see, I'm still trying to make up my mind just how to do this. No, we'll have the Laserscan where it is for now; although you're quite right, it *is* quick; I prefer the blade. I can be so . . . *creative* with a blade.'

'I remember.'

'And you're not so bad with the blade yourself – not so imaginative, but . . . effective.' Rohan put a hand to his cheek. 'Start talking.'

'They're in the city. There are three of them. They're all sick. Enjoy it, Rohan, that's all you're going to get.'

'Oh, I doubt that.'

'You won't get anything more from me. You know it.'

'Well now, think about this. I can get all the information I need from your friend . . . he *is* your friend, isn't he? Who would ever think Michael Merrick had a friend? A *friend*! And an illegal one at that. Why else did you want us to think he was nothing to you?'

'I told you – I met him in the woods. Hit him. Have you seen his jaw? Hardly call that the work of a friend, huh?'

'Is he a *close* friend, Michael?'

'You're the one with *close* friends, Rohan.'

'You know, Michael, you've broken so many rules I'm beginning to wonder if it might be more fitting to make you illegal and dump you in the city . . . let a few of them know you're a Watcher, of course . . .'

'You know what? I bet even *they* would take the binders off first.'

'Mmm . . . take Michael to the city . . . and let David Drum rescue him again? Maybe not.' Rohan bit his lip. 'Your *friend* is a Christian, isn't he? One of them? David Drum.'

'I told you, I met him in the – '

Rohan slapped a hand against the wall. 'Oh, Michael, don't make this tedious! Do you really want another broken collarbone, and all the rest of it?'

'Unbind me, Rohan. Make it more interesting.'

'Why are you doing this? Protecting them? Michael? Are *you* a Christian?'

'Christians forgive people. Unbind me. Let me prove to you how I feel about that.'

'We're getting nowhere like this.'

'Try something else then. You usually do.'

'Yes.' Rohan's pale eyes flashed. 'Good news, Michael! I suddenly feel generous. Perhaps I'll make it quick after all . . . if you get down on your knees and beg me. How's that?'

'Keep dreaming.'

'You think I'm dreaming? Kneel down.'

'No way.'

'Kneel *down*!'

'Take the binders off.'

Rohan suddenly laughed, and shook his head. 'Oh, you know, I'm glad you didn't die that night. I didn't realise how much I missed you! I wasn't glad when I first saw you . . . it was a huge disappointment for me when you turned up in the Deadlands . . . It really wasn't very convenient having you pop up like that. Not when you ought to be dead. I had many happy moments wondering what had happened to you . . . I mean, it was a *terrible* shame about Jay. But then, he was a lousy partner . . . I hate disloyalty, Michael, don't you? Had to let him go, I'm afraid . . . just couldn't assist.'

And Mike remembered the armoured car that hadn't given assistance on the night Jay had been killed. He had imagined that it had been part of a dream, a shadow, not real at all.

Mike stepped forward but the Laserscan was still there. Mike cursed the binders.

'I really thought the city scum had done it for me. Both of you at once. But they only got that half right, didn't they? Well, their mistake has some benefits, I suppose. Like this . . . I'm glad I didn't finish you in the Deadlands because I *really* want you to be on your knees . . .'

All Mike could think about was Jay. Staring into Rohan's soul-less eyes, he remembered his partner, dying in his arms.

'Beg me . . . beg me to make it quick.'

'You let Jay die.'

'Do it! On your knees! Beg me for your life!'

'Go to hell.'

Rohan hit him in the mouth – very hard.

'I liked that, Michael. I could get used to that.'

Mike could taste blood. Rohan stood up very straight and sighed in his affected manner.

'Can't see why you're so reluctant . . . you should be feeling very privileged. You're the first among many, you know, Michael. Everyone will kneel to me.' And he announced, with a smile, 'I am Auran.'

'You,' said Mike, 'are mad.'

'I will be worshipped. Father knows it. The gods have ordained it.'

'Let me guess. Father told you that you were special.'

'Don't you mock me! You'll never see my glory. All I've got to do is wipe out David Drum and his kind. Personally. By my own hand.'

'To make sure they're all dead . . . he's clever, Father. I'll give him that. He can't even trust the Watchers with it . . . and the great benevolent Father can hardly do it himself. But he can trust someone so totally obsessed. So totally under his power – as you.'

'The gods speak to Father. They have told him – '

'The World Council speaks to Father. He's just their lackey . . . like the rest of the government. A lackey with a special . . . what did you call it? . . . *mission*.'

'Lackey! Father? How dare you? He is far greater than you know! The gods have given the secret to Father . . . the secret of eternal life . . . and he's going to give it to me!'

Now it was Mike's turn to laugh. 'You really are mad, aren't you?'

'Don't laugh at me, Michael . . . I'm warning you.'

'You're crazy.'

'Get down on your knees!'

'Ever wondered why Father's so frightened of the Christians?'

'Frightened? What are you talking about?'

'Yeah, he's afraid. Why is that? Can you figure it out? Because I'm beginning to. And not just Father . . . must be the whole World Council. They must think the Christians have got something really special . . . something they haven't got – some sort of power. And you know, they're right. The Christians *are* powerful. They've got something that can change you right here, deep down inside.'

Adams kicked Mike's legs from under him.

'No one will stop me. I'll find David Drum, if I have to personally take out every Unclean piece of filth in the city.'

Rohan straddled him from behind; the Laserscan was gone, and the sharp tip of Rohan's knife was at the nape of Mike's neck.

'And it's payback time for my face.' Rohan was whispering in Mike's ear. 'Watchers are meant to be proud of their scars, aren't they? But not me, I'm afraid. I've never been too *keen* on that scar. And I never forgot who put it there . . . in fact, I've got an idea. How about this for a start, Michael? Wouldn't it be interesting if you had a scar to match mine? Time to start begging, I think. Don't you?'

This was it. No escape this time. No way out.

'Oh God!'

'Speak up – are you begging me yet?'

'God!' Mike gasped, into the cold floor. 'God! Help me!'

25

Running

Everything seemed to stand still.

Silence. Nothing moved. Nothing.

Mike turned his head and looked. Rohan was still astride him, holding the knife. But his face ... the expression ... it was as if he had had a sudden shock, seen something too terrible to contemplate. His mouth was hanging open and his eyes, staring.

And above him – a girl with a bloodless face, her hand rigid as she let go of the hypodermic that was sticking into him.

The knife dropped from Rohan's fist.

When the girl spoke her voice was dry and cracked and deathly.

'That's for Jay ... and for me.'

Rohan Adams struggled to his feet and, as if in slow motion, grasped the sides of the girl's head as if he was going to kiss her.

'No!'

Mike realised this was no kiss; it was a lethal grip. Mike knew what Rohan was trying to do – one swift move and her neck would be broken. The binders on his arms made it impossible for him to get a hold of Rohan's rifle – but he could grab the knife.

But it was over. The last of Rohan's strength hadn't been enough to do it. He slumped to the floor.

Juno was hysterical now. And here was Tristram, helping Mike to his feet.

'Did I ever criticise your timing, city boy? I take it back.'

'Come on. We've got to get out of here.'

'That's not going to be too easy! Get the rifle . . . and the knife . . . get the keys to these binders! That orderly – '

'It's OK, Mike. We took care of the orderly.' Tris showed the Watcher a set of electronic keys.

'Took care of him? How did you manage that?'

'Juno gave him what I ought to have had . . . a hypo full of something to make him – '

'What did she give Rohan?'

Tris unlocked the binders. 'I don't know.'

As soon as Mike was free, he snatched up the rifle and aimed it at the still form of Rohan Adams.

'I think he's dead, Mike,' said Tris.

'Let's make sure.'

'There's no time. We've got to move.'

It felt good to be holding a rifle again. Power! It gave Mike such a rush he hardly felt the pain in his shoulder.

Juno's hysterics had subsided into quiet sobbing.

'Move away, Juno!'

'I've killed him!'

'Mike! There are people coming.' Running feet were pounding along the corridor.

Mike swung round, the Laserscan pointing at the door. But the footsteps were hammering past. Someone was screaming about a dead doctor.

'Let's go!'

'What about the girl, Mike?'

'What?'

'She saved our lives. Well . . . if we do actually get out alive, that is.'

Mike glanced at her, and then at Rohan.

'Mike, we can't leave her.'

Then a strange thought flipped into Mike's mind: he could do something for Jay that would be better than avenging his death by killing a hundred of those city people, and Rohan Adams too. After all, nothing would bring Jay back, so revenge meant nothing. But he could do something right now for Juno, Jay's Juno, the girl he'd loved . . . something that Jay would probably have approved of.

Mike shouted to the girl. 'Come on!'

She wasn't listening. She had folded up on the floor beside Rohan, still crying.

'Do you know what he's done to me? Do you know?'

She's a liability. She'll slow us down . . . we haven't got a chance if we take her . . . but Mike's thoughts were interrupted by a sudden clear picture of Jay, lying in that filthy city . . .

Mike strode decisively over to Juno, and yanked her to her feet.

'You're coming with us! Come on! Do it! Do it . . . for Jay.'

'They're all piling into that office, Mike.'

'OK, Tris. Run!'

'Where to?'

'Just *run*, Tristram!'

Tris grasped Juno's hand and they all ran the length of the corridor.

'OK – service elevator at the end of the next corridor. Get out at street level.'

'And then what?'

'I don't know, city boy! Let's find out!'

'Uh-oh! Coming up the corridor, Mike . . . Watchers.'

'Stay back.'

Val and Rico were too startled even to reach for their rifles as Mike stepped out and levelled the Laserscan at them.

'Drop the rifles. Get into the laundry room. Fast!'

Tristram picked up the weaponry and then, inside the laundry room, watched the door as Mike smiled at his fellow Watchers.

'OK, guys. Your car still at the back entrance?'

'Mike! Come on. We always thought Rohan was crazy, targeting you.'

'Shut up, Rico, and answer the question!'

'What's happening here, Mike?' demanded Val. 'Why are you turning on us?'

'Your car – back entrance?'

'No one can blame you for anything . . . you're not illegal. You've got the Code . . . we didn't know what Rohan was playing at. Mike, we've got no problem with you.'

'Yeah, Val, but I've got a problem with *you*.' The rifle was in Val's gut. 'Car – back entrance. Confirm it, now!'

'Yeah, yeah! Relax, Mike! It's us, you know?'

'I know.' Mike smiled again. 'Strip, guys.'

'What!'

'Strip.' Mike turned to Tristram. 'OK, city boy. Here's your big chance.'

'Chance? What do you mean?'

'You're going to get to be a Watcher – for real.'

'I've worn this gear before, Mike.'

'Oh yeah . . . got to find out how you came by that. I'll hear that later. For now, put this on.'

Five minutes later, they were on their way again: two Watchers with an apparently sick female prisoner. And two angry men tied up in the laundry room with wads of dirty clothing stuffed in their mouths.

'OK, Tris. Be cool. Don't look at anyone. Get your hand on that rifle.'

'All right, all right.'

'Pity I couldn't give you a crash course in how to use one.'

'I know how to use one.'

'And how did you find that out?'

'Long story.'

'I'll hear that later, too.'

Mike looked with satisfaction at the Laserscan in his own hand.

'Now, that's a weapon.'

'You think? Give me the slingshot any day.'

Mike and Tristram walked calmly past a group of rushing medics who were shouting about Doctor Stone. No one seemed to recognise Juno; anyway, it was a fact – nurses became suddenly Unclean and illegal just like anyone else.

The service elevator at the end of the corridor led up to street level, and now Mike knew exactly what they were going to do. The warm air of early afternoon enfolded them like a blanket as they walked out of the back entrance, and headed for the armoured car.

'Hey, a new car,' said Tris. 'Just what we need.'

'Don't get too confident. We're not out of this yet.'

Mike shot Tristram a quick look as he opened the back of the car and pushed Juno in.

'Still praying?'

'You bet.'

They climbed into the car. Mike started it up and they roared away from the MedCent, turning out on to a side road that led to the highway. It was painful to drive, but the adrenalin surging through him blanked out most of it.

'I can't believe we just got out of there!' exclaimed Tristram.

'Don't get excited. We've got to get past the guard at the end of this road before we can get on the highway. And that'll be a problem because he'll check us out . . . he'll check identification details. Better keep praying.'

They slowed down at the barrier, and a guard appeared from the building at the side of the road. Mike grinned out of the open window.

'Merrick! Merrick – is that really you?'

'Hey! Looks like it, doesn't it?'

'Well, I'll be – we all thought you were dead in the city!'

'Yeah . . . that's what you were meant to think.'

The guard smiled. 'Ah, I *see*!'

'You do?'

'Oh yeah.'

'OK.' Mike revved the engine. 'Raise the barrier.'

'Ah . . . well, I've got to do my job. Don't want to become illegal and have you boys dragging me off to the city!'

Mike laughed, and Tris noticed his finger on the trigger of the Laserscan which was lying on his lap. 'Well, yeah, that'd be a shame.'

'Let's have your identification details, then, Merrick.'

'No, let's not do that.'

The guard had the rifle in his throat.

'Merrick! What's going on?'

Mike got out of the car.

'Stand still for scan check.'

'I'm legal! Merrick! What's this about?'

Another guard was coming out of the building.

'You want to be involved in this?' Mike shouted. 'You want to be illegal too? Get away from that building! Don't contact anyone! Stand against the wall, and spread your legs!'

The second guard obeyed, immediately.

'OK,' said Mike, to the first guard, 'raise that barrier or I'll de-Code you right now.'

'You know I can't do that . . .'

Mike's voice was low. 'Do you know what they do to guards in the city? Huh?'

'All right! OK, OK! Man, I've only just come on shift
. . . I don't need this!'

'The barrier.'

The guard's hand was shaking so much he could hardly
press the right button on the device he was holding. But
he did, and Mike thanked him with the kind of back-
hander he'd given Tris.

As the barrier rose, Mike ran to the car. But he'd
forgotten the second guard.

'Mike!'

That was Tristram's voice, somewhere close by. In an
instant, Mike turned, saw the guard had a weapon trained
on him – and realised he had no time to level the Laserscan.
Careless, careless, careless! This slip was going to cost him
his life. And then – the guard was on the ground.

'Still slinging rocks, city boy?'

'You complaining?'

'Where did you have that slingshot hidden?'

'You don't want to know.' Tris hesitated before he got
back into the car. 'Did I kill him?'

'Guards have thick skulls.'

They were racing through the barrier now.

Juno's hands were on the grille. Her wan face, washed
out and utterly defeated, stared at them both as they rolled
on to the highway.

'Where are we going?'

'Better ask *him*,' said Mike.

'Keep on the highway.'

'To where, Tris?'

'I'll let you know.'

'Still don't trust me?'

Tristram just smiled. Then he said, 'You did the right
thing back there, Mike.'

'When?'

'Getting Juno out.'

'My partner's girl. It was for Jay.'

'You know, you've spent a lot of time trying to persuade us you've got no emotions, Mike. But you cared about Jay, didn't you?'

'Cared? He was my *partner*. And –'

'And?'

'And he was . . . very young.'

'So's the girl. We'll look after her.'

'Yeah.'

'So, Mike – how does it feel?'

'How does what feel?'

'Your first rescue . . . and from the Towns, too! We don't usually get anyone from the Towns, Mike. Far too dangerous to even try.'

'Dangerous?' Mike checked the rear-view. 'Yeah, that's the word. Keep praying, city boy . . . pray that we don't have a whole load of Watchers on our tail when they find Val and Rico. Shouldn't have left them alive . . . and then they'll find the guards too . . .'

'Please . . . where are you taking me?' Juno asked. 'Mike?'

'To the Deadlands,' said Tristram. 'Don't worry. You'll be safe there.'

'Safe?'

Mike's eyes kept flashing to the rear-view. 'Yeah, if we don't get stopped.'

'We won't,' said Tristram, confidently. 'It'll be all right. David Drum never gets stopped on the highway.'

'Never? Armoured car – behind us!'

Tristram glanced at the side-view mirror and spotted the armoured vehicle speeding up behind them. Mike gripped the Laserscan which was across his knees. But the car overtook them, and shot away into the distance. Tris breathed a sigh of relief and Mike relaxed his grasp on the rifle.

'All right, Tristram. I'd like to know exactly where we're going. Tell me.'

'You're coming, then . . . coming back?'

'Do I have a choice – this time?'

'I don't know. Do you?'

Did he?

Mike mulled that question over as he drove along that highway in the glittering sunshine. He began to play a scene out in his mind: the extermination of the Christians was of such unimaginable importance to the highest powers. If he wiped them out, he would probably be more richly rewarded than he had ever imagined. Who would care about what had occurred during his escape from the MedCent? Who would care about Rohan Adams? Mike could say it was all part of a mission: would anyone argue? He could cut Cain in on the deal; or leave him out entirely, it wouldn't matter. He could turn the whole situation to his own advantage. He felt a sudden kick. That old steel was still there after all; that feeling of the power of fear and life and death, of being a Watcher, *wasn't* gone: he'd known it as soon as he'd had that rifle in his grip again. He could crush any weakness of feeling that had slipped in when he was with the Christians, injured . . .

Couldn't he?

'I can't wait to see Shanna's face,' said Tris. 'She must think we're dead. And Con . . .'

The fantasy Mike had been having about wiping the Christians out and getting some reward for it vanished away like the thin vapour reaching into the sky from the processing plant. He couldn't do it now any more than he could do it before. Things had changed; *he* had changed, inexplicably. He'd been right when he'd told Adams about that power. The thought of Shanna . . . then of Constance, Gideon . . . the charged, crowding, intertwined and complex feelings . . . caring, warmth, *goodness*. All the Credit in the world couldn't buy it.

Tristram noticed the Watcher had fallen silent. He began to feel a sense of foreboding. It intensified as soon as they reached a quiet stretch of highway, and Mike pulled the car over to the side of the road, stopped the vehicle and got out.

'Why have we stopped?' asked Juno.

'Good question.' Tris eyed the Watcher walking round the front of the car.

'OK, city boy. Out.'

'Mike?'

'Forget the slingshot. Come on.'

Tristram got out of the car, feeling his heart rate shoot up.

'What's happening, Mike?'

'I'm going to kill you. What do you think?'

'What!'

The Watcher's face broke into a half-smile. 'You really don't trust me, do you? Come on . . . Tristram, my shoulder's giving me trouble.'

'So?'

'So, you drive.'

'You want me to drive?'

'You know the way. And besides,' said Mike, getting into the passenger seat, 'I'm not the driver. Never was.'

'We're not Watchers!'

The irony of that remark hit Tris as he revved the engine. It seemed to hit Mike, too, and he fell silent again.

'Hey – look at that.' Tristram fixed his eyes on the road. There was something live, moving on the highway just ahead of them. It took off into the sky as they approached.

'Man, that's unusual,' said Tristram. 'Don't see many hawks on the highway this close to Town. I guess they don't like the smell of the Vermalyde from the plant!'

It had been feeding on the carcass of a rodent.

The hunter, feeding on death.

Mike watched the bird soar up into the clear blue sky, heading away from the Towns, the city, the processing plant . . . and as it disappeared from sight, a question flew around Mike's brain.

Could he really – *really* – align himself with the hunted – for all time?

He could get Tris to stop the car. He could go back to the Towns. He could face whatever was coming to him . . . maybe Cain would do something . . . But then, Mike would have to tell all he knew about David Drum.

'Mike? You OK?'

'Uh-huh.'

'Good to be out of the Town.'

'You know, you're right.'

'Yeah?'

'That world stinks, Tristram. You said it yourself.'

26

New Things

It had seemed endless, this tiring trek to the place they'd long agreed they'd head for first, in an emergency.

It was another beautiful morning. But the brightness didn't seem right. It should have been dark, black, stormy, raining. The great weight of misery lay like a heavy stone right inside Shanna's very being.

It was an old fort. Yes, an ancient ruin, a pile of rocks that had once been a castle, half-hidden on a small, partly-wooded hill. They wouldn't stay there long; they were heading west. But Tristram had known they would be there, and they were going to wait a few days. No one said it, but they all knew it would be a pointless waiting, more a kind of grim memorial than anything promising real hope.

Shanna, standing with her arms folded on the cold stone, stared beyond the trees to the grassy slope, the thin dirt track and to the fields, and the broad shining river that wove and meandered its way to the sea. It looked like a thread of silver-gold ribbon, sparkling like something precious in the middle of all that nothingness.

And then she saw it. A black speck in the distance, like a piece of moving darkness.

'Oh no.'

Something was coming along the track.

Shanna's mouth was dry.

'Armoured car . . . armoured *car*! David! David! Watchers!'

He was swiftly beside her.

'Oh, God! God!'

'David!' Shanna was half-crying. 'Oh, David – what are we going to do?'

Constance, Sunny and Gideon were there now too.

'How did they find us?' Constance was a deathly white.

'Tris must have told them . . .' David could hardly speak.

The car stopped.

'Here it comes. We can't run – not any more. Only one way down . . . one way out . . . straight into them.' David put his arm round Constance. 'I'm sorry. I'm so sorry. I let you all down.'

'No, you didn't, David,' said Constance.

'I should have done more . . .'

'Two Watchers . . . and – there's someone else,' said Gideon, shielding his eyes. 'Looks like a girl.'

Sunny was leaning over the wall.

'It's Mike! It is! And Tristram!'

She turned and raced off down the steep stairwell.

'Sunny! Come back! It can't be them!' shouted David.

'It is – look, they aren't wearing helmets! You can see it's them!' Gideon's face lit up with sudden and complete joy. 'David! They're all right! They're all right!'

'Thank God . . . thank God!'

As Mike and Tristram and Juno made their way slowly – very slowly – up the grassy slope towards the trees, the others descended on them.

Oh, they were battered; Tristram's jaw was bruised, but Shanna hardly saw that as she wrapped herself round him. Mike was in some pain, and his face was cut and swollen. Sunny and Constance flung themselves on him simultaneously, and he seemed overwhelmed by that;

no one had ever been particularly pleased to see him before.

Gideon was slapping Tris on the back now, and David looked as if he would burst with sheer happiness and relief. They eventually peeled Sunny off Mike and she decided to welcome Tristram in an almost equally enthusiastic manner.

'So glad to see you, Mike!' Gideon embraced the Watcher. Mike wasn't too comfortable with that, but he was so pleased to see that Gideon was still alive that he let it go. And then there was Shanna.

There was a moment when they just looked at each other, and then her face was wreathed in smiles.

'I'm glad too!' She put her arms around him and hugged him. Mike's eyes were shut as he brought his left arm tightly round her back. And in the celebration and excitement, nobody noticed that the two of them stayed like that for rather too long.

* * *

'Look at that,' said David. 'Look at that. And tell me why I'm not afraid.'

All eyes were on the Watcher. The Watcher with the Laserscan, sitting by the river.

'Someone who risked their life to save us isn't going to take us out with a Laserscan rifle,' said Gideon. 'No way.'

David's face lit up in a smile. 'You've got it, Gideon, my boy. I tell you, and I make no secret of it, the events of the past few days have done something for my faith. Yes, truly.'

'Something's happening to Mike,' said Constance. 'I don't suppose he knows what. But it's good.'

'He's got a long way to go. He doesn't know it, but this is just the start,' Tristram said. 'But it is just that. A new start.'

The quietness of the camp was broken suddenly by a burst of laughter. Sunny was playing with Tris's dog. David sighed, and stroked his beard.

'*Will* he stay with us? But what else? He *can't* go back now.'

Gideon nodded. 'He'll stay.'

'God knows what the future holds. He always did,' said Constance.

'I wonder what her past held.' Gideon glanced at the blonde girl sleeping on the grass beside him. 'She looks like she's been through hell.'

Constance looked thoughtful. 'Mike says she's a nurse. I'm glad she's here with us.'

'She's pretty,' said Gideon. 'Pretty, I think . . . or she will be.'

'And there I was thinking you were going to wait for Sunny to get older,' said David, lying back and blinking at the sky, 'and marry her.'

Gideon was about to say something, but didn't. He looked perplexed. David laughed, sat up, ruffled Gideon's hair and said: 'Just teasing, my boy. Just teasing.'

Tristram got up, and walked over to the Watcher. He cast a stone into the river.

'You've definitely got a thing,' said Mike, 'about rocks.'

'I guess.'

'I haven't thanked you and your slingshot yet for saving my life.'

'Well, at least I managed to do it without breaking any of your bones.' Tris sat down beside the Watcher. 'And you saved me . . . and us . . .'

'No. Gave you some time. It's not over. They'll come after you – us.'

'Will they? You fed those Watchers some strange information. Maybe they believed it.'

'They'll come.'

'So we'll keep moving. And moving. And moving.'

'Yeah.' Mike ran a hand over the Laserscan.

'I've got a confession to make.'

Mike glanced at him. 'You better talk to Gideon or David. I'm not the type you confess to . . . believe me.'

'No, I think you are on this one. When I took the guard down – I thought I'd killed him. I mean, I don't know if I cared. I didn't think . . . I just wanted him down. Mike, I think maybe there's a bit of the city left in me.'

'Perhaps there's a bit of the city in everyone.'

'I don't know. I mean, Gideon – I admire him. He's got – '

'Guts.'

'What?'

'Gideon. He's got guts.'

'Like his father.'

'Yeah.' Mike gazed out across the river. 'Like his father.'

A few moments passed by before Tris spoke again. 'It took a while, but then it came to me. I know where I saw you before.'

'With your friend Mole.'

'No, before that. Seven years ago.'

'Oh?'

'It was just before they got me out. I was talking to Kurt about my escape. He said it was a whole new life, a new life on the inside, not just on the outside. He told me about a God who loved me, who wanted me. Me! I said, no one wants a city kid . . . I've done things . . . but Kurt said no one was beyond redemption. Don't suppose that makes much sense to you right now.'

'You'd be surprised what makes sense to me right now.'

'I saw you. And another Watcher. And then Kurt was dead.'

'Uh-huh.'

'I just couldn't place where I'd seen you before. Then I did, that day in the barn. But it wasn't until I saw Adams that I remembered everything. He must've been your partner back then.'

'Yeah. For a while, when he first became a Watcher. But we had a few . . . problems.'

'You targeted Kurt. You had that light. But it was Adams who did it. Not you. I knew that as soon as I saw him.'

Mike said nothing.

'Anyway, Mike . . . guess I thought I had to say that.'

'Yeah.'

Tris leaned back on one arm. 'So, you're going to stay with us? Mike? What are you going to do?'

What *was* he going to do? Stop fighting it; explore it, this change that had begun to occur deep inside him. New things were happening: things that scared him, things that worried him; and yes, things that excited him.

Something landed near them, and they both leapt to their feet, Mike still holding the Laserscan.

Sunny was giggling. She'd thrown a stick for the dog. It had come to rest just behind them. Shanna was involved in the game, too, and Gideon was watching them, and talking quietly to Juno, who was sitting up, rubbing her eyes. Mike's eyes met those of Shanna, and she smiled; then she smiled at Tris, and his face was a picture of total adoration. Life, thought Mike, might just get more and more complicated . . . very soon, too . . .

'Come on, come on!' Sunny cried. 'We've got to have some *fun* before we move on.' She ran over to them. 'Come on, Tristram. Throw some sticks for your dog. She likes fetching stones, you know. Did you train her?' She threw her hands into the air. 'It's such a *beautiful* day.'

Tris laughed, and reluctantly joined in the game.

'You too, Mike! We won't start the game without you!' Sunny was breathless. 'Come and play! You're not too old to play – are you?'

There was no double meaning in her words. It was nothing but a cheeky taunt.

Mike looked at Sunny. He looked at Shanna, and Tristram and the rest. Then he looked at the Laserscan which was in his hand. Only he knew. Only he had any idea how quickly and effectively and unthinkingly he'd very nearly reacted when the stick had landed behind him.

He was getting back to full strength.

So when he threw the Laserscan into the river, it fell a long, long way from shore.

'Too old? No, Sunny.' He smiled at her. 'I'm not too old.'